WANDER

Kevyn Morgan discovers that her father is not as dead as she had been led to believe for these past thirty years. Alex Morgan is living in the Caribbean searching for sunken treasure.

Confusing thoughts of abandonment and intrigue beset her as she prepares to sail *Wander* through the islands in search of the father she has never known. When she meets Sam, who seems to know and not like her father all that much., she realises she may not wish to get to know the man who disappeared all those years ago.

Together with the handsome treasure collector they uncover tales of smuggling, drowning, drug-running, and the mysterious sinking of boats.

The rough waters of navigating relationships with both Sam and Alex are nothing compared with the storm of danger she finds herself in while sailing through paradise.

A story of Intrigue and deceit ...

CW01459690

THE AUTHOR

Victoria Allman has been following her stomach around the globe for fifteen years as a yacht chef. She writes about her floating culinary odyssey through Europe, the Caribbean, Nepal, Vietnam, Africa and the South Pacific in her first book, *Sea Fare: A Chef's Journey Across the Ocean**

SEAsoned: A Chef's Journey with Her Captain, her second book, is a hilarious look at a yacht chef's first year working for her husband while they cruise from the Bahamas to Italy, France, Greece and Spain – trying to stay afloat. Both books have won The Royal Palm Literary Award - First Place for Travel. Her essays on travel and food have appeared in Dockwalk Magazine and Marina Life Magazine.

ACKNOWLEDGMENTS

No book is written alone.

Wander and I had the expert help of story editor extraordinaire, Marjetta Geerling; writing coach and seminar leader, James Scott Bell; story editor, Ramona DeFelice Long; copy-editor Amy Lingor; sailing expert, Michelle Purinton; beta readers and friends, Yaz Smit, Dennis Bailey, Thomas Combs, and Joseph Collum; and everyone in Joyce Sweeney's Thursday night critique support group. I would have stuck this manuscript in a drawer without the encouragement and support of author friends, Elaine Viets and mentor Deborah Sharp.

My husband, Patrick Allman, was thrilled that I found make-believe characters to write about instead of him as I had in my last two books. Although…he just so happens to be a blue-eyed, blond surfer and anthropology major just like the handsome Sam.

A special thanks goes to my mother, Alana, who encouraged me to read from a very early age and always believed the 'fiction' I told her while growing up. She spawned my love of books and stories, and I am proud to be giving a little something back.

Wander

A novel by
Victoria Allman

*For Jimmy, who introduced me to the Isle of Hope
and the concept of making memories*

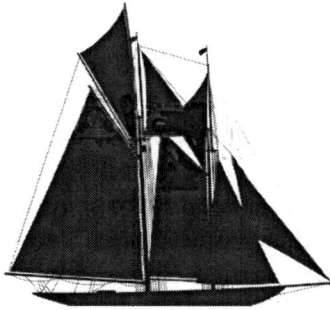

Copyright © 2014 Victoria Allman
Published by
CUSTOM BOOK PUBLICATIONS
First Edition

*All the characters are fictitious and any resemblance to real persons,
living or dead, is purely coincidental*

Chapter One

'I've been lying to you about Alex your whole life.'

Kevyn's head snapped up at her grandfather's words.

She stared at the man who had raised her and waited for more. Her father, Alex, had been dead for thirty years. What could Grandfather possibly have lied about?

They sat in matching slat-backed rocking chairs on his verandah overlooking the river of grass that wound its way along the coast of Savannah. A live oak draped with a tangle of Spanish moss cast a shadow over them, pretending to keep them somewhat cool. The air hung thick and muggy. A single line of sweat trickled between Kevyn's breasts. The fan above did nothing but keep the gnats away.

She leaned forward in her chair. 'What about?'

A picture of a tall, athletic-looking young man with short brown hair hung in her grandfather's back hall – a single image of her father in his teenage years and the fact he'd died when she was a baby, was all Kevyn knew about him. 'I promised your mama I'd never tell.' Her grandfather sighed as he pushed a piece of matted grey hair off his wrinkled forehead. 'You may hate me for keeping it from you, and she sure as hell is going to hate me for telling it, but it's time.' His words were as heavy as the air around them as he sat staring at the wake on the river from a Whaler that puttered past. 'I need to tell you the truth.'

Kevyn's stomach churned. 'About what?'

'Your father grew up here.' He waved his hand at the house of her childhood memories. She had lived with her mother in Savannah in various two-bedroom apartments around town, but every Sunday her mother would drive her out to the Isle of Hope and drop Kevyn off with her grandfather. 'He was quiet, like you. You have his green eyes and olive skin, you know.'

Kevyn sat on the edge of her seat. Was this just another of his rambling stories? He'd certainly been deviating lately, wandering through the past and forgetting about the present. 'He was a dreamer. Always reading books about African safaris or hiking in the Himalayas.' His voice cracked with his small, sad smile. 'I'd climb all over him about it.'

Kevyn took her grandfather's hand. She was surprised to feel it shaking. He was tough, indestructible, but with each new day his eighty-two years were starting to show. 'I wanted him to go to law school. To make something more of his life, have it easier than I did. He wanted to join National Geographic and see the world.' He looked her in the eye.

'But I didn't want him tramping about and told him to forget all that nonsense.'

'Sounds like you were just trying to protect him.' She could feel his knuckles through his paper-thin skin as it shifted under her grip. He still had the same silver hair and goatee that she knew from her earliest memories, but his once electric blue eyes full of life were fading to gray.

'I was gone a lot while he was growing up. I spent more time on the shrimp boat than in the house.' Tears welled up in his eyes. 'By the time I was ready to be a father, well… he was walking out the door.'

Kevyn's breath caught and she swallowed the flood of emotions that threatened to burst from her chest. 'Where'd he go?'

His hand once again waved in the humid air. 'Everywhere.'

'He traveled?' They never spoke of Alex. She had no idea he had stepped foot outside of Savannah. Kevyn had always dreamed of taking her sailboat to other places; perhaps she was more like her father than she'd thought.

He nodded. 'One day when he was about eleven, I took him to Ossabaw Island to see where the German U-Boats were spotted during World War II. When he was old enough, he returned every weekend on his boat to dive the area. He was determined to find sunken ships.'

'Did he?' Kevyn tried to hide her building excitement as she let go of his hand and sipped at her glass of sweet tea. When she was little she would ask about her father, but Grandfather would clench his jaw and change the subject and Mama always turned away without answering. Later, Kevyn realized that her questions were followed by one of her mother's long drinking bouts. She soon stopped asking all together.

'No ships. He was mostly free diving in the shallows. But he did find coins from a Spanish galleon.'

Kevyn sat straighter in her chair, not sure if this was just some rambling story or not. 'Pirate treasure?'

'Pirates got some of it.' The late summer sun hit the old coin her grandfather pulled from his pocket. It was not rounded like a regular coin, but jagged on one edge. It looked like someone had filed the edges to a sharp point. He handed it to her. 'Mostly they were ships coming up from the Caribbean.'

'And he *found* one of these ships?' Kevyn rolled the coin in her hand. It was lighter than she expected and cool to the touch, as if the cold ocean still held it in its grasp.

'He didn't find the ship.' Her grandfather pointed to the coin. 'But he found a lot of what washed up close to shore, like that doubloon.'

Kevyn couldn't believe what she was hearing. Without any stories of her father growing up, her child's imagination turned him into a hero

3

and an adventurer, but her adult mind had settled on the fact he was just a young man who'd died a tragic but common death. Images from *Indiana Jones* films filled her mind.

'What did he do with it?'

'He bought an underwater metal detector and took his boat out every day that summer. Alex scoured the whole area and took what he found to the shed.' He motioned to the one-room shack overlooking the marsh. For the last half dozen years Kevyn had used the building as her own little shop, a place to restore antiques.

'He never told anyone, but he spent his nights polishing and restoring all the coins and jewelry he found. Finally, he brought your grandmother out back and gave her the thickest gold necklace I'd ever seen.'

'You mean he actually found buried treasure?'

'Sunken treasure,' her grandfather corrected. 'I didn't believe him. Sounded like a lot of hooey to me.' Shifting uncomfortably in his chair, he looked Kevyn straight in the eye. 'I called him a liar and a thief. I threw the necklace back at him. I thought he had to be doing something illegal to have it in his possession.' Casting his gaze down to the wooden porch, her grandfather's voice was barely audible as he continued, 'We fought something fierce and he packed a bag and left that night. He was just sixteen.'

'Where'd he go?'

'He bought a used shrimp boat with his treasure and went hunting for more ships. He was gone for twelve years.' Reaching down, he lifted up a stack of yellow aged postcards from beside his wicker chair and handed them to her. 'Your grandmother received a postcard every couple of years.'

Kevyn thumbed through the stack, picking out names like Dominica, Trinidad, Merida – locales she'd dreamed of sailing to one day. Turning one over, she stared down for the first time at her father's handwriting, running her fingertips over the messages. *Grilled lobster on the beach. Swam under a waterfall.* These were her father's words--her father's life.

Her grandfather cleared his throat and took a deep breath. 'Then, one day, I was sitting on this front porch and he just came walking up the drive. He was wearing a Navy jacket. Turned out he'd done a tour in 'Nam.' His voice dropped to a whisper. 'We hadn't even known he was there.'

Shaking off the memory, he began again, 'He just walked up the lane and said 'Hello, sir,' shook my hand and kissed your grandmother on the cheek. She poured him a glass of sweet tea and that was that. We

4

waited for him to open up and tell us what had happened over there but he never offered any stories. It was a time when many young men came back disillusioned so we didn't want to pry and we could tell he didn't want to talk about it. He'd spend all day on his boat and all night in the shed but we thought that was his way of coping with whatever it was he saw over there.'

'I didn't know he was in Vietnam.' Kevyn suddenly felt as cold as the coin. 'Mama never told me anything about him.' Her voice dropped. 'Neither did you.'

Grandfather lowered his eyes. 'Being over there changed him.' He went back to staring out over the marsh. It had been a dry year and the grass was more golden than green. 'Or, maybe I never really knew him.' His gaze shifted to the azalea bushes in the corner of the yard; the flowers of spring were long gone. 'When he met your mama and she got pregnant we hoped he'd forget the war and all this treasure hunting nonsense and live a happy, normal life.'

'And that didn't happen?' Kevyn already knew the answer. No happy ending was possible after he died.

Her grandfather shook his head. 'You'd have trouble believing it now, but your mama was once a beautiful, strong woman who would've kept Alex on his toes. But something took him over, maybe fear, maybe memories, and he left.'

Kevyn's mouth went dry. 'But...Mama said he died in a car accident.'

The sigh was heavy and deep as her grandfather reached out for her shaking hand. 'No, Kevyn. Your father is still very much alive.'

'How could you lie to me?' Kevyn could barely speak through her anger and confusion.

Her grandfather stared at Kevyn's hand as it was wrenched from his. He looked as sad as he had in the days after grandmother had passed, leaving him all alone with this big house and, apparently, a heart full of regrets.

The sound of stones crunching under tires startled Kevyn as a car pulled into the driveway. Swiveling in her chair, she watched her mother slam the door of her Bronco and marched up the walk to the porch. Brianna's cheeks were even more sunken than the last time Kevyn saw her. Her angular jaw that reminded Kevyn of Kathryn Hepburn was locked in place, but her eyes had a hollow haunted look to them now, as if the life inside her had melted in the unforgiving Savannah heat.

'Mama, what are you doing here?' Kevyn couldn't remember the last time she had seen her at the house.

In her youth, Kevyn would stay here with her grandfather when her mother would drink too much. He'd take her out fishing off Warsaw Sound, or to a plantation west of the city in order to pick peaches. Neither she nor her grandfather would ever acknowledge what was happening; then, in a few days, her mother would appear in the long driveway and honk, signaling to Kevyn that it was time to return back to their life until the next time came around. But in all those times, her mother had never gotten out of the car.

'Ask him why I'm here.' Her mother stood at the railing glaring at Grandfather.

Leaning forward in his chair, he poured a glass of tea for her mother. 'I asked your mama to come.'

'No, James. You demanded I be present.' Her mother's hand shook just as much as his when she reached for the tea. 'Just like always, you're still running the show.'

'Are you going to tell her about my father?' Kevyn turned to her mother. 'Grandfather says he's still alive.'

Her mother's brown eyes flashed lightning at him. 'You told her?'

He held her angry stare. 'It's time she knew the truth.'

Kevyn's heart hammered in her chest. 'You knew, too?'

They certainly had never enjoyed the close mother-daughter bond, but Kevyn thought she would at least have shared this important bit of information. Kevyn remembered the time she came home from school clutching her first painting with the words, FOR MAMA printed in big block letters. With a cool gaze, her mother had hung it on the fridge, but crossed out MAMA and wrote BRIANNA in her careful cursive.

'We're not that type of family,' she had said.

And she'd been right. They weren't. Sometimes she was a mother, but mostly she remained Brianna, a taciturn woman of sorrow.

'You bastard!' Brianna slipped a hand into her purse and pulled out a silver flask. She poured a long stream of clear alcohol into her tea before refastening the cap.

'What the hell is going on?' Kevyn's voice rose, no longer willing to tippy toe around her mother.

'Alex didn't die in a car accident.' Her grandfather looked up at Brianna as he spoke. 'He left right after you were born.'

'He just... left?'

'Your mama vowed not to speak of him again. In fact, she refused to let anyone utter his name and I didn't have the heart to fight her.'

'Oh, so it's my fault? I lied to her?' The fire of hatred flared in Brianna's eyes.

Kevyn sat stunned, waiting to see if someone would laugh and this would all be a joke. She lowered her head, cradling it in her hands, and whispered, 'Dad's alive?'

'I never told you he died.' Brianna stared vacantly at the marsh, gripping the porch railing with clenched fists and bright white knuckles. 'When you were a little girl you used to say your father was magical and lived in a far-off land. I told you that wasn't true. I told you that he was a regular man like Joe, our neighbor at the time.' A wisp of hair fell over Brianna's left eye and Kevyn watched her hand tremble as she pushed it back in place. 'When Joe died in that car accident you changed your story and came up with the belief that your father had died the same way.' Her voice dropped to a whisper. 'It seemed better than the truth, so I never corrected you.'

'I was five years old!' Kevyn jumped to her feet. 'What kind of logical explanation could I have come up with? All the other kids had dads.'

Brianna spun to face Kevyn, the flame back in her eyes. 'Don't you yell at me! I'm not the one who left.'

Kevyn leaned in, speaking with a voice sharper than her jig saw. 'No, you're just the one who lied to me my entire life.'

Brianna's hand flew up and slapped Kevyn across the cheek. 'Don't talk to me like that!'

Kevyn's own hand shot to her face as the pain exploded inside her head. Her vision blurred as she covered her stinging skin. She couldn't believe this was happening.

'Brianna!' Her grandfather's voice boomed. He may have looked weaker than the man of Kevyn's memories but he still could command the scene. 'Stop this! It's time she knew.'

Both women glared at each other, unwilling to back down.

'You were always very imaginative.' Brianna squared her stance and gave a small bitter laugh. 'Dreaming of other worlds and exotic places.' She spat the words at Kevyn: 'You are just like your father.'

'How would I know? I've never met him!' Kevyn's face stung, a rage inside her began to burn. She lowered her hand to her hip and narrowed her eyes in order to match her mother's piercing look.

Brianna studied her daughter for a moment, as the light suddenly flickered from her eyes. 'How do you tell a five-year-old that her father abandoned her the night she was born?' Turning back to the marsh, Brianna drained her glass of spiked tea.

Kevyn suddenly wondered if this big secret was what led to all the spiked teas she'd witnessed Brianna drinking over the years. She collapsed back into her chair, and leaned over her knees to try and catch her breath from the wave of nausea that overtook her. Still alive?

'Why are you telling me this now?' Kevyn's heart thumped so loudly in her chest she felt certain they could hear the hollow noise it made as it seized, waiting an impossibly long time before it began to beat again. 'I've thought he was dead for thirty years. After all this time, why now?'

Her grandfather poured another glass for Brianna. 'Last week I got a call from an insurance man down in Florida regarding a boat, the *K Sea*. It sank between Puerto Rico and the Virgin Islands. He said there was a fire onboard and the boat didn't make it. Said he wasn't sure where he was now, but Alex was the one who called in the claim.'

The hard, cracked wicker of her chair gouged at Kevyn's hands where she held the armrests in her clenched fists.

'Alex reported the sinking to the coast guard but he disappeared before the insurance investigation was finished.' He leaned forward in his chair. 'It took some time, but they traced him back to me as next of kin.'

'He's in the Caribbean?' Kevyn's voice was strained as she tried to form the words.

'Thing is, that when I called down there, Customs wouldn't give me any information. They won't tell me whether he left the island or not.'

'So he could be there right now?'

The ice in Brianna's tea produced beads of condensation on the glass. Her thin fingers gripped it like a lifeline. 'You know, when I first met your father he told me he was a descendant of Captain Henry Morgan.' Brianna's cold, raw voice took on a mystical quality as she talked of the past. 'He told me tales of Caribbean pirate ships and sunken treasure. He was absolutely charming and at the time I thought it was romantic.' She was staring over the marsh again, talking to no one in particular. 'Turns out pirates aren't always seeking adventure. Sometimes they're running from one.'

'So he's chasing pirate treasure in the Caribbean?' Kevyn turned to face her grandfather. Brianna may have calmed, but Kevyn could still feel her mother's slap on her face.

'I don't know.' He shook his head. 'I called up an old friend of your father's in Lauderdale and he said he'd seen Alex over the years, but the last time was about two years ago. Doesn't know where he is now.'

'Pete?' Brianna's brown eyes glared once again at Grandfather. 'That figures. Those two were thick as thieves, both hightailed it out of here to chase adventure.'

'How would this Pete guy know where he was?' Kevyn ignored her mother's bitterness and stood back up. She needed to move, to try to restore the feeling back in her limbs. As she walked back and forth in front of her grandfather, she carefully avoided the corner where Brianna stood refilling her glass from the flask. 'You just said he hadn't seen him in two years.'

'He said Alex always stopped in when he was in town but he hadn't seen him since the *K Sea* went down.'

'So, where is he?' Kevyn couldn't believe that in the past thirty minutes she'd learned her father was alive, but now no one knew where to find him. This is unbelievable. It felt far more like a soap opera than her real life.

'I don't know.' Grandfather grabbed her hand as she passed. 'Kevyn, I know this is a lot to take in right now. I'm sure you're mad as hell that we've been lying to you, but I'm telling you the truth. Your father is alive. I don't know where, and I know I have no right to ask this of you... but I'd like you to go find him.'

'What? Me?' Kevyn stared with disbelief into her grandfather's pleading gaze.

'No!' Brianna's face was all hard angles. 'Don't bring that man back into our lives.'

Kevyn saw the fury in her eyes and felt her own anger soften. She swallowed hard, 'Why, Mama? What really happened?'

'Happened?' Brianna waved her hand like a brushstroke, once again erasing the past. 'Nothing happened. There wasn't time for anything to happen. He was gone too quick. Your father fled when the waters got rough and he certainly doesn't deserve rescuing now.'

Grandfather clenched her hand tighter. 'You're a good sailor, Kevyn. You spend as much time on his old sailboat as he did. If there is anyone who can find him, it's you.'

'I wouldn't even know where to start.' Her mind raced as she suddenly caught what he said. 'What do you mean, his old boat?'

For her eighteenth birthday her grandfather had given her a dilapidated thirty-two foot sailboat, and for the next two years Kevyn had scraped the hull of the flaking paint and varnished the teak interior. She'd made the boat seaworthy and then moved onto it. It was her home. 'That sailboat was your father's. I gave it to him before he began searching for treasure. It was the boat he took out to Ossabaw every day looking for gold.'

'Let me get this straight.' Kevyn heard the sass in her voice but didn't care to correct it. 'You want me to sail my boat down to the Caribbean, to God knows where, pick up a man I don't know, who left me alone with Mama, and bring him back here to you?'

'I wish there was a way I could save you the pain. But, yes, I want you to go find your father. He may not have been a father to you, but he did what he thought was best for you and your mama at the time.'

'By leaving us? By making me think he was dead all my life? Do you know what it feels like to think your father is dead?'

She stormed back and forth across the verandah. Sweat ran down her neck and soaked her tank top. But she no longer noticed the heat; she was burning far hotter with rage than the weather around her. 'To always be afraid to mention him? Look at Mama. It's two-thirty in the afternoon and she's already on her third drink. Don't you think he's responsible for that?'

'You try being left with a newborn and see if you handle it any differently.' Brianna slammed her glass on the rail.

Her grandfather held up his hands in an effort to stop the looming fight. 'I know how it sounds, and I surely don't blame you for being mad. But he felt he had to go. He was a broken man, if he stayed you could've ended up hating him a whole lot more.'

Kevyn spun on her heel. 'I sure as hell would have liked the opportunity to try that scenario.' She regretted her words instantly but held her ground.

'I'm so sorry, Kevyn.' He dropped his head to his chest. 'I know this is my fault. If I hadn't chased him out of the house all those years ago, maybe he'd have felt this was home and stuck around.' The look of shame in his eyes caused Kevyn to take a deep breath and calm herself down.

Taking a knee in front of the man who had shown her love all her life, Kevyn spoke calmly, 'Even if I wanted to find him I can't just pick up and go. I have a job. I can't afford to just sail off into the sunset.'

Kevyn had lived in Savannah her whole life, but if she was honest with herself, she didn't have many ties. Her mother's drinking had alienated her from friends at school, being always too embarrassed to bring anyone home. She'd been married for half a minute but that was long over, and these days she spent more time alone on her boat than out with friends.

'I've got some money put away.' Grandfather looked up at the house and the acre of land it sat upon. 'House's been paid off for a while now. Taxes keep risin' but I've got more than enough to see me through. It'll all go to you one day anyway.'

'I don't want your savings.'

'I know you're too proud to take a hand out.' He sighed heavily. 'So that's why I'm going to hire you. This is a job. Please go find my son and bring him back home.' His shoulders slumped forward and he looked every one of his eighty-two years.

Brianna shifted closer to him and laid a hand on his arm. 'I don't think you should ask her to do this.'

He looked startled by the show of affection. 'Alex might be in trouble, Brianna. His boat sank and he's disappeared again.'

'Serves him right.' She turned from him, the tender moment vanishing into the sticky air. Her back stiffened and her words became sharp as she spoke to Kevyn. 'You want to go find him, fine. Just don't be too surprised if you don't like what you discover.' She snapped her purse onto her shoulder. 'I've got to go to work.' She marched off the porch without even a goodbye.

Kevyn couldn't believe she was leaving.

Brianna stopped at the bottom of the stairs and, without turning around, spoke over her shoulder, 'You're a damn fool if you go chasing after that man.' She stalked back to her car. Gravel spat from the Bronco's tires as she roared down the driveway.

'I guess leaving is how all the members of this family deal with problems.' Kevyn's fury at her mother relit. She was no longer the scared little girl who shrank from her mother's drinking; she was a grown woman who could decide for herself whether she wanted to go find her father.

Kevyn stuffed her father's coin into the front pocket of her shorts. Picking up the plate of lemon coconut squares, she stormed into the kitchen and let the screen door slam behind her. Her grandfather had little time to eat this afternoon with all the talking he had done, so she wrapped them and placed them on the counter as she tried to control her breathing.

She removed the plate of pecan tarts from yesterday and brushed the few remaining crumbs into the garbage. She washed and dried the plate and tucked it into her bag to fill the next day. It wasn't much compared to all the love and support her grandfather had showered her with throughout her life, but the baking plus the hour they spent together on the porch each day before she went to work in the shed was something he looked forward to. Of course, usually their conversations were a little less world spinning than this one had been.

Pulling his favorite mug from the cupboard, she dropped a single tea bag inside and filled the kettle, setting it on the stove for when he was ready. It was a routine she performed daily, and allowed extra time for her mind to go over all that was said. *My father isn't dead. He's spent his life searching for treasure. He fought in Vietnam. He escaped a sinking boat and disappeared. He's not dead…*

Her anger slowly subsided as the truth began to cement itself in her. She couldn't remain mad at her grandfather. She just felt numb, incredulous, as if this whole afternoon had not just happened. It had to be a dream she would wake from soon.

Leaving the kitchen, she walked into the antique parlor and picked up a blanket her grandmother had crocheted long ago. No one had sat in there for years. Grandfather spent all his time on the porch or in his study reading. He really didn't have anything in his life any more but Kevyn.

She took the blanket out to the verandah and wrapped him up tight. 'How come you're not mad? He abandoned you, too.'

He squeezed her hand. 'Girl, when you get to see as much as I have in life, you realize that things are rarely as one-sided as that.'

'But why now?'

'Look at me, Kevyn.'

Kevyn raised her head and met her grandfather's gaze.

He reached out, stroking her cheek with his work-worn thumb. 'I may not have much time to make amends.'

'Don't say that.' Kevyn shook away the thought. 'You're the strongest man I know.'

'Not for long.' He leaned his head closer to hers. 'I'm old. I'm not going to be around forever and I want to see my son one last time before I go. Please do this for me.'

Kevyn could barely breathe. Her grandfather had never asked her for anything.

'Just think about it,' he whispered.

'I don't have to think about it.' She wiped a tear from her cheek. 'I'll go find him... for you.'

*****

Chapter Two

Wander was an old thirty-two foot sailboat built in the sixties. It had sat vacant in her grandfather's yard for years before Kevyn began fixing it up. Although she lived on her for the past ten years, she had little experience sailing her in open waters. *Wander* had not been out much past the border of Georgia, but neither had Kevyn, so their first adventure would be all about learning together.

Athens, her calico cat, strolled out on deck when Kevyn returned. Rubbing his flank along her calves, he lifted his head to be scratched as Kevyn bent down, scooped him up, and nuzzled her face in his soft fur. 'It looks like we're going to sea, kiddo.'

Kevyn knew she needed help getting *Wander* ready for the trip. She called the shipyard in Thunderbolt and booked a slip at the yard with the manager. 'Billy, I need her to be able to cover some serious miles.' Light streamed into the cabin as if the gods were giving her their blessing for a safe, warm trip. 'I want to make sure she can handle a long voyage.'

'I'll take care of 'er, darlin'.' The pride in Billy's voice was evident.

Kevyn had known Billy a long time. He had lived his whole life in Savannah and bragged about the fact he'd never been farther south than Cumberland Island and wouldn't step foot into Yankee territory north of the Carolinas. He'd once told Kevyn the closest he ever wanted to get to a big city was to see the Falcons play a home game on TV.

'Can she handle a trip like this?' Kevyn asked.

Billy had been the one to help when she first inherited *Wander* and had taught her how to sail. 'I won't let you leave 'til she's ready.' If anyone could help her get *Wander* prepared to cross the Gulf Stream safely, Billy could.

The next day Kevyn motored *Wander* down the Wilmington River to the shipyard. Standing by the wooden tiller, she looked out over the salt marshes and muddy waters she'd called home her whole life. She may not know the ocean, but she certainly knew the river like the back of her hand. If she wasn't cruising down it in *Wander*, she was kayaking it in the mornings or running its shores in the afternoon. Up ahead, a white ibis took flight. With three powerful flaps of its wings, it rose from the reeds and soared overhead to the branches of a distant cypress tree.

Kevyn drew a deep breath. The smell of the salt water and mustiness of the marsh co-mingled, producing the familiar scent that felt like home. She was both excited and terrified to be leaving and wondered what the tropics would smell like. Did all that sunshine and those palm trees smell brighter?

When the shipyard came into view, she maneuvered the boat to glide into the slip. Slowing her speed, she eased *Wander* into the slot.

Billy stood on the starboard side waiting to grab her lines. Reaching up, he tugged at the corner of his ball cap. 'Howdy.'

He used his right hand to motion her another foot further into the slip. His eyes darted between the concrete and the bow that curved under and away from Kevyn's line of vision. She trusted Billy to be her eyes and judge the distance properly, and as soon as Billy held his hand up in a fist, Kevyn tapped the throttle into reverse to stop the forward motion and sprinted up the side to the bow. She grabbed the eye of the line she'd snaked over the lifeline and swung it to Billy.

'She looks good.' He reached down to loop the line over the cleat on the dock as Kevyn secured the bow.

Hurrying to the stern to repeat the process with the next line, Kevyn then hurried around the side deck to check the placement of her fenders so she wouldn't rub against the concrete dock. Being a solo sailor was a lot of work.

She scrambled back to the cockpit and poked her head into the cabin. Athens lay curled up on the bench. His tan and black fur glowed in the late afternoon light streaming through the portholes.

'You going to ride the boat up?' She reached down to scratch under his chin, but he showed no sign of putting in any effort to get off the boat while it was lifted onto the hard. 'Suit yourself.'

Kevyn grabbed her coffee cup off the chart table and stepped back outside. 'Nice day for a boat ride,' Billy said, holding his hand out to help her off the boat.

While the yard workers were busy setting the straps to lift *Wander* out of the water, Kevyn told Billy all about her plans.

'Dang crazy idea, if you ask me.' He lifted an empty red Solo cup and spit; a dark line of chew hit the inside of the plastic. Billy had years of practice to perfect his aim. 'Why'd you want go digging up that fool?'

'You knew my father?' All these years and he had never said a word. She tried to think back. Had she never spoken about her father to anyone? It now seemed crazy that she'd never questioned the story of the car accident. Had her mother's drinking made her scared to mention his name even to the people she trusted?

'Everyone knows everyone in this town.' He kept his eye on *Wander* as it rose in the stirrups. River water poured off the hull and rained down on the concrete platform below. 'When your daddy was just a boy he came to me to learn to sail, just like you did. He was out on this boat so often and ran it so hard he had to bring it to me when it wouldn't keep up with him.'

It was strange for Kevyn to think of *Wander* as her father's boat. How fitting the name now seemed. All this time she thought the name was a private message to her, about what she should do with her life, yet all along it had been a message from him about his own dreams. She'd just never gotten around to it, while, from what Grandfather had told her, all her father *did* was wander through life.

'Back then I was working out of my house on the river and your daddy would come by with a pail of shrimp in exchange for my labor.' Billy reached into his back pocket, pinched off some more tobacco, and tucked it into his gum. He removed the John Deere cap from his head and scratched the top of his white hair. 'Shit, I was more of a father to him back then than your granddaddy ever was. Them two never saw eye to eye.' Billy glanced up at Kevyn then quickly lowered his eyes again. 'Guess I never did a good job with the responsibility part.'

'Why didn't you ever tell me any of this?' Frustration laced Kevyn's voice. She was sick of everyone thinking that she couldn't handle the truth. 'You could've told me when I asked you to help me with *Wander*.'

'Never saw any point in sticking my nose in anyone else's business. That was your mama and granddaddy's story to tell.' Billy pulled his Leatherman out and scraped a barnacle off *Wander's* hunter green hull; he wiped the dirt away with a rag. "Sides, Alex was different back when I knew him. He was a dreamer but still a real hard worker. He was out there every free minute looking for treasure.' He nodded in the direction of the ocean. 'After the war he was never the same. Came back with a look in his eye like he'd seen things he weren't gonna talk about.' Billy stole another quick glance at Kevyn then returned his attention to *Wander's* hull.

Anger danced in her. 'So? He got drafted,' Kevyn heard the petulant tone in her voice but didn't back down. 'Lots of guys had a hard time after Vietnam, but it's not like he didn't have a family to help him. Grandfather might have been hard on him but he and Grandmother loved him and would have helped him deal with what it was haunting him.' Billy threw down the cloth in his hand.

'Girl, you don't know what he saw.'

His harsh tone shocked her. He'd never spoken to her that way.

Bending down to pick up the rag, Billy spoke a bit quieter when he straightened, 'Alex never talked 'bout this with me, but word got back to the base here.' He twisted the rag in his hand. 'Alex was discharged after an accident involving a boat he was driving.'

'What kind of accident?'

Billy sighed. 'The boat collided with another Navy vessel. There were six sailors onboard. Four were killed, two were maimed.'

'That's awful.' She may not have known her father, but Kevyn couldn't imagine what he would have gone through in the aftermath of such a tragedy.

'One of the Marines was apparently his best friend. His name was Kevin.'

Kevyn's hand flew to her throat. 'I'm named after a man he thought he killed?' When she was a kid she hated her name. *Kevyn*. It was a boy's name. But the older she got and the more independent she became, she had grown to love it. Let people blink twice or have it cause an 'Excuse me?' from bewildered little old ladies. It was unique. And now, apparently, it'd come from her father. 'I reminded him of his dead friend.' The sudden sense of relief flowed over her. That explained it. Her father hadn't run from her; it was the guilt he felt about this other Kevin that'd made him leave.

'I don't think that's it.' Billy stared down at the brim of his hat in his hands. 'It gets worse.' His voice was barely a whisper as he rubbed a cloth on the back of his neck. 'There was a three-year-old Vietnamese girl found down below in a cabin. She drowned.'

Kevyn gasped. 'What was she doing there?'

'Don't know.' Billy stared at the ground. 'Alex swore he was taking her out of Vietnam to safety.'

'And was he?'

'Thing was, there was also eight bags of heroin on board.'

Kevyn closed her eyes and squeezed them tight. 'He was a drug smuggler?'

Billy shook his head. 'Nothing was ever proven. Apparently, there was a long investigation where Alex claimed one of the dead men loaded the drugs. Said he didn't know about them and the dead man couldn't defend himself.' Billy shrugged. 'Navy couldn't prove otherwise but Alex was discharged either way.'

Kevyn couldn't believe what she was hearing.

'I didn't have much contact with him after he came back, but I figured when he left again he'd gone chasin' his ghosts. By the time you came along, I figured you didn't need that kind of haunting, so I kept my mouth shut.'

'Does Grandfather know about any of this? Or Mama?'

Billy shook his head. 'I don't know. Your mama barely speaks to me since I was a friend of Alex's and I could never bring myself to talk your granddaddy about it.' His eyes reflected his apology. 'I thought I was respecting everyone's privacy.'

'It seems like everyone felt the same way about telling me.' Kevyn stared up at *Wander*, wondering if Alex's time in the Caribbean searching for treasure was a cover for more drug running? What other secrets had been kept from her all this time? And what exactly Grandfather's request to see him again was getting her into?

Kevyn had not much of a plan other than to set sail for Puerto Rico and find where the *K Sea* had sunk. Maybe she could locate someone there who knew her father or had seen him after the sinking had occurred. She'd studied the charts, and knew she could bounce down the coast of Georgia and Florida before heading offshore for some overnight passages.

Grandfather had mentioned her father's friend in Fort Lauderdale, so she would start there--with Pete. Lauderdale was four hundred and twenty nautical miles from Savannah and would be a good first run for *Wander* and herself in order to see if they both were up to the long voyage ahead.

Kevyn spent the next few mornings with Billy working on the boat. He insisted she check every piece of equipment on board and demonstrate to him how she would fix everything that could potentially go wrong.

'I'm not letting you leave until I know you'll be safe.'

In the afternoons, she gathered books about pirates and treasure in the Caribbean and was surprised by what she read. What she'd once thought were nothing but fairytales, like Peter Pan or King Arthur, suddenly became true. There really had been a Captain Henry Morgan who sailed throughout the Caribbean, and Kevyn soon found herself agreeing with her mother: all of the history did sound romantic.

'He wasn't just a pirate,' she told her grandfather on her last afternoon in Savannah. 'Captain Morgan was knighted by the King of Britain and made Lieutenant-Governor of Jamaica. The English considered him a hero.'

Grandfather's smile curled upward on one side. 'I bet the Spanish didn't agree. It was their ships he plundered.'

Kevyn thought for a moment. 'I guess it depends on which side of the story you're on as to whether someone is a villain or a hero.'

He sat quiet for a moment and then resumed rocking in his chair. Finally, his eyes twinkled to life. 'And I thought Captain Morgan's biggest claim to fame was having a rum named after him.' He didn't look so frail when he laughed. When he closed his eyes and listened to her stories, the wrinkles seemed to smooth. Maybe they were just melting in the heat, but Kevyn couldn't help but think she should stay right on the porch and never leave. After all, he was the one who'd looked after her and loved her. He was the one who'd stayed for her, and abandoning him seemed wrong; especially if Alex was running drugs instead of searching for treasure. Would Grandfather want him found if that were the case? Did she?

She pushed the thoughts from her mind. She wasn't about to break Grandfather's heart with Billy's stories of Vietnam until she was sure for herself that was what Alex was doing.

'Port Royal grew under Morgan's tenure from the wealth he brought along from his pirate days.' She was starting to sound like she believed he was her ancestor as well. 'Port Royal was home to a lot of pirates, but the whole city sank in an earthquake along with Henry Morgan's grave.'

'So much for checking DNA.' He rocked back and forth in a slow-moving sweep; even the chair seemed lethargic from the heat.

'You don't really think he's related, do you?'

'I wish we had a pirate in the family,' her grandfather chuckled. 'I could've used a bit of gold the years when shrimp were lean.'

The one thing she didn't speak of was the story Billy told her. She wasn't sure if she was keeping her father's heroism of trying to rescue a little girl a secret or hide his illegal smuggling, but Kevyn kept telling herself that with her grandfather's age, he couldn't handle the disappointment of knowing what Alex had done.

Truthfully, neither could she.

Later that afternoon, Kevyn stopped by Brianna's to say goodbye. She lived in a small, one-room apartment in a restored old house in the Historic District of Savannah.

Kevyn took a deep breath as she climbed the brick stairs. Her hand trembled as she gripped the wrought-iron railing not knowing what condition she'd find Brianna on the other side of the wooden door. She did not want a repeat fight.

'So, you're really going?' Brianna bucked the tradition of Southern-hospitality and turned from the door leading Kevyn into the kitchen without a proper greeting.

A quick glance around her mother's apartment revealed no family ties. Where Grandfather still hung a picture of his estranged son in his hallway, Brianna's walls were bare.

Kevyn flinched and turned to her mother.

'I have to go, Mama.' She stood by the kitchen table not bothering to sit down nor being invited to. 'It's about time I met my father, whether you want me to or not.'

Brianna's eyes flashed furious than softened. 'I never meant for this to be our lives.'

Kevyn nodded. 'I know it's been hard on you, Mama.'

Tears shone in Brianna's eyes. She took a deep breath, brushed them away with one hand and reached for her purse on the table. She rummaged around inside and pulled out a picture. She kept her eyes lowered, avoiding Kevyn's gaze as she handed it to her. 'If you do go, I guess you'll need this.'

It was a square Polaroid, wrinkled with well-worn, rounded corners. The quality was grainy but it showed a young man with a short military-style haircut sitting on a piece of gnarled driftwood.

Kevyn stared, fixated on the picture. Her grandfather was right; she did have the same olive skin tone, but the similarities ended there. She definitely looked more like her mother. Kevyn squinted in order to see her father's eyes, but the picture was taken from too far away to know for sure if they were the same color green as hers.

'Is there a picture of him and me together?'

Brianna shook her head. 'You're lucky I still have that one; I should have burned it a long time ago.'

Kevyn's heart jumped in her chest and seemed to settle in her throat. 'Are you alright with this?' She laid a hand on her mother's arm.

Brianna tensed. Neither woman was used to much physical affection. Her smile was sad. 'I should be the one asking you that question,' she said in a small voice as she turned from Kevyn and picked up a dishtowel. She refolded it twice before placing it back in the exact spot she'd grabbed it from.

Kevyn was glad her mother's back was turned while she wiped a tear from her cheek. It was the closest thing they'd had to a tender moment in years. 'I want to know why he left. What made him go?'

Brianna stiffened and whirled back to facing Kevyn. 'You think I made him leave?'

'No, I...' She tried to correct her words but bitterness fired out of Brianna too fast.

'Do you even know how to sail well enough to go find him?' Like a flash, the tenderness was gone.

Kevyn stung like she was slapped all over again. She clenched her fists by her sides. 'I guess we'll find out.' She grabbed the keys to her Jeep off the table and strode out the door with the barest resemblance of a goodbye.

*****

Chapter Three

Six o'clock came early the next morning as Kevyn rolled from her bunk and untangled herself from Athens curled up at her feet. Late Friday, Billy had given the okay to put *Wander* back in the water and her sailboat was now tied to the dock outside ready to go.

'Time for a change of scenery, kiddo.' Kevyn tried to straighten the quilt around the calico's prone position, but gave up when she realized there was no hope of hurrying him. 'What do you say we sail south today?'

Athens raised his head and licked her fingers. The scratch of his tongue felt like the sandpaper she used to smooth the grain of a piece of wood.

'I'll take that as a yes.' Kevyn stacked the books she'd been reading the night before and fastened the fiddle to keep them in place while out at sea. The cabin was small and keeping it organized was nearly impossible, but she went through the motions every day, even if it was just for herself. This time, her fidgeting with the organization of the cabin was to avoid wondering if her mother was right. Could she handle going to sea?

She wasn't sure but she knew it was time to find out.

She threw a fleece sweater over her head and ran a brush through her hair before gathering it into a ponytail and covering it with a ball cap. It was way too early to care about how she looked.

Opening the oak door that separated the two living areas on *Wander*, she walked into the main cabin to start the coffee. As it percolated, she flicked on the VHF radio to listen to the weather. NOAA called for seas of four to six feet offshore, so it wouldn't exactly be smooth sailing. But if she hugged the coast she'd be protected. She had checked *Wander*'s 30-horsepower engine yesterday, and Billy had already given her the okay on everything else, but still she dipped the oil stick and tightened the connections on the batteries just to be sure. Flipping her navigation lights on, Kevyn stepped outside to make sure they were both working and pulled the cover off the mainsail.

Just as she was about to attach the jib, Billy strolled down the dock. 'Thought you might need some help with lines, darlin'.' Years of smoking before he switched to chew had caused the gravel tone in his voice, but his eyes spoke only tenderness.

'Thanks.' Kevyn fired up the engine. 'I'll be back as soon as I can.'

'Fair winds.' Billy dropped the bowline and made his way back to the stern. 'You know who to call if you run into any trouble.'

Kevyn waved goodbye as she backed the boat out of the slip.

It was two hours down the river, which she planned to do under power before she got out into the ocean and raised the sail. She sat on the bench by the wooden tiller and sipped her coffee, watching Billy and the shipyard grow smaller with each passing minute. Clean shafts of light broke over the marshes. Ahead, a pelican flew low over the water, seeming to take the lead so that Kevyn would know the way.

Athens sauntered up the companionway and out of the main cabin, claiming his spot on the cushion beside her. He was more cautious than a boat dog who would be bounding to the bow, panting and happy to ride the chop, enjoying the spray in its face. Athens was a boat cat with indifference. His lackadaisical attitude meant he stayed safely in the cockpit or down below when they traveled. There was little fear of him being washed overboard.

'Just you and me, kid.' Kevyn reached down to scratch behind his ear, glad for the company.

It wasn't long before *Wander* made it to the mouth of the Wilmington River. Kevyn stood, grasping the tiller in her left hand, and steered into the ocean. When she was where she wanted to be, she cut the engine and turned the boat directly into the wind. Pulling hard on the halyard, she raised the main sail and turned the boat slightly in order to catch the wind and immediately begin the first leg of her journey.

The wind gusted stronger than she would have liked and *Wander* quickly picked up speed. It blew hard against her and blasted the hat off her head, sending it into the sea.

The taut sail pushed *Wander* through the water. The bow split the sea like a jig saw, as *Wander* heeled to starboard and flew across the water. 'Yeah!' Kevyn pumped her fists in the air and whooped with excitement. A smile spread across her face as she felt a surge of freedom. The wind whipped through her hair and blew the old Kevyn out of her body, allowing the wild and joyful woman a chance to breathe.

The day broke, creating a brilliant baby blue sky with fluffy white cumulus clouds that signaled a stunning day ahead even if the swells did make it slightly uncomfortable. She could have set the autopilot and relaxed, reading one of the magazines she'd brought, but this was the beginning of her adventure and she wanted to work for it. There would be plenty of days and nights ahead to use the autopilot if she was to sail all the way to Puerto Rico…or further.

She really didn't know how far, or to how many islands her search would take her. Kevyn hoped that when she reached Fort Lauderdale, Pete would have the answers that would steer her in the right direction.

The day passed quickly. Pleased with her progress, Kevyn raised the binoculars to look for boats one more time. Seeing an empty ocean, she headed down into the cabin with Athens following close behind. She grabbed the opener out of the one drawer used for utensils and opened a can of soup, which she dumped into one of the two pots she had on board and set it on the gimbaled stove to heat. She opened a can of tuna for Athens and placed on the floor, as the calico wound around her ankles on his way to the bowl.

'You're easy to please.'

Kevyn scrambled up the two wooden companionway steps and stuck her head out the hatch. She scanned the horizon before retreating back into the cabin to make a sandwich. She spread hummus on a slice of wheat bread and was reaching for a tomato in the vegetable basket when a loud boom resounded throughout the cabin.

The room shuddered and rose up under her feet, knocking her off balance and sending her hips smashing into the stainless steel corner of the stove.

Wander's forward motion slowed to a crawl. The pot flew across the counter and slammed into the bulkhead. Tomato soup sloshed up and out, splattering all over the wall and creating a bad special effect from a horror movie. Kevyn clung to the rail along the stove and tried to regain her balance. 'What the hell?'

Athens hunched his back and hissed. His claws dug into the leather upholstery of the dining banquet.

This time, Kevyn bolted up the stairs and searched the horizon wildly. There was no boat in sight, but it felt like *Wander* had hit a brick wall. 'What happened?'

No one answered.

A gust of wind filled *Wander's* sails as the boat picked up speed.

Out of the corner of her eye Kevyn spotted a round shape, a quarter the size of *Wander's* hull, floating on the surface of the water. It looked like a huge, flat fish head with a ruffled tail. Two fins stuck out like airplane wings on either side and one pitch-black, unblinking eye stared up at her as *Wander* sailed past. Is that what she hit?

As if the prehistoric looking mass had awakened from being stunned, it flipped its flimsy body into a corkscrew and an elongated fin sliced out of the water.

Kevyn stumbled backwards and tripped over the tiller. She fell onto the port cushions as she watched the Jurassic fish submerge and swim away, seemingly unscathed.

Her heart pounded. Her palms were wet. Her throat was dry.

Only eight hours out of Savannah and Kevyn already wondered if she should have left home at all.

Kevyn leaned out over the water to get a better angle on the hull. Salt spray-soaked her t-shirt and splattered her sunglasses. She was unable to see any damage but that did not mean the impact of the immense fish hadn't broken something.

Scanning the horizon, this time looking directly into the sea as well, Kevyn scurried down below to check the bilges. If there was a gash somewhere under the waterline, they would be filling with water.

Everything looked dry so far, but the pressure of *Wander* pounding through the waves could change that at any moment. With an immense amount of trepidation, Kevyn returned to her post by the tiller, curled her knees to her chest and waited to see what would happen next.

It was a long, sleepless night of worry and watching. By the next day, however, Kevyn felt slightly more secure. Her first night at sea had been somewhat of a nightmare but she was still afloat. She may not have slept, alternating between watching for lights and checking the bilges for leakage, but adrenaline and excitement flowed through her veins. If the wind held, she still had another day and a half to get to Fort Lauderdale. She felt better about surviving the first night without any major problems. Maybe the fish hadn't brought damage to *Wander's* structure.

It started out as a beautiful day. The water around her was bluer than Kevyn had ever seen before, matched only by the sky above. Two white terns chased each other overhead, as Athens kept Kevyn entertained. He crouched beside her, completely transfixed by the birds flying circles above them. Like a leopard stalking his prey, his head followed their every move.

'They're forty feet in the air. What do you think you're going to do?' She leaned forward and grabbed the jib halyard to raise the sail. Athens barely noticed the movement, as if keeping an ever watchful eye on a dinner he was praying would fall to the deck.

She pulled at the line but it didn't budge. She tried wrapping the halyard around the winch but got nowhere. There wasn't even any give in the line.

'Pffft,' Kevyn blew a deep breath out. She lifted her hand to her brow to shade her eyes and squinted up at the top of the mast. The bright sunlight blinded her, not allowing her to focus in order to identify the problem. The halyard must have tangled somewhere in the rigging.

Kevyn checked for nearby traffic and then set the autopilot. Hoisting herself up on to the cabin top, she headed to the mast, keeping her weight low for balance. With one hand she held the boom; the other held on to the boat for support. The day may have been bright and new, but the wind was still strong and the seas rough enough to keep her cautious. She shifted her weight to her heels and looked up to the top of the mast where the head stay was attached. The change in perception made her dizzy and she lost her balance and veered backwards. As the rubber soles of her Sperry's slid on the wet surface, she skidded into a crooked full split on top of the foredeck. Both hands slammed down on the top of the cabin in order to stop the slide. Every muscle in her body tensed as she clung to the topside. It suddenly felt like she was playing *Twister* with *Wander* acting as the game board.

Reaching back up to the mast to straighten herself, Kevyn felt *Wander* lift out of the water. The wind had picked up. With her right hand she jiggled the jib halyard and watched it clank and slap against the steel post. She still couldn't tell where it'd tangled or what had been the problem, but it now felt like it was free and loose all the way up to the top of the mast.

She skidded back into the cockpit on her bottom and turned *Wander* into the eye of the wind. Pulling on the halyard, the sail rose unencumbered, as she tugged hand over hand until the luff of the jib became smooth and taut along the leading edge. *Slap, slap, slap* – the material cracked in the wind. Kevyn secured the halyard and sank back down on her bench before turning *Wander* away from the wind and easing the leeward jib sheet. With the increased sail area, the boat then flew across the water.

'It wasn't pretty, Athens, but the jib is up.' She smiled, reaching down and scratching behind his ears. 'I can do this.'

Athens lifted his head but didn't look as if he cared one iota about how many sails were up. And Kevyn sailed on, wondering who would care—or even know—if she *did* get into trouble out here in the vast emptiness of the ocean.

By afternoon the skies were no longer clear. Since lunchtime the weather had gotten progressively worse, and now low hanging clouds threatened to rain. Throughout the afternoon the howling winds had increased in velocity. Kevyn shifted in her seat, scanning the horizon for an indication of what Neptune had planned for her future.

She knew she had to lower the jib and stow it, but leaving the cockpit and going back to the bow was not something she looked forward to. Since the weather had turned and she was alone, she decided to put on her safety harness and clip in to the jack lines before going forward again. At least if she stumbled this time, she would still be tethered to the boat.

She released the halyard and scooted along the top deck to gather the material. The weather deteriorated rapidly as she stuffed the sail into its bag. With only one hand to work with, it was slow and awkward. Her earlier mishap had scared her, so she didn't dare let go of the boat.

As she finished cinching the sail bag, the rain began. Water hurled from the sky; the main sail flapped madly as the wind whipped in from a new direction signaling the onslaught of the storm. The spray off the crest was blinding and all Kevyn could taste was the salt on her lips.

She retreated to the cockpit, dragging the bag behind her. She didn't want to risk flooding the forward v-berth by opening the forward hatch to stow the sail in its proper place.

Soon waves filled the cockpit, soaking every inch of her skin. Heading below, Kevyn put on her foul-weather gear and checked the bilges one more time. But the increased slamming of the hull through the water hadn't created any problems…yet.

Athens cowered in the corner of her bunk; his hair stood straight on end, alert to danger. He wasn't used to being at sea in a storm any more than she was. 'You better stay down here,' she advised.

His claws dug into her comforter anchoring him in place as she headed back outside.

Wander pitched at an unnatural angle, unaccustomed to the turbulent ocean thrashing around her. Dark grey clouds blocked the horizon, and steel-colored waves formed much too close together. The wind picked up to a face-stinging force as Kevyn struggled with the sheets to maintain proper sail trim.

The skies darkened to an ominous shade of grey. The front was moving fast, too fast to run for cover inland. Kevyn's only choice was to ride it out. She reefed the main sail to reduce the amount of mainsail she had up and once again clipped herself in to the harness for safety. Most of all, she didn't want someone to be obligated to come looking for her, too.

She brought her hand up and rubbed the St. Christopher medal pinned to her jacket. Years before she'd found it in the shed at her grandfather's, and ever since that day she'd never left the dock without the patron saint for mariners protecting her.

'Keep me safe,' she said into the wind.

Wander rode the steep waves skyward just to drop, bow first, off the face. Up and down she rode through the chop, like a rollercoaster without the predetermined route of the track. The violent sea sent huge sheets of water up and over the cockpit as the hard rain lashed her face. She felt small and powerless, unsure whether she should stay on deck or take cover below.

Every muscle in her body tensed. Her heart seemed to beat a heavy metal song inside her chest as the adrenalin raced through her veins. Should she have left the jib up for stability, or was she right to have brought it down? She wasn't sure.

Batches of white foam washed over the decks while a rush of water swooshed down the side. The main sail snapped in the increasing winds. Kevyn knew she had to lower it to avoid ripping the material, so she reached forward and released the line. It didn't budge. She pulled harder but it, too, was jammed.

'Ugh!' She slammed her hands down on her thighs and screamed in frustration, 'Not again!'

She took a deep breath and fought her way to the mast, crouching low along the deck. Heaving herself up to a standing position, both arms hugging the mast, she held the boom and shook the main halyard. The sail finally untangled and she pulled it down, sending buckets of water that'd gathered in the slack canvas down upon her head. It seemed to take three times as long to flake the sail under the weight of the water. And just as she was securing the sail ties around the boom, *Wander's* bow rode up the face of a larger wave and smashed down with a shudder. A river of water barreled over the topside, catching Kevyn's feet and pulling them out from under her. Her legs gave way and her body twisted as she crashed forward. A loud *thunk-thunk* sounded through the driving rain as she smashed her head, first on the boom and again on the cockpit sole.

'Ow!' She reached up and placed her fingers on the side of her temple. Pain shot through her forehead, as balls of light burned bright, blurring her vision. She pulled her hand in front of her eyes to search for blood, but the pelting rain made it hard to focus.

She tried to get up but her head felt light. *Wander* seemed to be spinning from far more than just the angry waves. She slumped back down in the corner and braced herself against the side as another surge of water poured over her.

Shutting her eyes in the darkness, Kevyn concentrated on holding herself in place. *This,* she thought, *is no way to end my first voyage.*

She had no business being on the water when it was like this. A million more things could go wrong between here and the Caribbean, and suddenly Kevyn wondered if this trip was perhaps cursed from the start.

Her right hand was wrapped around the sail and held aloft like a Raggedy Ann doll. She pulled herself up and hugged the boom as yet another wave sideswiped her. She looked to the sea to time her move, and as soon as the next wave hit she opened the hatch to the relative safety of her cabin. Quickly she secured the hatch so a waterfall would not follow her inside. *Proper watch be damned!*

Stripping off her wet weather gear, Kevyn wrapped herself in a sleeping bag. She wedged her body into the corner of her bunk and snuggled up with Athens.

He hissed and nipped at her hand as a sharp crack of thunder exploded outside. Lightning lit up the cabin through the porthole and the rain hammered down, echoing like tribal drums right before the sacrifice was made.

Athens shook with fear. Kevyn did the same. She anchored herself with her feet, bracing her body so she would not slide around, and began her second long night of riding out the storm.

There wasn't any sleep for Kevyn that night. She switched positions, from being clamped into her bunk to gripping the outside hatch of the cabin while she scanned the turbulent sea for lights from any nearby boats. The last thing she wanted was a collision in the middle of the night. Her grandfather had already answered a call about one boat sinking and she'd be damned if he would receive another.

The clear skies of morning and the calm water were a stark contrast to the previous night's weather. At some point in the early hours the waves had subsided and the winds had died down.

Kevyn still shook as she surveyed the boat for damage. She untied the sail and inspected the canvas for tears. The sheets needed untangling and she picked up the pile of papers that'd scattered with the jerking of the boat. She switched on the VHF radio to check the weather for the coming day and contemplated her position on the chart. She was just north of Palm Beach and would make Fort Lauderdale, if Poseidon cooperated, by late afternoon.

She navigated *Wander* closer to the shoreline. Even with the calming seas of a new day, she felt far safer being close to land. And the rising sun reflecting off the glass of the multileveled hotels and condos lining the beach like glitter brought her a sense of relief. She was no longer in the middle of the ocean alone. She could now at least see land.

She was still too far out to sea to pick up a cell signal in order to call and say she was all right, but there was no one to tell anyway. She didn't want to worry her grandfather and she certainly didn't want to tell to her mother she *had* run into trouble on the water. She'd handled everything that had been thrown at her but her voyage was far from over and there were many more miles of possible problems to prove her mother's disbelief in her abilities correct.

'Athens, I just want you to know that I'm alright.' She reached down and rubbed behind his ears. 'How about you? You all right? I promise I'll try not to put you through that again.' She pulled out another tin of tuna and offered it as an apology for taking him into the storm.

His quick response to the dish led Kevyn to believe that he'd already gotten over his fright and had forgotten all about it. She only wished it was that easy for her.

'What do you say we spend a few days on dry land before attempting another crazy night like that again?'

By afternoon, four red and white stacks on the skyline appeared in Kevyn's binoculars, signaling the approach to Port Everglades. She dropped her sails once again and turned on the motor. Billy had warned that the Intracoastal Waterway in Fort Lauderdale was a tricky thing to maneuver; there were bridges to sail under and sand bars to run aground on, so Kevyn made sure to focus.

On top of that, heavy traffic zoomed in and around the river; many of the drivers she'd meet would have been drinking all day in the hot sun. Lauderdale was famous for its party atmosphere. Spring break or not, it had an allure that invited a crazy mix of people, and Kevyn didn't trust herself, or others, enough to sail haphazardly; she wanted the increased control that the motor provided.

Wander didn't produce a wake as they cruised the channel. The only sign they'd just passed was the clear sheen of water where the boat's hull blocked the wind from producing ripples on the water. It was calming. Kevyn sighed with relief that the first leg of her voyage was over. Feeling the tension and anxiety drain from her body, the aching muscles took over. She hadn't realized how physically exhausting sailing for long stretches could be.

Ahead, the Seventeenth Street Bridge spanned the skyline stretching from one side of the river to the other. Concrete posts rose out of the water to support the bridge above. Kevyn had checked the waterway guide and knew there was plenty of room to transit the bridge but still the perspective from where she stood looked tight. She lined *Wander* up to head down the middle of the passageway and instinctively looked up as she approached to make sure her mast cleared.

There was a slight current pulling *Wander* off course and Kevyn refocused on the boat's path, correcting it with her steering. She motored straight ahead, alternating her attention from the course to the top of the mast and the approaching bridge. The sky above was blue, the hard grey concrete rough and unforgiving. She held her breath as the sky disappeared. And when she cleared the bridge as the guide had said she would, Kevyn heaved a sigh of relief.

She was halfway through the pillars under the bridge when a slick black speedboat with red lightning bolts stenciled on the side zoomed into the channel ahead, ignoring the 'No Wake Zone' sign. Loud music thumped out of its speakers and vibrated over the water. The driver twisted in his seat and lowered his mirrored glasses to watch his two bikini-clad passengers behind him shake and grind to the beat.

Kevyn edged *Wander* farther starboard to give them room to pass, but the man barely slowed down or even turned his attention from the girls. He wasn't looking where he was going and was pointing straight at her. 'Hey!' Kevyn shouted, hoping he could hear her over the hideous music.

The man turned his attention back to where he was headed and twirled the steering wheel to the right with one hand, while giving her the finger with the other.

'Nice,' Kevyn muttered under her breath.

The boat passed on her port side. Its speed created a wake that rocked *Wander* and pushed her even closer to the starboard pilings. Still shaken from last night's storm, Kevyn now feared a collision with the bridge instead of the speedboat and pulled hard on the tiller to readjust direction. *Wander* over-corrected by turning sharply and heading for the outside pilings.

Kevyn fought the panic rising in her. She was now lined up to clip the far edge of the concrete on the wrong side of the channel. Adrenaline rushed back through her veins as she pushed in the opposite direction to avoid collision. If there were someone behind her they would have thought she was drunk, weaving back and forth over the invisible line through the center of the bridge.

The storm may be over, but she wasn't out of danger yet.

*****

Chapter Four

Kevyn pushed the tiller as far as it would go and *Wander* passed the concrete blocks of the bridge and wooden rub-rails within inches of an accident. She wiped loose tendrils of hair from her face and blew out a deep breath. She would be glad when she was once again tied to a dock. Her hands shook as she steered *Wander* to the right of the forked waterway once again, and tried to ignore the laughing she swore she could hear coming from the speedboat behind her.

Awe filled her as she passed by the houses on her way to the marina. Elegant one-story ranch houses sprawled out on perfectly manicured lawns lay on either side of the waterway, interspersed with two-story mansions boasting marble columns and French glass doors. Kevyn thought they looked more like the Palace of Versailles than actual homes. Every property she passed was grander and more elaborate than the last, each with a private yacht or colorful speedboat parked at the dock.

On one property, a woman in a barely-there black and gold, animal-print bikini lounged on a white overstuffed sofa by a turquoise-tiled infinity pool. A glass of champagne sat on a marble table beside her; the bottle rested in a sterling silver bucket to her right. She lowered her dark Jackie O' sunglasses and watched Kevyn sail past with a look of sheer boredom on her face.

Kevyn laughed. After all, compared to the yacht parked at her dock, *Wander* probably looked like a poor relative who had no right to sully the waters of wealth. But who the hell drank champagne poolside in the middle of the day? *No one in Georgia*, Kevyn thought. *That's for sure.*

She picked up the handset again and hailed the marina to confirm her dockage. Knowing she was only going to spend a few nights here, she splurged to get dockage in the central location of Bahia Mar. It was close to the beach and not far from the dive shop Pete owned. At six dollars a foot it was expensive, but at this point, all Kevyn wanted was to be tied up safely no matter what it cost.

The marina manager gave her *Wander's* slip assignment and told her there would be a dockhand waiting there to help. Sure enough, a man in white shorts and polo uniform stood on the pier halfway down the long dock as she approached. Forward of the dockhand was a shiny white yacht with three decks towering above sea level. Behind him sat another shiny white yacht with a helicopter resting on the bow. Kevyn estimated she had to squeeze *Wander* between sixty million dollars worth of boats.

She slowed *Wander's* speed and hopped up on the foredeck.

Reaching down, she swung two fenders over the starboard side and jumped back into the cockpit to set two more fenders along the back edge of the hull. Then, grabbing a hold of the tiller, she checked behind her for traffic. With none in sight, she slowly lined up her approach and maneuvered *Wander* alongside the dock, slipping between the obvious signs of wealth.

She threw the dockhand the bowline and hurried back to repeat the process with the stern.

'Nice docking,' the kid said. 'We don't usually put sailboats here among the yachts, but it was our only open slip. I'd never hear the end of it, if it didn't go well.'

Kevyn smiled. She may not be an ocean-crossing veteran, but she'd docked *Wander* a thousand times before.

Finally she felt like she could breathe again. This is what *Wander* was used to, being tied to a dock. For the past ten years she'd been used more as an apartment than an actual sailboat. Kevyn thought about all that had happened since she left Georgia a few days ago. She'd been anxious, and at times, terrified, but now, looking back, she'd been exhilarated, too. The sailing was exciting, the adventure unknown. A flame had lit inside her. She hadn't felt this alive in a long time. It wasn't smooth sailing but she'd handled it.

Raw energy pumped through Kevyn. Whether it was nerves or excitement she did not know. But, she didn't want to sit around waiting to see what would happen next. With light still left in the day she hooked up a hose on the dock and began washing down *Wander*. The storm had left its mark in every tight little corner, and she didn't want the corrosive salt water doing any damage.

It felt good to stretch and move. She wasn't used to being still for so long. Bending forward to reach the lower part of the boat's hull, she exposed her legs, and it took no time at all before the dockhand reappeared to offer his help.

'I don't need help washing down, but I could use directions to the nearest bar.' She coiled the hose at her feet.

'Depends on what you're after.' The twenty-something, dark-haired dockhand grabbed the hose from her. His biceps flexed as he curled it up to his shoulder. 'The Elbo Room is just around the corner on the beach. It's a little raunchy, but famous for spring breakers and anyone trying to find some action.' His smile revealed the dimples of youth. 'Not a good place for a woman alone...I'd be happy to go with you.'

Kevyn laughed and politely declined.

'My favorite spot,' he continued undeterred, 'is The Treasure Trove. It's just a block away. It's more of an old-timers bar. Open atmosphere, cold beer – you'll find more fishermen and divers in there than college kids.' He tried to sound authoritative, as if he was far removed from those young impetuous students.

'Sounds perfect. Thanks.' Kevyn went below to give herself a quick wash as well. Running a brush through her hair, she selected a clean T-shirt to wear. Surveying her two tiny drawers she realized she'd better use the marina's laundry before she left for the islands. She didn't have much with her, and it might be the last chance for a proper cleaning before she reverted to hand washing and sea breezes in order to dry.

She looked in the tiny mirror hanging above her sink. Her skin had already darkened another shade with the past few days in the sun.

'I'll be back in a while,' she said, running her hand over Athens' back and giving his tail a gentle pull as she opened the companionway to step outside. He raised his sleepy head an inch. The heel of the boat combined with the storm had made it hard for him to get his normal twenty hours of sleep a day, so he was making up for it.

Kevyn stuck her head back into the cabin. 'Don't wait up.'

The night air was still warm, but a moist ocean breeze blew as Kevyn made her way out of the parking lot to The Treasure Trove. The soft-packed sand beach lay just across the A1A highway.

It was twilight, yet the street was full of bumper-to-bumper, slow-moving traffic. A souped-up black muscle car cruised past, blaring heart-thumping bass through its open windows. Next came a convertible, where three young blondes bounced to the stereo's beat behind a driver wearing a flashy gold watch and designer sunglasses despite the darkening sky. Maseratis, Ferraris, Porsches, and BMWs all cruised by in a line of luxury. Kevyn had never seen so many exotic sports cars in her quiet Georgian life. Florida may only be a state away but it was a whole different world here.

The bar was set back from the strip. Windows opened to the street and strains of the Allman Brothers drifted out, along with the stale smell of beer and fried fish. It felt more like home than the opulence she had witnessed since sailing into the Lauderdale cut.

Taking a seat at the bar, Kevyn ordered a bottle of Corona.

'Just get in?' the bartender asked.

She nodded. 'How'd you know?'

'Most of our customers are either regulars or come in from the boats. I haven't seen you in here before, so I figure you're new in town.' He drew a draft as he spoke, and winked. 'Besides, I saw you on the dock a few hours ago.'

'Small world.'

'Even smaller town. Working here you get to see everybody pass by these windows.'

He waited for the foam to subside before topping off the pint. 'We get bodybuilders from next door, chicks in bikinis from the beach, Harley riders, and divers from the operation across the street.' He nodded to the guys in dive t-shirts sitting at the table by the window. The one facing Kevyn read, *Divers Like to Go Down*.

The bartender delivered the draft and returned to his position behind the bar. 'In the past five years, I've seen it all.'

'You remember all your regulars?' Kevyn asked.

'Most are hard to forget. Our famous regular was Mel Fisher; you're sitting in his chair. He used to come in here all the time while he was hunting the *Atocha*. Talked nothing but treasure for years. One day he hit the mother lode and found the wreck off the Marquesas. Guy's a legend around here.'

'I'm actually looking for another treasure hunter, one who's far less famous.' Kevyn slid the picture her mother gave her across the bar. 'That was taken thirty years ago.'

He studied the picture for a few seconds then shook his head. 'Hard to tell. That could be anyone now. Who you need to talk to is Sam Strider over at Deadman's Chest. He buys anything those guys pull up, and knows everyone in the game around here.' He handed her back the picture. 'Guy's a walking encyclopedia on pirate history.'

'Thanks.' Kevyn returned the photo to her pocket as the bartender went back to wiping down tables.

The place had emptied out; the only man left was hunched over the far end of the bar, guarding his beer with a prison elbow stance. He looked up at Kevyn with shifty eyes and smiled a lecherous grin.

She tried to ignore him and finish her beer as quickly as possible.

'I'll buy your next one, sweetheart.' The man's voice sent a shiver down Kevyn's back. He was bald on top with a long fringe pulled back in a ponytail – a fifty-year-old's attempt at a mullet. Why did she always attract the creeps?

'No, thanks. I'm on my way out.'

'Aw, it's early. Where's a pretty little thing like you going to?' His speech slurred.

'Give it a rest, Lemon.' The bartender returned. 'No scaring away my customers.'

'Just askin'. No need to worry. I ain't gonna bite.' Lemon smiled like a lizard. 'Unless she asks me to.'

Kevyn shivered again. 'Probably not.' Reaching into her jeans, Kevyn searched for a ten to throw on the bar.

'Hey, no need to run away,' Lemon sneered. 'I told you I ain't gonna bite.'

'Don't worry about Lemon. He's just leaving.' The bartender fixed the man with a hard stare. 'Aren't you, Lemon?'

'Yeah, yeah…I know. You 'bout to cut me off anyway. I seen this before.' Lemon tilted his head back and finished his beer, slamming the bottle back on the bar. Pushing the stool aside, he weaved past Kevyn and tried to whisper in her ear, 'I'll see you around, sweetheart.' He stumbled out the door and down the street.

'Nice regulars you got.' Kevyn popped the wedge of lime into the neck of the bottle the bartender had just placed in front of her.

'Lemon's not so bad. He used to own a dive shop down the street, but, like many 'round here, he invested in some dive boat that never showed up and lost everything. Not sure if that's what started the drinking, or the drinking drove away the boat, but he's been in here ever since.' The bartender shrugged. 'I cut him off earlier and earlier these days, but he still keeps coming back.'

'Why's he called Lemon?' Kevyn wasn't really interested, but she couldn't think of any other conversation.

'After a lemon shark. He's got mean yellow eyes and ragged teeth. I'd steer clear if I were you.'

'Good advice for sharks of *all* kinds.' Kevyn held the bottle of Corona up in salute. 'Thanks for the information. I'll go see Sam tomorrow.'

Kevyn walked back to *Wander* and fell into her bunk. Exhausted didn't begin to describe how she felt after the long days and nights at sea. Even her eyes ached, and her limbs weighed heavy. She didn't have the energy to wash her face or brush her teeth, so she curled up in the tight space around Athens.

The moment she shut her eyes, she saw waves crashing over the deck and flooding the cockpit of *Wander*. She bolted upright, her heart in her throat, wide-awake, as the storm replayed in her mind. Maybe she wasn't as comfortable with this new adventure as her earlier energy surge had made her feel. She could have died on the ocean alone with no one to search for her.

Pushing back the comforter, knowing there would be no sleep coming anytime soon, she walked into the main cabin, flicked on the overhead light and poured herself a glass of sangiovese.

At the table, she pulled out a notebook. The first page had a chart with Alex's name dead center. Underneath her father's name, she had jotted a few notes.

Alex Morgan:
-K SEA sunk off Puerto Rico
-chasing treasure -???

Pete Daniels' name was listed on the right; Lauderdale dive shop was all that was written under his name. Kevyn added Sam Strider to the left with a notation of treasure expert. Looking at all the white on the page, Kevyn realized she had very little to go on. She shut the book and stared at the chart of the Caribbean laid out in front of her. There were a whole lot of islands for a man who didn't want to be found to hide on, and she had no idea where to start.

The next morning was even brighter. Kevyn woke early for a run along the beach and immediately noticed that the scene had changed significantly from the night before. Gone were the short skirts and low-cut tops. Gone were the cars cruising in circles. Gone was the loud music and party-going crowd. In their place was a group of sixty-year-old men gathered at an outdoor patio for coffee. Two men with bodybuilder physiques jogged past Kevyn with a white poodle on a pink leash wearing a diamond collar struggling to keep up. Along the beach a tractor raked the sand creating the picture-perfect ocean view.

She jogged along the water's edge for a few miles before her mind went back to the men and their early morning coffees. They reminded her of her grandfather. Missing home, she looped back and crossed the street to St. Barts to grab a non-fat latte. Smiling, she walked over to the group of men.

'Hi, anyone know where I can find Deadman's Chest or The Dive Tank?'

'Deadman's is a few blocks north on the left-hand side; you can't miss it.' The man who spoke wore checkered golf pants and a wool sweater. Even though this early in the morning the temperature was already well above seventy.

'The Dive Tank is the stand-alone building between the swimming pool and Las Olas Boulevard.' The second man, although also wearing a sweater, had braved shorts with knee-high black socks to cover his legs. 'You just missed Pete.' He turned to the group. 'He's in here every morning with us. Always has a story to tell about a tourist mistaking a grouper for a shark or some such thing.'

They all laughed; two began to cough with the exertion.

'Pete Daniels is actually who I'm looking for.'

'He was on his way to open the shop. Should be there by now.' The third man wore similar golf attire and a straw hat. None of them looked strong enough to swing a club, let alone walk nine holes of a course.

'Thanks. Enjoy your game.' Kevyn lowered her sunglasses. Still, she squinted as she walked back into the fierce sun. The glare seemed to intensify off the white sand.

Walking the two blocks to The Dive Tank, Kevyn thought about what she would say when she met Pete face to face. It seemed ridiculous she only had a thirty-year-old photo to show him. How exactly was she supposed to explain that? *I'm looking for my daddy and he might look something like this?* It all sounded so silly.

A bell chimed as she walked in the front door.

A gaunt man with a skeletal face materialized behind the counter. 'Mornin'.' His grey hair was cut short and neat. His leathery skin hung from his bones, and he had the grizzled look of a man who had spent his life out on the water.

Kevyn smiled politely, but wasn't ready to embarrass herself quite yet by asking about her father, so she wandered over to the mask and fins on display. Picking up a mask, she turned it over in her hands trying to summon the courage to begin her hunt. This, Pete Daniels, had known Alex. They'd been friends. Therefore, he should have stories about her father and know exactly what he was like. Absentmindedly, she picked up another mask.

'Those Mares masks are top of the line. They have great visibility and a good seal. Won't let any water in, as long as your hair is out of the way.' Pete had come up behind her while she'd been thinking. He walked with a slight limp, but other than that he was in great shape for his age.

He must be the baby of the coffee group, Kevyn thought.

'I can give you a good deal on that particular mask you're holding if you get a pair of fins, as well.' He leaned in front of her and picked a black pair off the shelf. 'What are you, an eight?'

'Eight and a half,' Kevyn replied.

'Try these on.'

Kevyn sat down on a bench and kicked off her sandals, stalling for time. She wiggled her foot into the equipment; it was tight and took some prying to stretch the rubber around her heel. She held out her leg to examine the foreign extension.

'Tight is good.' Pete held the second fin out to her. 'You don't want to slip out of them in the water.'

'I need a wetsuit, too.' This delay was going to cost her a fortune.

Kevyn maneuvered her other foot into the rubber and stood up. She tried lifting her feet to walk, but it came out more like a shuffle. She instantly felt like a penguin.

'You'll get used to them.' Pete held out his hand to steady her. 'You gonna dive around here?'

'I'm headed down to the Caribbean.' Kevyn sat back down so she wouldn't embarrass herself.

Pete hesitated, quietly studying her face. Helping her take off the fins, he turned and grabbed a black and teal full-length suit from a rack. 'You ever dive before?'

'A little. Nothing serious. Not much diving in Savannah.' Kevyn felt more confident talking when Pete's back was turned. She shut her eyes and took a deep breath. 'Actually, I'm on more of a search than a dive trip. My name is Kevyn Morgan.' She opened her eyes to see Pete's reaction. 'I'm looking for my father... Alex.' Pete didn't flinch.

'I know.' He handed her a pair of gloves. 'I knew it was you.'

Kevyn sat, stunned. 'How? Have we met?' She thought back to everyone she'd met at her grandfather's house over the years, and she was pretty sure she would have remembered this man.

'No, but you look just like your mama. It's hard to miss.' Pete's voice grew soft. 'Anyway, James called last week to tell me you might come down.' He hobbled over to the counter.

'You know mama, too?' Kevyn felt her face heat where the slap had made contact.

Pete nodded. 'I get back to Savannah sometimes and I stop in on Brianna every now and then.'

'I didn't know that.'

'I owe it to your daddy. See, him and me came down here in an old shrimp boat he'd bought. Just two sixteen-year-old kids who knew nothing 'bout nothing.' The corner of Pete's mouth turned up in a nostalgic smile. 'That thing had more rust on it than paint, more holes than welds. I spent the first three days running up the stairs bailing water 'cause the bilge pumps didn't keep up.'

'You made it, though.' Kevyn thought it sounded adventurous until she remembered her trip. Adventure and terror must go hand-in-hand, she thought. But, maybe at sixteen they were more experienced sailors than she was at thirty. Maybe they didn't mind the terror.

Pete leaned down and thumped his fist against his thigh. 'Yeah, but my bum knee sure hurt like hell. I never told Alex this, but I sure was glad to make shore.'

'I know how you feel.'

'We were here 'bout six months before Alex wanted to head south again. But, I just couldn't do it.' Pete rubbed his leg as if he could massage away his disappointment. 'I stayed and he went on his own.'

'You didn't go to Vietnam?' Kevyn tried to put the story Billy told her together with Pete's description of their voyage south.

37

'Nah, knee wouldn't let me do that.' Pete lowered his eyes and stared at the floor. 'Couldn't pass the physical.'

'Do you know what happened to him over there?' With each new piece of information about her father, Kevyn felt like she was stripping away layers of paint on an old headboard. The only problem was she wasn't sure if she'd find strong and straight grains underneath or a rotted piece of wood when all was said and done.

Pete shook his head. 'Your daddy came back here after 'Nam and we headed to Savannah. This time in my old truck. We lived with your granny and granddaddy until Alex met your mama, but he never said much 'bout his time over there.'

If the story Billy told was true, she couldn't imagine them all sitting around the dining room table discussing transporting heroin or a little girl's drowning. Where was he planning on taking her? How did he avoid military jail time? There was a lot she or her grandfather didn't know about Alex's travels. 'Did Grandfather tell you about the *K Sea*?'

Pete nodded. 'I told him then that I didn't know much. Last time I saw your daddy was probably two years ago when he blew into town to sell some pottery.'

'Pottery?' She was surprised Alex was involved with something so crafty and homemaking as that. Was it just a front for what he was really shipping into the States?

'Not the Martha Stewart kind.' Pete's laugh was gruff. 'Stuff he brought up from the ocean floor.'

Kevyn mulled it over. That made more sense and fit into the evolving story she was learning of her father's life. 'Who'd he sell it to?'

'Usually he sells direct to Deadman's. Sam buys most of his stuff here in Lauderdale. I think he's used Jimmy down in Key West before, and there's a guy in St. Thomas that buys some, but here I think it's just the Chest." Pete placed the fins and mask in a mesh bag. 'Alex comes in here and buys his equipment. He hangs out here with us for a few days and then leaves town without a word of where he's going.'

'Sounds familiar.' There was acid tone to Kevyn's voice.

Pete put down the bag, reached over the counter and grabbed her hand. 'You've got every right to be mad. Hell, I ain't saying Alex is an angel, but he's got his reasons for what he did.'

Kevyn snatched her hand from Pete's grasp. How did everyone know about her father but her? Pete seemed to know he'd run out on her, so who else did? They all must be having a good laugh at how silly she was for not knowing.

'Yeah, well he didn't think they were important enough to tell anybody,' she snapped. 'He never bothered to explain his reasons to me.'

Pete looked down at the counter. 'You're right, and it ain't none of my business.'

Kevyn wiped the back of her hand across her cheek and straightened her spine. Outbursts weren't going to get her anywhere. 'Do you have any idea where he might be?'

'Last time he was here he was all fired up about some wreck. Said it would blow the Fisher boat out of the water. He was here looking for backers to stake a claim. He was all secretive about the location, but he was telling grandiose stories about what he could bring up.' Pete chuckled. 'Alex always was one for adventure but he's real good at exaggerating, and I didn't take his stories too seriously. He was here maybe a week, in the store every day talking about this new wreck. Then one day he just didn't show up.'

'He vanished again.' The bitterness crept back into Kevyn's voice.

Pete ignored it. 'The guy you should talk to is Sam Strider at Deadman's. He may have heard from him after he went south. My guess is he'd need to keep selling stuff in order to finance his operation.'

'He's next on my list.' Something struck Kevyn as being off. 'How's he looking for treasure if he isn't on the *K Sea*?'

'Guess he found another boat. As I said, he was still all talk when he was in here. He could have found a backer and another boat and just sailed on to anywhere. Sorry, I'm not much help.' Pete fiddled with the tubes of sunscreen on the counter. 'I've known Alex a long time. He's a good guy, your father, when he's not off running after something. Even then he has an energy 'bout him that you can't help but fall for his stories and tales.' Pete paused, lost in his memories. 'I'd like to help you find him, but I haven't heard much.'

'Thanks, Pete.' Kevyn smiled, trying to make up for how she had behaved earlier. It wasn't this man's fault her father had left her and her mother alone. 'What do I owe you?'

'On the house.' Pete handed her the dive bag full of gear. 'As I said, I owe Alex.' He grabbed her hand again. 'I figure, least I can do is outfit his daughter so she can go find him.'

On impulse, Kevyn leaned over the counter and kissed Pete on the cheek. Stubble from the day before scratched at her skin. 'I'll let you know what I find.'

Kevyn left the store feeling better than when she'd entered – not as foolish about her search. She still had no idea where to start looking, but at least Pete hadn't told any more stories of smuggling or drowning.

*****

Chapter Five

Deadman's Chest was easy to find. It seemed that everything Kevyn needed was located just blocks from the marina.

The blinding sun glared overhead as she entered the shop. Once inside, she pushed her sunglasses to the top of her head, pinning her hair back, and squinted to adjust to the change in light.

The shop was small. A pitted anchor lay on its side by the door and sun-bleached wooden bookshelves lined the walls. A sword that looked like it was used once upon a time for dueling was mounted on the far wall over a glass display case.

A blond man who Kevyn assumed was Sam Strider stood behind that display case. Beside him hung a framed ancient map of the Caribbean lined with a myriad of drawings – from a cloud blowing the north wind to a sea serpent swimming in the southwest corner. The words, 'Here Lies Monsters', were scripted in the corner.

'Morning.' His smile produced sun-streaked crevices around his blue eyes, and his shaggy hair waved naturally off his face. He looked relaxed and comfortable; a state Kevyn never felt.

Once again, Kevyn didn't know how to start this conversation. Why did she feel so nervous asking about her father? She ran a finger over the glass display and stared down at the array of gold and silver coins that looked just like the one her grandfather had given her.

The man picked up two and laid them on the counter. 'These coins are from 1679. They were found off the coast of Ecuador at a wreck site of a South Sea Armada called the *Santa Maria De La Consolacion*.' He held out a coin for Kevyn to look at; his fingers brushed hers. 'The ship was running from six different pirate ships when it struck a reef and began to sink off the shore of Isla de Muerto.'

'Isla de Muerto?' It sounded familiar but Kevyn couldn't place it.

His smile turned mysterious as the dimple in his chin deepened. 'The Island of the Dead.'

She looked down at the coin in her hand. 'Are they real?'

'You bet they are.' He placed the treasure back into the display. 'I only stock authentic artifacts in this store.'

'This is your store?'

'Sam Strider,' he said, holding out his hand. 'Owner, buyer and part-time counter boy.'

The warm grip held her hand a moment longer than in a normal introduction, and Kevyn's stomach flipped. She felt herself flush and looked away, cursing herself for acting silly over a good-looking man. What was she, *twelve?*

Sam cleared his throat and rearranged the coins in the display. 'You haven't been in before?'

'No. I just got to town last night. Sailed down from Savannah before heading off for the islands.'

'Big trip. How long are you in Lauderdale?'

'Just a few days. I need to fix a few things on the boat and talk to some people before I journey south. You're actually one of the people I need to talk to.'

'Well, you got me.' When Sam smiled his cornfield-blue eyes seemed to dance like the waves around *Wander*.

'Pete, at The Dive Tank, said you've purchased treasure in the past from a man named Alex Morgan.'

Sam's eyes immediately darkened to storm-filled seas. 'Yes.' He snapped the coin case shut and slammed a stack of papers onto the counter.

'I'm trying to find him.' Kevyn didn't know what had changed, but Sam was not the same happy man he was when she'd walked in.

'Alex hasn't been in here lately.' He turned his back and grabbed what looked like an old rum bottle. He lifted it to his lips and blew the dust from its neck before using the corner of his shirt to wipe it down.

'Pete says he was in town a couple of years ago.' Kevyn couldn't think of the right questions to ask. She wasn't a detective, after all. Nor did she have the probing personality of a reporter. She didn't quite know how to get him to tell her about Alex, especially since he clearly didn't want to talk about him. 'Maybe you saw him?'

'Yeah. That was probably the last time he was in.' His voice hadn't thawed.

'Do you know where he is now?'

'No.' Sam continued to polish the stout bottle, not exactly encouraging her questions.

'Do you know anyone who would?'

Finally looking Kevyn in the eye, he sighed. 'Look, I know Alex. He usually rolls into town every couple of years with a new bag of goodies. He's been one of my more regular sellers. Let's just say that he has an uncanny ability to find new wrecks and treasure. He simply blows through town to sell some of what he's found and immediately heads back out again. He's never here long, and he never says where he is headed.'

'Sounds like you know him well enough not to like him,' she said with a huff. The distaste in Sam's words offended her but she didn't know why. Kevyn didn't know Alex and shouldn't be insulted by Sam's attitude, but she felt like she had to defend him.

'Alex tends to leave a wake of destruction when he's in town.'

Kevyn couldn't argue with that. Her mother and grandfather had said the same thing.

'The guy's good at what he does. Brings in a lot to sell.' Sam rummaged through the display case in front of him. 'This is an old find he had.' He pulled out a similar looking coin to the one Kevyn held in her hands. 'It's a shield type cob he found while working on a salvage site in the Bahamas. The name of the ship was never discovered, so there isn't much known about it.'

'He found a shipwreck?'

'Not exactly. He was working with a salvage operation that found some treasure. He's worked a few sites since I've known him, but he never sticks around long enough to salvage the whole thing. He starts the project and after a few months he moves on, leaves the work for his crew to finish up, and heads to the next site he's read about.'

'How does he know where to look?'

'That's the hard part.' The venom from earlier mellowed while Sam continued. 'It's a big ocean out there, lots of sand to cover up a ship and lots of years and storms to scatter the pieces. Alex listens to the stories, does his research, then takes out a boat equipped with big metal detectors and blowers to move the sand and clear the bottom. A lot of it is mainly research – studying maps, water currents, sailor's logs and old documents written in Spanish. Mostly, I say it's luck.' Sam sounded excited when he spoke about finding treasure. 'Alex seems to have that luck. He's been involved with more sites than any salvager I know.'

Kevyn studied the coin and twisted it in her fingers. Only an inch and a half in diameter, it was thin and worn away, but she could still see the designs on one side. A cross and shield were raised from the surface along with the number twenty-four.

'See the 'M' here?' Sam pointed to a faded mark that Kevyn barely recognized as a letter. 'That means the coin was minted in Mexico.'

'You sure know a lot about this stuff.'

Sam placed the coin back in the case. 'Anthropology major. I studied Spanish cultures for years in college at the same time as I was working in a dive shop to put myself through school. The two went hand in hand and led me to a salvage operation in Mexico for a year. That's where I realized I liked the stories and research more than those monotonous dives. A lot of time you come up with nothing but sand. I moved here after that and opened the shop as a way to keep involved and have more time for the research end of things.'

'You ever do any of Alex's research?' Kevyn asked.

'Some. Not here in the shop, but in Key West.' Sam looked at her. 'Why are you asking about Alex Morgan, anyway?'

She took a deep breath. 'I'm Kevyn Morgan, his daughter.'

'Oh.' There was a long pause. 'I see.' Sam offered nothing more, and the silence grew awkward.

Kevyn twirled the ends of her hair around her finger while she thought of something to say. 'His boat sank last month off Puerto Rico and nobody's heard from him since.'

'No police report or hospital records?' Sam asked.

'None I know of.' Kevyn bit her lip. She actually hadn't thought of calling any hospitals. She'd tried to get information from customs in the islands but had gotten nowhere. 'Authorities say Alex wasn't on the boat when it went down, so I'm trying to retrace his steps and find out where he could be.'

'You're headed to Puerto Rico on your boat?'

'I guess.' Kevyn switched from playing with her hair to chewing on her lip. 'I don't really know where else to start.' God, it sounded ridiculous when she said it out loud. What was she doing?

'You must be worried sick.'

'Not really.' She looked down at the coins. Kevyn felt strange talking about her family secrets with a stranger. 'I don't know the man. He took off when I was born. I thought he was dead up until last week.' Kevyn didn't want to go into the whole story so she stopped right there.

Sam clenched his jaw. The look of steel returned to his eye. 'That figures.'

'I just want to find him for my grandfather, to let him know that he's okay.' Kevyn lowered her eyes and stared at the coins in the display in front of her, unable to look Sam in the eye. Her last statement was a lie. If she were honest with herself, her search was as much her need to find out why he left, left her, as it was about Grandfather's request to see his son again.

'That's a big step, to go from thinking he's dead to searching for a missing man you never even knew.'

'Yeah, well, the search isn't going so well. Pete doesn't know where he is; you haven't seen him; I'm not sure where to go next.' A wave of doubt washed over her. It was a long shot thinking she could sail down here and find a man she'd never met. 'I was hoping you'd have some answers.'

'I can't tell you where he is, but I do know some of the places he's been and who he deals with.'

'I'd appreciate anything you can tell me.' Kevyn's eyes felt hot and she prayed she wouldn't start crying.

'Listen, I didn't mean to upset you. Let me make it up to you.' Sam grabbed his keys from the bench behind him. 'You had lunch yet?'

She swallowed her tears. 'Not yet. There's not much left on board after the trip down.'

'Well, come on then. I know a great place to grab a fish sandwich, and while we eat I'll tell you all I know about your father.'

While Sam called one of his employees to cover for him, Kevyn looked around the store. There were the requisite pirate t-shirts with slogans like: *Beatings Will Continue Until Morale Improves* and *Pillaging, Drinking, Flogging and Wenching…Just Another Day at the Office*, as well as a few plastic swords and plush parrots for the treasure hunter extraordinaire.

'They're mostly for the tourists,' Sam called over his shoulder. 'Lots of people buy a t-shirt or coffee mug as a souvenir. Only the stuff in the cases go to serious buyers.'

'You get a lot of people interested in treasure?' Kevyn picked up a clay skull and turned it in her hands.

'Some people develop an interest while they're down here. They get caught up in the sun and sea, but there are quite a few enthusiasts who have actually studied the history of when the Spanish explored this part of the world.' Sam held the door open for Kevyn as they stepped back out into the fierce light.

Kevyn lowered her sunglasses from the top of her head. Her hair fell free and forward onto her face. Running her fingers through the mass like a comb, she gathered the locks in her hand and tied a loose knot at the back of her neck.

Sam shook his head, giving her an incredulous stare. 'I never understand how women can do that.'

As they strolled back down A1A, Sam made small talk as they passed high-end hotels that sat right beside the t-shirt shops and tattoo parlors. It was a strange mix of money and tourist kitsch. It didn't take long for Kevyn to recognize they were headed for The Treasure Trove.

Turning away from the beach toward the Swimming Hall of Fame, Sam placed his hand on the small of Kevyn's back and guided her through the door.

The place was mostly empty. A young blonde wearing short shorts and a tank top flashed a bright smile and waved from behind the bar. She hardly looked old enough to be serving alcohol.

'Hey, Sam. Grab a seat. I'll be with you in a minute.' The girl ran a knife through the last of the limes on her cutting board and scooped them into a plastic container.

'I guess you come here a lot.' Kevyn followed Sam to a table near the window.

'Yeah, it's close by and serves the coldest beer in town.' He pulled out a stool for her.

'Great clientele, too.' Kevyn climbed up onto the tall chair. 'I was here last night. Had a bit of a run-in with a man named Lemon.' Folding her arms in front of her, Kevyn leaned on the table.

'You talk to *him* about Alex?' Sam sat back, slinging his arm around the back of the stool beside him.

Kevyn looked up surprised. 'No. I didn't realize Lemon knew him.' She kicked herself for missing the opportunity to find out more about her father.

Sam pushed the bar menus to the side as he leaned forward. 'Lemon used to own a dive shop in town but he wasn't much of a businessman. There was a rumor he did more smuggling than diving. This was the eighties, when Florida was the gateway to everything that came up through the islands. It wasn't until the nineties when things started to tighten up around here,' Sam pushed the saltshaker back and forth on the table. 'A couple of years ago, Lemon was under investigation by the police and had to go legit with the dive shop. Thing is, he was really bad at it and the bank eventually took the shop. He's been here, sitting at The Trove bar, ever since.'

Kevyn was confused. 'What does that have to do with Alex?'

'I used to see Alex in Lemon's shop a lot a few years ago. I guess he was using his dive equipment.'

'That's strange.' Kevyn frowned. 'Why wouldn't he use Pete's equipment? They were friends. He even put money into The Dive Tank.'

Sam shrugged and shifted in his chair, all the while keeping his focus on the saltshaker in front of him. 'I don't think Pete puts up with any shifty business.'

'Is that what Alex is up to?' Kevyn had no reason to think otherwise, but in her naïveté she didn't want to imagine her father smuggling. She knew he had cracks in his veneer but didn't want to think of how deep they ran.

'I don't know. I stopped doing business with him a while ago.' His voice had a hard edge when he spoke of her father and Kevyn truly wondered why Sam disliked him so much.

Before she could ask, the smiling waitress bounced over to their table. Her ponytail actually lifted from her shoulders as she walked.

Kevyn couldn't help but notice that the front of her shirt did the same as she threw her arm around Sam's shoulder, and leaned in close to give him a big hug.

'Hey there, handsome. I've missed you!' She shot a look at Kevyn to make sure she got the hands-off message, and kissed Sam on the cheek.

'Elle, this is Kevyn, Alex Morgan's daughter.' Sam disentangled himself from the girl's attention.

'Really? Is he in town?' She placed her pink-polished, manicured hand on Sam's broad chest and pushed herself off him, but hovered close in order to mark her territory. 'He hasn't been in lately.'

Kevyn did her best not to roll her eyes at the girl. 'No, but I'm looking for him. Do you know how to contact him?'

'It's been a few years since I've seen him around. He used to come with Lemon and have a few beers, but he hasn't been in for a while.' She hadn't taken her eyes off Sam the whole time she spoke.

'That's what I'm hearing from everyone.' Kevyn said.

Elle didn't acknowledge her. 'Something to drink?' she asked Sam.

'Two Coronas and two grouper sandwiches.' He handed her the menus. 'If you think of anyone else who would know Alex, let us know.'

'Sure thing, hon.' Elle leaned in close to Sam to make sure he got a full view of her cleavage before turning her head toward Kevyn and smiling a, you-can't-compete-with-this, smile. Straightening, Elle turned on her heel and retreated to the kitchen.

'I don't think she likes me sitting here,' Kevyn said when Elle was out of earshot. 'I don't want to mess anything up for you.'

'Who? *Elle?* Don't be ridiculous. She's like that with everyone.' Sam brushed away the flirting. It was true he hadn't turned to look at Elle's cleavage, nor had he returned her kiss when she greeted him, but it was hard to imagine he didn't notice.

'Usually there are just guys in here and she's the belle of the ball. She makes better tips if she acts like that.' He sounded like someone who put a great deal of thought into the way people acted instead of just taking them at face value. 'Since everyone in here is a regular, she builds a relationship with a lot of them.' He shrugged, like it was the most natural thing in the world.

'You're not in a relationship with her?' *God, I sound like a teenager,* she thought.

'No, she can't really hold up a conversation.'

Kevyn laughed. She'd had dates like that before. They were extremely painful and short-lived.

Elle returned with two beers and placed one in front of Sam, offering him a full-lipped pouty smile. The other she slammed on the table in front of Kevyn, just hard enough for it to bubble up the neck of the bottle and start foaming over. Elle turned away pretending not to notice.

Kevyn mopped up the mess with her napkin. 'You sure *she* knows she's not in a relationship with you?'

Sam shrugged. They made small talk until their sandwiches arrived and sat together eating quietly. Kevyn was lost in thought again, wondering how all these people seemed to know her father, yet the person with his DNA floating around inside her didn't have a clue about the man he was. She was jarred out of her thoughts when Sam asked what she was doing the next day.

'I'm not sure. I'm at a bit of a standstill until someone comes up with some information to go on. So far, everyone I've met knows Alex but hasn't heard from him. I'm not sure where to turn next.'

'Well, I was thinking about taking my boat out for an early morning dive. Why don't you come with me? I can show you a little of what Alex does on a daily basis.'

Kevyn's head snapped up. 'You'd do that? I didn't get the impression you liked Alex.'

Sam's eyes lit with a smile. 'I don't. But spending the morning on my boat with a beautiful woman is something I very much like.'

Kevyn blushed and bit the side of her lip. 'I'm not much of a diver. I took lessons a couple of years ago, but I don't get much chance to practice.'

'No problem. It's supposed to be calm tomorrow so we can do a shallow, easy dive close to shore so you'll feel comfortable. I'll pick you up at the marina at nine.'

'Don't you have to work?'

'Ginny can cover the store. It's a quiet time of year anyway.'

'Okay, nine o'clock.'

Kevyn walked back to *Wander* grinning from ear to ear…until she realized that Sam had never told her another thing about her father, or how in the world she would find him.

*****

47

Chapter Six

On the stroke of nine Sam pulled his center console up to *Wander*. His Oakley sunglasses hid his blue eyes, but Kevyn could see his smile broaden as he approached.

The Quiksilver board shorts and t-shirt that advertised a ski slope in Colorado framed his physique, causing Kevyn to blush as she stood on the top deck holding the stay. She had dressed in a forest green t-shirt and khaki shorts over her bikini. Although not really sure what an appropriate outfit would be for an early morning date, Kevyn breathed a sigh of relief to see Sam in similar garb.

'Nice boat.' She caught the line that Sam threw her and tied off his bow.

'I was going to say the same to you. What's that, a Pearson?' Sam obviously knew something about sailboats as well as diving and history.

He tied a line from his stern to a cleat along the side of *Wander*. 'I haven't seen a tiller-driven boat in a while.'

Kevyn shifted her gaze to the cockpit where most boats of *Wander*'s size held a wheel. 'I couldn't bring myself to upgrade when Billy and I refitted her. I wanted to keep it as original as possible.' Kevyn jumped down into the cockpit. Athens crawled through the cat hole in the hatch and wound figure eights around her ankles.

'You've kept it in great shape. Your boyfriend do the work?' Sam asked, as she handed him her bag of gear from Pete's shop.

Kevyn laughed, pleased Sam was asking if she were single or not but amused that he thought she was involved with Billy, a grey-haired, dip-chewing man over twice her age. 'No boyfriend.' She turned back to the boat to make sure she hadn't forgotten anything. 'Friend of the family, I guess you could say. Billy runs a shipyard in Savannah and is always on my case to bring *Wander* in so he can work on her. He's shown me how to replace the engine, install a GPS and helps me paint the hull every couple of years. I think it's more a labor of love for him.' Locking the hatch, she gave Athens one last nuzzle. 'He taught me to sail when I was eighteen.'

'Aren't you nervous taking her down to the Caribbean?' Sam held out his hand to help Kevyn into his boat.

'A little. I had some trouble getting here. I hit a huge sunfish just outside Savannah.' Kevyn was laughing now, but the fear that rushed through her at the time was still fresh.

'You aren't the first person to hit one. They float on top of the water to soak up the heat.'

Sam was laughing now, too. 'Just be glad it wasn't a whale sleeping on the surface. They'd do *real* damage to a boat this size.'

'Hopefully it wasn't an omen for the rest of the trip.'

'Ah, you have a true sailor's belief in superstition.'

'Maybe. But, as soon as I get a clear weather window I'll head out again.' She grabbed the stainless steel bars that wrapped around the drive house to steady herself. 'I plan on island hopping most of the way, so I should be able to skirt the outer rim all the way down. I won't be too far from land if there's any more trouble.' It was a statement that she kept repeating in her head the last two days to calm herself.

'Maybe you should head down to Key West first.' Sam reversed and pulled his boat away from *Wander*. 'There's a museum down there where Alex used to spend a lot of time.'

Kevyn stood at the side of the console. Sam moved farther to the right and offered her a seat on the bench beside him. Their bare arms touched as she settled in behind the protection of the Plexiglass screen, sending a tingle of excitement down her spine.

'Really? Pete didn't mention Key West.' Kevyn brightened with the first real bit of information she'd received. Maybe she was wrong about Sam not wanting to help her.

'There's a woman who runs the museum there that knows Alex pretty well.'

'Then I'll make that *Wander's* first stop.'

Sam shook his head. 'I'd drive down to the Keys and then sail from here, if I were you. Key West is only a four-hour drive from Lauderdale on a good day. Then you're in a better position to shoot over the top of Bimini and head down the east side of the Bahamas.'

'Good thing I've got you advising me. I could use some local knowledge.' The drive through the Keys was supposed to be beautiful. She wished she had her Jeep down here to make the drive.

They motored slowly along the same route Kevyn had come in on, past the mansions and branches of the river. Each canal led to more mansions and even more boats. For a moment Kevyn imagined that this was what the waterways of Venice looked like, minus the lavish houses and adding hundreds of years of history to the sights.

The storm had passed; only a light wind blew through the canopy of palm trees that lined the waterway. They motored under the Seventeenth Street Bridge easily and without incident, and were out of the port and into the Atlantic before Kevyn even realized it.

Pushing against the throttle, the boat picked up speed. The bow rose out of the water and leveled off as it planed across the surface, making Kevyn feel as if she was flying. It was a different sensation from her sailboat, but exhilarating all the same.

Kevyn's hair whipped in the wind, the spray of sea salt showered her body and the warmth of the sun baked her skin. Behind them, white foam marked their path, while straight ahead the water was flat and clear. Kevyn had hoped to ask more about Alex this morning but the roar of the engine prohibited much talking.

'This is the spot for lobster,' Sam shouted over the engines. He eased off the throttle and the boat slowed as they puttered over the area for a moment while Sam studied his GPS. When he found the location he was looking for, he asked her to drop the anchor.

Once the boat drifted back and settled against the chain, he shut off the engines and applied sunscreen to his arms. Passing the tube to Kevyn, she applied a coating to her chest and arms, but when she bent down to rub the lotion into her legs she caught Sam watching her. Immediately she smiled, embarrassed, and straightened back up. It had been a long time since she'd had any male attention.

'You okay with your gear?' He handed her the mesh bag from Pete.

Kevyn pulled the wetsuit and fins out of the bag. 'I guess we'll find out how much I remember.' Pulling her t-shirt over her head, she dropped her shorts on the deck. She could feel Sam watching her again as she stepped into the wetsuit and wiggled it up over her hips.

Sam was doing the same routine; the tight fabric showed off his wide shoulders. Kevyn tried not to stare, but his sculptured form sure wasn't how the shrimpers back home looked standing on the decks of their boats.

As she fiddled with her fins, Sam sat down beside her, reached over and wrapped his arms around Kevyn's neck.

She looked up, startled, wondering if he was about to kiss her. Instead, he yanked at something behind her and she felt a tug on the neckline of her wetsuit. *Was he trying to take it off?*

He smiled wide. 'You still have the price tag attached.' He brought the small square of cardboard around for her to see.

Her face flushed from more than the roasting sun. 'There's no doubt I'm a novice, is there?' Kevyn tried to recall all she'd learned from her dive class ten years ago. It wasn't much. 'I might be a little rusty.'

Sam looked up from the tank he was fitting and smiled. 'Don't worry. I'll be right beside you.'

Turning the air on her tank to flow, Sam checked the gear to make sure everything was tight and secure. As Sam's hand lingered on her hip, goose bumps popped along her arm. She hadn't felt this way in a very long time.

Sam clipped her dive computer into place so she could easily see how much air she had, as Kevyn lowered her mask over her eyes and nose.

Reaching over, Sam removed a strand of hair that had gotten stuck in her mask. His fingertips brushed her cheek. 'I'll meet you in the water.'

Kevyn placed the regulator in her mouth and took a deep breath. Putting one hand across her chest and the other over her mask and regulator, she looked at Sam and nodded.

'Clear.' He signaled that it was safe for her to enter the water.

Leaning back, the weight of the tank pulled her over the side of the boat with a splash. Entering the water like a turtle stuck on its back, Kevyn twisted underwater to right herself. Bubbles streamed from her regulator clouding her view, and she kicked with her fins. Breaking the surface she fanned her arms to tread water as she filled air into her BC, the vest she wore to help keep her afloat.

'You okay?' Sam asked.

Kevyn removed the regulator from her mouth and held it above the water. 'Yeah, I forgot how bulky this stuff is.'

'You'll get the hang of it,' he said with a wink. He pulled his mask over his eyes and rolled into the water. Slowly, like an underwater Olympian gymnast, he surfaced headfirst. Looking around, he raised a hand to the top of his head, signaling Kevyn that all was okay.

Grabbing Kevyn around the waist, he helped fill her BC with his other hand. 'Ready to see what's down there?'

'Let's go find us some treasure.'

Sam laughed. 'You think it's that easy, do you?'

Kevyn tried to shrug but wasn't sure she pulled it off while wearing the inflated vest. 'Maybe it runs in the family.'

He laughed and made a thumbs-down signal.

Nodding, Kevyn replaced the regulator as they began their descent. She copied Sam's actions: clearing her ears by gently pinching her nose and blowing; stretching her neck from side to side to adjust to the pressure of being underwater. Looking around, all she saw was blue. Sam floated directly in front of her. His eyes behind the faceplate of his mask pierced her gaze for the entire descent, as he held on to her BC jacket with one hand to help steady her.

Rays of sunlight slanted down from above as they disappeared into the depths. Fine particles of silt floated all around, creating a distorted vision of baby blue liquid.

Sam checked once more that she was okay and motioned to follow him. He reached out and grabbed her hand as they began to swim into the abyss. It only took a few kicks of her fins for the reef they approached to come into view. It snaked along the sandy bottom of the ocean floor. Kevyn stopped kicking and stared.

Multi-colored fish swam in and out of the coral in haphazard motions. They hadn't been in the open water lying fifty feet behind them, but here they gathered in multitudes. Dark blue and black fish darted in front of Kevyn's mask, as tiny fish with violet fronts and golden rears flitted about looking like two different fish stuck together. Kevyn recognized them from hours of watching her favorite nature shows, but had never seen them in the wild. Had she known this was part of her father's world she would've paid more attention in biology class.

Kevyn glanced over her shoulder to see where they'd come from when a flash of silver caught her eye and the air from her regulator suddenly seized in her throat. A menacing three-foot barracuda stared at her with steely grey eyes. Her whole body shuddered at the sight of its pointed teeth and under-slung jaw. It looked well beyond mean as it stalked behind them.

She squeezed Sam's hand. When he turned to look, he seemed to laugh behind his regulator. He smiled at her, completely ignoring the predator, and pointed to a spot between two outcrops of coral where two antennae stuck out of a dark hole. Shining his light directly into the gap, he revealed a brown, spotted lobster propped up on its thin legs at the entrance, while its mate cowered in the corner.

Kevyn stole another glance behind her and swallowed down her fear. If Sam wasn't worried about the barracuda and could turn his back on it, then she would try to do the same. This was his world after all; he must know what he's doing.

Reaching into the hole slowly, Sam caused the lobster to back up as he scooted his hand behind its body and jerked it from its hiding spot. Bucking like a bull, the lobster tried to get away, but was stuffed into the mesh bag clipped to Sam's vest. With lightning speed Sam nabbed the other and added it the bag.

He reached out for Kevyn's hand again and swam down the reef toward the boat. The barracuda followed.

Black and grey angelfish with their bright lemon yellow stripes and a few blue parrotfish meandered past them. The slender forked tail of yet another flashed a brilliant blue.

Kevyn enjoyed being in the water and eventually got used to the trailing barracuda. She wondered if her father ever got to enjoy the fish and coral around him, or if he was so focused on the gold that he'd missed the beauty of the ocean all his life. .

Once they returned to the anchor line, Sam repeated his earlier maneuver of looking Kevyn straight in the eye as they slowly made their way to the surface.

They surfaced at the rear of the boat. This time Kevyn knew how to fill her BC with air so she could float easily, and then removed her mask and regulator.

'That was great!' Kevyn exhaled, wiping the hair off her face.

'No gold, but we *did* nab dinner.' Sam laughed, taking off his fins and flinging them into the boat. He climbed up the swim ladder and reached down to help Kevyn. 'Are you up for a lobster dinner tonight?'

'I think I can manage that.' Kevyn grabbed a towel and wrapped it around her body.

'My condo is small but there's a great view of the beach.' Sam removed his wetsuit, toweled off, and pulled a t-shirt over his head.

'Sounds perfect,' Kevyn said, trying to keep her eyes averted from his well-defined abs.

Sam lugged the heavy dive tanks to the rack set up along the transom, and twisted his upper body as he effortlessly lifted each one. The t-shirt stretched tight across his shoulders, accentuating his muscles.

This man isn't all about the research, Kevyn thought.

Sam dropped Kevyn off at *Wander*, promising to return at seven.

It was early afternoon when she stepped from the shower to run some errands. She caught a cab and went up Seventeenth Street to pick up a few groceries and stop in at Bluewater Books to get the charts she needed for the Caribbean. She returned to the marina by four and was loading her bags onto *Wander's* deck when she looked up to see Lemon walking down the dock.

He wore a Budweiser t-shirt that was ripped along the bottom and had a large grease stain across his belly. A green plaid work shirt with the sleeves ripped off barely covered the rag, and cut-off jeans and flip-flops completed his ensemble.

'This your boat?' He ran one hand through his long hair, slicking it back from his face with the grease it held from days of not washing it.

Kevyn shuddered, not wanting him to know where she lived. 'Hey, Lemon.'

'Nice lines.' Lemon lowered his sunglasses and looked over *Wander* like it was a used car.

Kevyn half expected him to kick her fenders.

'*Wander*.' He made it sound sleazy.

Kevyn ignored his comments. 'I was actually going to walk over to The Trove later to look for you.' She held her hand out, but quickly retracted it when she realized she would have to touch him. 'My name is Kevyn. We weren't properly introduced.'

'My lucky day,' Lemon sneered. 'The other night you didn't want anything to do with me. Today you come to find me.' His smile revealed a mouthful of rotted and nicotine-stained teeth. Kevyn thought he looked more like a snake than a shark.

'I was told you had business dealings with Alex Morgan.'

Lemon's eyes narrowed. 'You were told wrong,' he said. 'I ain't never doing business with him again. And if I ever see him 'round here, I'll make sure he can't do business with no one *ever* again.'

'Guess you aren't his biggest fan.' Kevyn bristled at his reaction.

'I ain't got no time of day for that maggot, and if you was smart you'd keep your pretty little head away from him, too.' Lemon tried another smile on Kevyn, but it came out more like a scowl.

'You don't know where he is, then?'

'If I knew, he wouldn't be there long.' Lemon raised a bushy eyebrow. 'What do you want with him, anyway?'

Kevyn didn't want to give away any personal information to the guy. 'He's a friend of the family. Thought I'd look him up while I was in town,' she lied.

Lemon reached out and grabbed her arm. He squeezed tight and leaned in close. 'You know where he is?'

Kevyn jumped back, wrenching her arm from his grasp. 'Get your hands off me!'

Lemon's laugh was the creepiest thing Kevyn had ever heard. 'I ain't gonna hurt you. I just want to find Alex, too.'

Kevyn took a step back. 'Why?'

'We're old friends, Alex and me.' Lemon's laugh turned into a snide sneer. Nothing about his statement felt sincere or friendly.

'If that's the case, and you think of where he might be, let me know.' Kevyn turned to step aboard *Wander* and escape from Lemon. 'I'll be here for a few days.'

'I can think of better things to let you know about than Alex Morgan.' Lemon reached out and ran a finger down her arm.

Kevyn shook off his touch, jumped aboard and hurried downstairs, closing the hatch behind her. It was time for another shower.

*****

Chapter Seven

Sam pulled into the marina parking lot in an old steel blue Mustang Coupe with the windows rolled down. His shaggy blond curls were given extra volume by the wind. He'd changed from his shorts and t-shirt into a sapphire blue polo shirt that highlighted his eyes.

Kevyn was glad she had taken the time to blow-dry her hair and put on a maroon sundress with a low neckline. It swirled around her body, reaching her calves, and made her feel like a girl, a neglected feeling while tinkering in her workshop or scrubbing barnacles from *Wander's* hull. She had few opportunities to dress up in Savannah, so this was a novelty. She'd applied a thin coat of mascara, and a dark gloss moistened her lips. Kevyn wasn't sure if this was a date or not, but she wanted to look good all the same.

'Wow, you look great.' Sam slid across the leather seat and kissed her on the cheek. His lips lingered a second longer than a standard hello.

Kevyn tried to hide her smile and play it cool but she felt like her whole body was beaming.

'I hope you like wine. I picked up a bottle of viognier and a pinot noir from Oregon for dinner.' He shifted into reverse and pulled away from the curb.

'Great minds think alike.' She pulled out a bottle of her favorite sangiovese from her bag.

It wasn't far to Sam's condo. He lived in an older development along the northern end of the beach. The building was painted bright white over the stucco and was highlighted with sea blue molding. They rode the elevator to the seventh floor.

Sam led the way into a beige living room with white tiled floors and a sliding glass door that opened to a large balcony overlooking the beach. The windows were bracketed by linen drapes strung through a cocoa-colored rod as thick as a baseball bat. The material mirrored the parchment of an antique map that hung on the wall above a worn leather couch. Suspended from the ceiling was a collection of old Japanese glass fishing balls that rounded out the decor.

Sam dropped his keys into a carved wooden bowl on the side table. 'Make yourself at home.'

Kevyn wandered over to a shelf filled with hardback travel books, recognizing many of the titles. She glanced around the room; a white longboard rested in the corner. 'You surf?' The answer was obvious. The board was clearly patched in spots and had a well-used look.

'Nowhere near as much as I'd like to.' Sam set the bottles of wine on the island that separated the kitchen from the living room. 'You have to drive north to get really good waves here. Lauderdale is blocked by the Bahamas, so waves don't have a chance to develop.'

Kevyn handed him her bottle of wine. The knuckles of his right hand grazed hers and she felt her body heat rise. 'I thought Florida would be good surfing.'

Sam shook his head. 'On the odd day, if the swell is just right, a little something can develop. I push it and jump in the water, but it's more just to get wet. My days of big wave surfing are long over.'

'Big waves?' Kevyn raised an eyebrow.

'Before I switched to Spanish cultures I spent some time at the University of Hawaii studying Polynesian history. There was a group of us who would surf early morning before class.' Sam pulled two large wine glasses from a rack on the wall. 'Dawn patrol.'

The kitchen was small with just one counter. Red and yellow peppers sat beside a mini pyramid of dimple-skinned avocados. Emerald green bunches of cilantro lay beside the vegetables. Its distinct smell wafted through the air. 'I thought we'd make tacos out of the lobster tonight.' Sam opened the bottle of viognier and poured a glass for Kevyn. 'Cheers!'

She held out the glass to clink against Sam's. He wasn't like any bachelor Kevyn knew in Savannah. Looking at the stainless steel refrigerator and gas stove in the kitchen, she suddenly wondered what it would be like to cook here instead of in her galley for a change. Billy had upgraded her galley nook so she could live on board, but no matter how modern her equipment, it was still a very confined space.

Sam raised his glass, holding it by its stem, and swirled the deep golden liquid around in the bowl. He held it up to the light for a moment and lowered the rim to his face. Instead of drinking as Kevyn had, he held the glass at a forty-five-degree angle and took a deep breath. Taking a tentative sip, he didn't swallow right away, but held the liquid in his mouth and moved it around with his tongue.

Kevyn stood still, captivated as she watched him perform the ritual. It was a sensual act; there was something very primal and intimate about the moment. Blushing, Kevyn looked down at her own wine glass.

'Relax for a few minutes while I get dinner started.' Sam picked up a chef's knife and began chopping fresh tomatoes, onions and chilies, while a pot of water came to a boil on the stove. Salting the water, he added two lemons before dropping in the lobster tails. As quick as they were added to the water, Sam used a pair of tongs to pluck them from the aromatic liquid. He picked up a pair of kitchen shears and began splitting them, pulling the jelly-soft meat from the shell. Slicing it, he placed it back inside the shell before pulling a bowl from the fridge and topping the tails with an herb paste. Placing them in the oven to roast, he tossed a salad before making fresh guacamole.

Kevyn stood across the island counter mesmerized by the show.

'Would you like to stick with wine or should we switch to lime daiquiris?' Sam warmed tortillas in a pan on the stove.

'I'll stick with wine,' Kevyn said. 'I'm not much for hard alcohol.'

'Better get used to rum, at least, if you're headed to the Caribbean.' Sam topped off their glasses and grabbed the salad bowl to set dinner out on the balcony.

The aroma of food and cologne mingled together as he leaned down to place her wine glass in front of her, and she smiled to herself. She'd *never* been on a date like this before.

Kevyn raised her glass. 'Thank you for taking me today and for cooking. This looks fabulous.'

'My pleasure,' Sam said, bowing his head at the compliment. 'It's nice to have someone to cook for again.'

Their glasses clinked with a crisp sound that Kevyn imagined came only from good crystal. 'Where did you learn all this?' She motioned to the platters in front of her. The green of the Caesar salad stood out bright against the royal blue and marigold hand-painted Mexican pottery. The coral-colored lobster tails sat beautifully arranged on a bed of green with the vibrant red tomatoes and contrasting cilantro in the fragrant salsa looking like a painting.

'As I said, I spent a lot of time in Mexico.' He shrugged like this was a normal, everyday occurrence.

Kevyn smiled. 'I just came from three days at sea eating cereal and cold cuts. *This* is amazing.'

Digging in, Kevyn's taste buds exploded. The Caesar was laced with lime; the salsa was rich and hot and filled her mouth with flavors; and the lobster practically melted when she bit into it. The meal was more than a work of art; it was heaven.

'I've never had anything like this,' she said. It was a far cry from the deep-fried and boiled seafood of Savannah.

Sam grabbed the second bottle of wine. As he poured another glass, his fingertips grazed Kevyn's bare shoulder, electrifying her body.

'Tell me about being an anthropologist.' Her voice was nothing but a whisper from his touch.

'Not much to tell. It's the stories of other lands and other cultures that I like.' Sam pushed his chair back from the table and crossed his ankle over his knee. 'But I never pictured myself locked away in a library all day.' Staring out over the railing at the sea below, Sam gazed at the dusty purple sky – the color that appeared just before all went black. 'I have a captain's license and dive tickets, but that seemed more like recreation than a career, so I bought Deadman's to be able to interact with people. I still get to do the reading and hear the stories, but I also get to talk to people and go out diving and exploring when I want.'

'Sounds like you have the perfect set-up.' Kevyn wished she felt as comfortable with her own life.

'The store practically runs itself and I have great help, so I can escape when I want and travel or start new projects. But Deadman's keeps me coming back.'

'It keeps you grounded while you run.'

'I'm a not much of a runner.' Sam stared into his wine glass. 'My heart is here.' Again, he shook his head. 'Being my own boss allows me to move around instead of keeping to someone else's schedule.' Leaning forward, Sam helped himself to the last tortilla. 'What about you? What do you do when you're not chasing after men you don't know?'

'I'm not much of a runner, either. I want to be, but have never done it. I've lived in Savannah my whole life.' It was Kevyn's turn to look away. She stared over the balcony's railing to the ocean beyond. 'I've worked at different jobs here and there, but nothing has really caught my attention for long. I've taught violin, worked a vegetable stand… even guided kayak tours through the marshes.'

She trailed off; the list was really too long to recite. 'Lately, I've been restoring antiques for dealers. That's my favorite job. People call and ask me to refinish old pieces they have, or I rummage through the plantations and historical homes in Savannah and find all these forgotten pieces that just need some love and attention. I take them back to my workshop and bring them back to life before I sell them to the dealers in town.'

She mimicked Sam, attempting to swirl the last of her wine in her glass. It sloshed around clumsily instead of the graceful movement he produced. She set the glass back on the table and stayed quiet for a beat or two. Her life didn't sound all that purposeful now that she said it out loud. She loved her job but was a little surprised at how easily she'd left it behind to start this search for her father. Maybe she wasn't as committed to it as she thought.

'Sounds like you are a treasure hunter, too, just on land.' Sam reached over to refill her glass.

'I never thought of it that way.' Kevyn stared into the ruby liquid. '*Wander* was really my first restoration job. When I got her, Billy and I had to strip all the wood down and replace the rotting boards before we put her back in the water. He taught me how to caress the wood and bring out its best qualities. After that, pieces of furniture seemed like a natural progression.'

'What happened to that job?'

'Nothing happened to it. I can go back to it when I get home.' She turned to watch the thin sliver of moonlight reflect off the waves. 'I'm just not sure I want to.'

'You think you'll head back to Savannah if you find Alex?'

She nodded. 'My grandfather wants him to come home.'

'And what do you want?'

Kevyn thought for a moment. 'Seems like either way I go back, with or without my father, I'll be a different person. Before now, I was Kevyn Morgan whose father had died when she was young. Now, I'm Kevyn Morgan whose father abandoned her because he couldn't be bothered to get to know her.' Kevyn looked away again, embarrassed that she wasn't cool and collected, the way she wanted to portray herself to Sam. 'Maybe it's time to become a new Kevyn Morgan.'

Sam got up from the table, grabbed Kevyn's hand and pulled her out of her chair. He clenched her hands in his and held them close to his chest, drawing her body against his own. He ran his hand through her hair and met her gaze. 'Kevyn, you might not know Alex but I do.' His body pressed into hers. 'He's been running ever since I've known him. Are you *sure* you want to catch up with him?'

Kevyn looked deep into Sam's eyes trying to decode the secrets behind what he was saying. 'I don't...I don't know.'

'I'm just saying, you might not like what you find.'

Sam let go of her hands and wrapped his arms around her. He pulled her close and kissed her shoulder. The stubble on his cheek scratched and tickled when he kissed the groove between her neck and his collarbone. She squirmed with delight. Heat rose in her body. By the time his lips found hers she was positively on fire.

Sam pulled back and looked into her eyes for approval. Bending his head, his lips touched hers in a kiss that made her knees go weak and her toes curl.

Kevyn took a step back and caught her breath. The warmth of the wine swirled through her.

Sam's eyes sparkled when he smiled down at her.

'I've been thinking about what you said about Key West. I liked your idea about driving down and wondered if you wanted to come with me to look for my father?'

Sam's smile disappeared. He dropped his arms from her waist.

Kevyn's stomach knotted. Did she read the sign's wrong? 'I mean, only if you want to. We could, um, go for a day.' She chewed on her lower lip. 'Of course, I would understand if you can't... what with work and all. I mean we really just met, but I guess I'd like it if you'd come.'

Sam's face darkened like the clouds had in the storm. 'You don't want me looking for Alex.'

Kevyn's smile faltered. That wasn't the answer she'd expected. 'Not if you don't want to. I mean, I know you don't like him...' Her sentence trailed off. All of a sudden Kevyn wasn't sure what Sam wanted.

'Alex and I don't see eye to eye on certain things.' The muscles in his jaw clenched tight.

Kevyn looked down at her dress and realized she may have misunderstood why Sam had invited her to dinner. He didn't seem to care about Alex at all. Maybe he did not want to help her find him.

'I just thought you might like to go for a...um...' Stepping away from Sam and into the living room, she spotted her purse in the hallway and stepped closer to it. '...go for a drive. I hear it's pretty there. I don't have a car. You do. That's all.' Kevyn knew she wasn't making any sense. Reaching down she snatched her purse and hugged it close to her chest, now feeling silly in a low-cut dress.

'Kevyn, wait.' Sam reached out to grab her arm, but Kevyn pulled away. The doorknob jabbed her in the back, and she twisted her hand around to grab it.

'What I meant to say was...' She prayed the door was unlocked. 'That I didn't know where in Key West I was going.' She curled around the door as it inched open. 'I'll just ask Pete.'

'Kevyn, wait,' Sam repeated.

Kevyn kept babbling as she stepped into the hallway. 'No, that's okay. I've got to get going. I've got lots of work to do on the boat in the morning. Thanks for dinner.' She backed out of the condo and held the door as a barrier. 'I'll see you later.'

'Kevyn, wait!' Sam said a third time, but she pulled the door shut before he could stop her.

Hurrying down the hallway she stumbled and turned her left ankle. But, now staggering, she kept right on going. Why was she wearing heels? She wasn't used to walking in them, much less fleeing. Punching the elevator button, Kevyn looked down, embarrassed, at the dress she wore.

The elevator plummeted as fast as her spirits while she tried to figure out just why Sam hated her father so much.

Wander never looked more inviting.

Kevyn had jumped in a cab and returned to the marina before Sam could stop her. She'd heard him following and calling her name but had ignored him, too embarrassed to face him. She'd found the cab idling outside his building.

She hurried down the dock and kicked off her heels before jumping aboard. She unlocked the hatch with keys from her purse. Athens jumped from the bed. Kevyn scooped him up and squeezed him tight. She buried her tears in his soft flank.

'Just you and me, kiddo.' She ran her fingers through the fur on his head. Her polished fingernails stood out against his caramel and black tones. Embarrassment rose again. It had been years since she had painted her nails.

Kevyn curled up in her bunk, snuggling Athens close and repeated her earlier statement. 'Just you and me.'

The next morning, she awoke early and headed out before anyone had started work on the dock. She walked along the beach where the sand and surf met and stared out at the ocean, watching it turn from grey to robin's egg blue with the rising sun. Soft gentle waves washed up around her ankles. The bottoms of her feet ached with muscles she wasn't accustomed to using as she trekked through the sand.

Going to dinner last night with Sam was silly. Good-looking man or not, Sam was not the reason she was here. She was supposed to be down here searching for her father, not running around, chasing after a man. It was time to get back to her quest. And if Sam was a dead-end, she would have to go back to Pete and see if he knew anything more. Pete was Alex's best friend after all. He must know something more that would lead her to him.

She ran out of beach at the inlet and headed west through a beachside community of wooden bungalow homes and stately ficus trees. Royal Poinciana's canopied the road exploding with fiery orange flowers and feathery green leaves while wide-leaved banana palms acted as fences. She wound her way through the quiet neighborhood, enjoying the change from the rumble of cars along A1A. By the time she hit the ocean road again, she decided to take a chance that The Dive Tank was open early.

Pete was hauling air tanks from one location to another when Kevyn arrived. His sun-leathered skin draped loosely from his gangly frame. He wore a tank top with the slogan *I'll be at the Dive Bar* splashed across the front. He looked up and smiled as the door chimed.

'Mornin', darlin'' Pete might have been living in South Florida, but he hadn't lost his Georgia drawl. 'What can I do for you?'

Kevyn collapsed on the fin-fitting bench. 'Can you please tell me about Alex?'

Pete turned from the tanks and studied her. 'What do you want to know?'

'I think you're the only one who knows him well enough to know what he's doing and where he'd go after the *K Sea* sunk. You seem to be the only person I've met who even likes him.'

'Hey now, I never said that.' Pete snorted and laughed at the same time. 'There's times your daddy drives me just as crazy as everyone else, but you're right, I've known him a long time.' Pete sat down on the bench beside her. 'You know, when I came down here after spendin' time with Alex and your mama back home, it was the late seventies. Things were pretty crazy 'round here. I wasn't naive. The folks back home had been runnin' grass in the shrimp boats, but here...' Pete shook his head. 'Here they had graduated to cocaine from Colombia. Everybody with a boat or a plane was bringing it in. They called 'em cocaine cowboys.'

Kevyn fiddled with the strap on her purse. *Was Pete going to tell her that her father was a drug smuggler?*

'Alex was a lot younger then and a lot more eager. He was researching a lost galleon off the shores of Colombia and spendin' a lot of time down there.' Her hand clenched the purse strap.

'On one of his return voyages, the DEA was waitin' for him. His boat was impounded, and he was under investigation for months.' Pete leaned forward, resting his elbows on his knobby knees and stared at his hands interlaced in front of him. 'During that time, this store wasn't doing so well. I'd just opened and business was slow.'

Please don't tell me this. Please don't tell me this.

'Alex came by every morning to help me lug gear 'round the store. Each night as I counted the till, there was always an overage.' Pete smiled at the long ago memory. 'Some days it was enough for me to buy dinner, some days it covered the rent.' He turned to look Kevyn in the eye. 'We never talked about it, but all the time he was being hounded by the cops he was worried 'bout me and helpin' me.'

Kevyn let out the breath she'd been holding for far too long. 'Was it drug money?'

Pete shook his head, no longer looking Kevyn in the eye. 'I don't know. The cops never found anything, and his boat was eventually cleared to leave port. I never asked him 'bout it, and I never will. Far as I'm concerned, your dad helped me out of a jam.'

Pete got up and started fiddling with a display of snorkels. 'I'm not sure where he is now, but if I could, I'd help him same as he helped me.'

Kevyn got up and laid a hand on his shoulder. 'Thanks, Pete.' She felt proud of her dad for being there for an old friend. 'I needed to hear a good story.'

Pete smiled and went on with his work.

Kevyn tried to ignore the fact that just because Alex wasn't caught did not mean the money had not come from smuggling cocaine.

The blinding sun beat down as Kevyn walked back down the dock at Bahia Mar.

As she kicked off her shoes on the dock and was about to step on board *Wander*, she noticed the hatch was open a crack. Her throat constricted; her feet became anchored to the spot. She knew she'd secured the padlock on her way out this morning and she always double-checked. But now it hung open from the door part of the latch, not connected to the frame at all.

Taking a deep breath, she grabbed the rail for support as she hoisted herself aboard. She knew it had been a bad idea to reveal to Lemon which boat was hers.

'Lemon! If that's you, I've already alerted security.' She hoped her voice didn't sound as shaky out loud as it did in her head. When no answer came and no form appeared, she reached down and grabbed the boat hook hanging on the bulkhead and took a step closer to the hatch. Her hands now shook as much as her voice as adrenaline rushed through her. 'Lemon?'

Out of the corner of her eye Kevyn caught a movement on the bow. She raised the boat hook over her head like a baseball bat.

Sam's hands shot in the air. 'Don't shoot!' A smile danced on his lips. 'I'm unarmed.'

Kevyn's heart pounded so loud she could barely hear his words. Placing her hands on her knees, she bent at the waist to try and catch her breath. 'You scared the hell out of me!' She glared up at him. 'What are you doing here?'

Sam held up *Wander's* sail cover in his left hand. 'When I picked you up to go diving the other day I noticed there was a tear.' Sam's smile was part schoolboy-innocent, part hand-in-the-cookie-jar-I-hope-I-am-cute-enough-to-forgive-me. 'I thought I'd help you fix it.'

Kevyn wasn't sold. 'How'd you get in?'

The smile turned to full-on-caught-red-handed. 'Your cat let me in.'

She narrowed her eyes. 'Try again.'

Sam raised his hands in mock surrender. 'I used your spare key.'

No longer scared, Kevyn's freight turned to suspicion. 'How'd you know where it was?'

Sam put down the sail cover and hopped into the cockpit beside her, pointing to the cushions on the portside bench. 'It wasn't hard to find. My wife used to hide her spare key in the same place. If I were you, I'd switch it to the anchor locker,' he said, his eyes dancing with his smile. 'You never know who wants to break in and repair things for you.'

Kevyn knew he was trying to make up for last night, but she was still embarrassed and mad--or hurt; she really didn't know how she felt. And why was he sneaking on her boat while she wasn't there? But as strange as the moment was, she couldn't help but pick up on what Sam said. 'You're married?'

Sam shook his head. 'Was.'

'Divorced?'

'Widowed.'

Kevyn didn't know what to say. She guessed Sam was only a few years older than she; far too young to be a widower.

Without waiting for the standard apology Sam went on, 'We used to have a sailboat and Beth hid our spare key under a cushion, as well.'

'Do you still have the boat?'

'No, she's gone, too.' Sam's smile faded. Just like the night before his eyes clouded and his demeanor changed.

Kevyn stood straighter. 'Sam, I'm sorry. It's none of my business.'

'No. I'm the one who's sorry…about last night.' Reaching out, he grabbed her hand. 'I didn't mean to upset you.'

'I wasn't upset.' She tried to pull her hand from Sam's now uncomfortable grip, but he held on tight. 'I just don't know what to think about my father.' She looked into his eyes; the cool blue of the ocean. 'No one seems to have much good to say about him. Pete's the only one who even seems to like him, and I don't know anything about *him*.'

Sam squeezed her hand. 'Well, how about we drive down to the Keys and find out some more?'

It was Kevyn's turn to smile. 'You want to come with me?'

'Just let me call the shop.'

*****

Chapter Eight

Ginny agreed to cover Sam's extra shifts and stop in to feed Athens at Sam's apartment. It didn't take the cat long to explore his new home. Kevyn felt a twinge of guilt seeing how much more room he had to run around in compared to the cabin of *Wander*. He wound around each door of Sam's apartment discovering new rooms, but ten minutes later he was curled up in the sunlight streaming through the patio doors.

By early afternoon they were on the road headed south. Jimmy Buffett played on the stereo.

Kevyn wrinkled her nose. 'Little cliché, isn't it? To be in South Florida listening to 'Margaritaville'?'

Sam reached over and turned the volume up. 'Clichés become clichés for a reason. Just wait. By the time you sail through the islands you'll understand everything Buffett sings about.'

They drove the slow road, down A1A, along the beach to Miami, passing in and out of neighborhoods, strip malls and shopping centers. Sam pointed out the traces of old Florida in Surfside where wrought iron gates and brick driveways led to houses with large bay windows and barrel tile roofs. These homes had character and felt far more Spanish in style than the faux-mansions in Lauderdale with their marble columns and white stone statues decorating the manicured lawns. This area had charm, while still exuding wealth.

Next came the neon bridges and high-rises of Miami. Kevyn hadn't realized how diverse Florida was. Seems her Sunshine State image had been formed from commercials for Disney World and episodes of *Miami Vice*.

There wasn't much conversation during this part of the drive. Kevyn was too wound up in seeing the city for the first time, although she did feel guilty that she was having such a good time when she was supposed to be looking for Alex. She told herself that she had to go to the Keys to get more information, but she felt a little like she was cheating her grandfather. He'd given her a lot of money to find Alex, and he was counting on her to bring him home. He wasn't getting any younger, and she couldn't waste any time.

Sam drove with his arm resting on her seatback. Kevyn's stomach returned to flip-flopping when he stroked her hair with his fingertips and told her about a time he'd driven to Key West.

'It was right after Hurricane Wilma in '05. I packed up a trailer of water and clothing that people donated to the Chest and drove down here to help with the rebuilding efforts. It took me sixteen hours to get through with all the traffic and chaos. I stayed for a month, helping put things back together again.'

Sam smiled, and Kevyn couldn't quite remember why she'd run out the night before. He may not like Alex, but he was helping her find him. And, he'd led such an interesting life that she found herself truly intrigued and wanted to know more about him.

'Did your wife come down here with you?'

Sam dropped his arm from her seatback and clenched the varnished wood steering wheel. He stared straight ahead, oblivious to the passing scenery. 'Not that trip,' he said, his smile long gone.

Kevyn's throat caught. 'I'm sorry. Had she already passed?'

Sam gripped the steering wheel tighter, not answering.

Kevyn blew out a breath and stared out the window as they worked their way south. She didn't know what to say. Do widowers want to talk about their former life, or keep it buried? She rarely thought of her own marriage, it had been over so quick. But, she knew loosing your wife was an ocean away from leaving your husband because you'd gotten married for the wrong reasons. She wondered how she died but was now afraid to ask.

She ran her fingers through her hair and gathered it off her shoulders into a ponytail. Like her Jeep back home, long hair, lipstick and the roof down didn't mix. It seemed like a carefree sunny drive through the Keys; top down, radio on, but the atmosphere inside the convertible had just turned arctic.

The car was silent; too silent, even with the wind whipping past. The anger and emotion Sam struggled with seemed to crackle around him.

'How about a late lunch?' Sam finally broke the tension as he turned off the main highway.

They drove down a tree-lined road that seemed to stretch on forever. Alabama Jack's was exactly what Kevyn pictured a bar in the Keys would be. Motorcycles lined the entrance in a long row like dominoes waiting to fall. An open-aired wooden patio over the waterway looked out to the mangrove swamp, and a collection of fishing buoys and nets hung from the ceiling. Strains of The Eagles' 'Take It Easy' came from a five-man, steel guitar band in the corner.

'You aren't in the Keys until you've had a rum-runner at Jack's.' Sam directed her to a table by the water. His earlier darkness seemed to have faded.

'I guess I know what I'll order then.'

The waitress, a waif of a girl in tank top and cut-off jeans, took their order for conch fritters and grouper sandwiches. When she returned with their drinks, the sweet thickness of the frozen juices gave Kevyn an ice-cream headache. She winced, not knowing if it was brain-freeze or the three shots of rum that got to her first. 'Is this amount of alcohol even legal?'

'A rum-runner is standard here. Coming down to the Keys is like stepping into America's loading zone.' Sam sat with his left ankle crossed over his right knee sipping at his drink. 'During prohibition these islands were used by rum runners to bring the liquor up from the Bahamas, then drugs started arriving from the Caribbean and South America. These days the largest import is refugees from Haiti and Cuba.'

Kevyn ran her finger over the condensation on the glass, creating lines in the moisture. 'Pete said something about a boat of Alex's being tied to the dock on suspicion of smuggling.'

Sam nodded.

'And he may have been running heroin in Vietnam,' she continued cautiously.

'Lots of stories of people doing both those things.'

She sighed. There was definitely something that Sam was keeping close to the chest. 'Grandfather sent me down here to find Alex and bring him home. But how am I going to tell him he's been down here smuggling drugs for the past thirty years?'

Sam remained silent.

'Maybe it would be better if he went on thinking his son was diving in the tropics completely carefree,' she said.

'You don't know he's smuggling.' Sam didn't sound strong in his defense of Alex.

'I don't know he's not. I don't know anything about the man. All I know is that I can't tell Grandfather any of this.'

'We aren't going to make Key West by dark. How do you feel about an afternoon kayak through the mangroves? We could watch the sunset at Lorelei's, share a slice of Key lime pie, and finish the drive tomorrow?' Sam asked as they left Jack's.

'How could a girl say no to that?' Kevyn's earlier thoughts of not chasing after Sam and concentrating on only the search for her father sailed from her thoughts.

Sam rented two sunlight-yellow sea kayaks from Florida Bay Outfitters in Key Largo and paddled out over tidal flats into the mangrove forests. They glided along a creek maze canopied by mangrove trees with roots that anchored them like twisted tines of a fork stuck in the water. The overhead branches blocked the diminishing rays of the sun, creating a shifting pattern of sparkling light, as the herons waded in the shallows by the hammocks in search of fish for dinner.

The repetitive swish of her paddle entering the water lulled Kevyn into a warm and happy daze – or maybe it was the residual rum in her bloodstream. Either way, she loved kayaking. She might be new to diving, and not a seasoned long-haul sailor, but this was something she'd done often. She felt comfortable paddling on the water, and the strange desire to impress Sam with her ability pulled at the corner of her thoughts.

Sam's kayak glided ahead of hers, and for a moment she watched the muscles in his back contract as he stroked. Her pulse sped from the sight and she leaned forward to dig harder in order to catch up. Her gaze followed the paddle as it entered the water ahead of her body to her right. But suddenly, out of the corner of her eye, she spotted a dark shadow.

A large grey mass surfaced right where her paddle had been.

'Oh!' She shifted in the narrow cockpit, worried she would hit it like she had the sunfish.

Her kayak rocked with the motion and rolled left, then right.

'Oh,' she cried again as it rolled upside down, submerging her in the warm water. *So much for impressing Sam with my kayaking skills.*

The dark object beside her moved, sending ripples under the water. She felt its presence and knew she shouldn't make any sudden movements.

The spray-skirt she wore around her waist and cinched tight to the kayak held her in place, upside down in the murky water. Holding her breath, she let go of her paddle and felt her way along the lip of the opening to the release. Pulling hard on the loop, she felt the material of the skirt give way. She pushed herself out of the upside-down kayak and kicked to the surface. Beside her, a grey snout broke the surface of the water just as she took a gulp of air.

'Sam?' She treaded water trying to locate him.

She didn't have to search far. The tip of his kayak barreled down on her at a fast pace. A look of fear was cemented on his face. 'Hang on!' Terror laced his voice and he paddled harder.

'I'm okay,' Kevyn called back, but it didn't look like he heard her. He kept streaking across the water.

Kevyn felt the hard plastic rub against her upper arm as the boat glided past. Sam reached over the side and plucked her from the water, pulling her up onto the deck of his boat. It was a wonder the narrow kayak didn't tip as well.

'Are you alright?' He leaned forward and held onto her lifejacket with both hands. It was a little overzealous of a rescue.

'I'm fine.' Kevyn pushed the wet hair out of her eyes

'You scared me!' Sam's hands moved over her body checking for damage. His touch sent shots of electricity tingling through her body. Even if the treatment wasn't a romantic gesture, Kevyn liked the feel of his hands on her body.

'Are you sure you're okay?' he asked again, the panic still evident in his voice.

'I may not be able to handle a storm at sea but I think I can handle a dip in the water.' She pointed at the manatee that nosed its way over to them. 'I was just startled, that's all.' She slipped back into the water beside Sam's kayak. She looked at the cow-like creature floating beside her; it had large grey wrinkles like a walrus and tread water with its flippers. A deep and ragged scar ran from the top of the manatee's head to its shoulder blade.

'These guys are pretty harmless, nothing to be afraid of.'

'I wasn't afraid,' Kevyn replied. 'You were the one acting like I was drowning.'

Sam pulled some sea grape leaves off a low hanging branch and waved them in the water. The giant mass glided sluggishly over to Sam's outstretched hand. He raised his massive head out of the water and munched on the offering. Sam rubbed its head like you would a dog, before it sunk into the brackish water and disappeared from sight.

'You are a soft touch, Sam Strider.' Kevyn swam back to her own kayak and began the process of flipping and draining it, both bewildered and amazed at the exchange she'd witnessed, not to mention perplexed at the severity of Sam's reaction to her supposed danger. Did he really think she needed rescuing?

Kevyn's nerves sizzled when Sam pulled up to the hotel. They had not talked about the logistics of this trip. Jumping out of the Mustang, he circled around the car to open Kevyn's door.

Once inside, neither of them uttered a word as they walked toward the woman behind the counter. Sam took the lead. 'A room for two, please.'

Kevyn's stomach flipped. *I guess I know what that means.*

'With a king-sized bed, sir?' The woman looked up at Sam, her fingers poised over the keyboard in front of her.

'Two doubles, if you have it.' Sam didn't look back at Kevyn when he replied.

What does that mean? Kevyn thought as she followed Sam down the hallway past door after door of people who knew where they were sleeping that night...and with who.

The tight room barely fit the two double beds. Sam paused in the doorway, and Kevyn bumped into the back of him.

'Sorry,' she started as he spun around to face her. 'I wasn't paying attention.'

'Excuse me,' he said at the same time.

Nervous laughter twittered out of Kevyn. Sam looked stricken for a moment but soon, he too, was laughing.

'Ridiculous, isn't it?' He reached down and grabbed the battered duffle bag from her. 'I feel like a teenager. I didn't want to be presumptuous, though. Especially after the other night...' His fingers caught hold of Kevyn's hand, putting an end to her laughter. 'It's been awhile since I've done this.'

Kevyn took a big breath of air and looked into Sam's blue eyes. 'Me, too.'

Dropping the bag in the small space between the beds, Sam used his free hand to brush a strand of Kevyn's hair off her shoulder, lightly kissing the curve of her neck.

'If it's okay with you, I'd like to try this again.' Sam raised his head and met Kevyn's gaze.

She smiled and nodded. Her nerves were still dancing the samba. 'I'd like that.'

Sam wrapped an arm around the small of her back and lowered her to the bed.

Kevyn felt as if she was leaving the troubles of the journey behind. Her breath caught in her throat as everything faded from concern.

Kevyn's eyes flew open at first light, momentarily confused about where she was. A thin white sheet covered her naked body, and a pile of pillows lay on the floor; thrown out of the way the night before. The bed was larger and much softer than her bunk on *Wander* and filled with Sam beside her.

She looked over her shoulder at the man who had been a stranger to her just a few short days ago. He lay on his side, curled behind her with one arm cinching her close. His breath was warm and welcoming on the back of her neck, and the feel of his muscular chest caused her temperature to rise once more.

Kevyn shifted in order to memorize every wrinkle, every sun-crevice, every dimple line he owned. It'd been a long time since she'd woken up with a man and she tried not to wake him. She wanted to enjoy the feeling of Sam holding her tight for as long as possible. But sitting had never been Kevyn's strong suit. Within minutes she squirmed. All she wanted to do was reach out and run her fingers through his thick, wavy hair.

He moaned in a half-sleep state and tightened his hold on her waist.

Kevyn kissed his shoulder and slid across the bed in order to go get coffee.

Sam opened one eye, reached out and grabbed her. Pulling her back across the bed, he pressed his body against hers.

'You're not going anywhere.' His kiss was fierce.

Kevyn wound her arms around his neck and kissed him back with a savage lust she didn't even know she possessed.

All thoughts of coffee fled her mind.

It was late afternoon by the time they made it to Key West. Sam drove her down the fabled Duval Street. Commercialized t-shirt shops, jewelry stores and raucous open-air bars lined the street. The familiar logos of Banana Republic and Starbucks flew by.

'It's not what I expected.' Kevyn watched a man in electric purple spandex pants walk a dog that was dressed in a leather vest and wore Blues Brothers glasses perched on his furry little nose. 'I thought it would be all flop houses, Cuban cafes and cigar makers.'

'Hemingway's Key West days are fading fast.' Sam pulled up beside a Jeep, the same black color as Kevyn's back home, and for a second she felt like her old life was fading just as fast as Hemingway's island image. 'Those things are still here, but you have to know where to search. Biggest thing these days are the tourists.' Sam parked the Mustang, got out and came around to open Kevyn's door.

This time she wasn't nervous. In fact, she was fighting the sudden urge that had risen inside her--the urge that wanted nothing more than to find another hotel.

Sam caught her hand in his and steered her to the heart of historic Old Town. There they walked down narrow streets, past grand old Victorian houses and Key lime-colored cottages. People were everywhere.

Sam directed her to Mallory Square to watch the sun settle down for the evening over the Gulf of Mexico. They entered the gathering of people to see a group of buskers juggling fire on one side and a man performing magic tricks on the other.

A tattooed man with a grey mustache and ponytail blew into a conch shell to signal the beginning of his act. 'Welcome to the Conch Republic,' he called out to the crowd. His steel grey eyes lit with excitement as he walked a high-wire tightrope and juggled bowling pins at the same time. The crowd erupted into applause. The colorful street theatre felt like a carnival – Key West's definition of a live circus.

A mime pantomimed, giving Kevyn a bouquet of flowers. She accepted with a dramatic curtsey as Sam held his arm out regally to steady her.

'Look, Sam.' Kevyn pointed to a fortune-teller roaming the square.

The woman walked with difficulty; the curve of her back seemed to pull one leg higher than the other when she stepped. Wearing a midnight-black and blood-red scarf wrapped around her long grey hair, large gold hoops swung from her earlobes as she approached them with awkward determination.

Sam whispered in Kevyn's ear, 'We're about to be told we'll have two kids and a lifetime of happiness.'

'Let me read your cards, sweetie?' the woman asked.

'I don't really believe in that stuff,' Kevyn started to say, but the woman already had her by the hand and was directing her to a clearing where a table was set with a purple velvet cloth. From somewhere in the depths of her flowing black dress the woman produced a worn pack of tarot cards. She shuffled the deck and placed them on the table in the shape of a cross. Her practiced frown appeared as she tapped a three-inch, yellowed nail on the first card.

'This is the Six of Swords.' An Arthurian looking man in tights and short shift stood, rowing a canoe-like boat with a long pole. 'This card means you are setting off into the unknown.'

Kevyn laughed at the relevance of the crone's statement. Between her budding relationship with Sam and her search for Alex, her whole life was one gigantic unknown at the moment.

'This next one is a Major card. The Tower. It means an unforeseen catastrophe and abrupt change.'

Kevyn stopped laughing. Weren't these things supposed to be positive?

The woman tapped yet another card. 'There is, The Fool. He's in the reversed position, so he's telling you that there'll be missed opportunities and aimless wanderings in your future.' She turned another card over. 'The Ten of Swords speaks of conflict, destruction and loss.'

Loss of the *K Sea?* Loss of Sam? Loss of the belief that her father was dead? Kevyn wasn't sure what the woman spoke of.

The fortune-teller picked up the last card to show Kevyn. 'But this is the one you want to hear about.'

Kevyn peered at the card. On it was a man and woman holding hands in front of an angel who wore the head of a lion. Crowns of fig leaves rested on their heads, and their clasped hands made them look like they were being married.

'The Two of Cups means love. It's the card of romance.' She looked up at Sam and smiled. 'I presume that means you, young man.'

She returned her gaze to Kevyn, grabbed her hand and spoke feverishly – her voice was grave. 'I see a voyage in your future where you will meet danger. You will fight with pirates and find great treasure deeply hidden.' Scooping up the cards, the crone tucked them back in the folds of her skirt. 'That'll be ten dollars.' The intensity had passed.

Sam pulled a bill out of his pocket. 'I'll give you twenty if you change that to 'sailing off into the sunset with a handsome stranger'.'

'Only the cards and the girl know what the future holds. It's all inside her.' The woman squeezed Kevyn's hand, digging her fingernail into the skin between Kevyn's knuckles. She had a firm grip for such an old woman. 'The next card in the deck was Death, child. There's a change about to occur in your life.' Nodding her head solemnly, she backed up until she was engulfed by the crowd.

Sam rolled his eyes. 'Pirates and lost treasure. The stories of Key West have clouded her spiel. The only other thing she needed to add was being forced to walk the plank.'

Kevyn stared at crowd where the woman had disappeared. She rubbed her sore knuckle. The woman had left her mark both on Kevyn's skin and, more importantly, her mind. Travel and change had been picked – all things that'd happened in the last week – so she wasn't completely off base. But what did loss and catastrophe mean?

'She was incredibly intuitive to know that love was in the air,' Sam added with a wink. 'I, at least, am in serious lust.' Leaning in, he planted a kiss on Kevyn's lips. 'Come on, let's grab a margarita and watch the sunset.' Catching her hand, he led her back through the crowd.

Kevyn took one last look at the wall of people into which the fortune-teller had dissolved and wondered what else in her fortune was about to come true.

*****

Chapter Nine

The dim light filtered through the louvered shutters and woke Kevyn the next morning.

They'd rented a cottage on a quiet side street. Bougainvillea and frangipani trees from the lush courtyard rested right outside the window and filtered the light so that fishnet-like shadows painted their forms. Sam had awoken earlier and sat propped up against the puffy pillows.

Kevyn stretched lazily under the thick white comforter. 'Early riser?'

'Couldn't sleep.' Sam stared into the corner of the room.

'Another morning waking up next to you.' Kevyn rolled onto her stomach and propped her head on her hand. 'I may never go home again.'

Sam ignored her teasing and swung his feet to the hardwood floor. 'I'll make coffee.' There was little emotion in his voice.

'Not so fast.' Kevyn grabbed him around the waist and pulled him back into bed. 'Some things are more important.' Rolling on top of Sam's chest to hold him in place, she kissed him good morning. 'Coffee can wait.' Without smiling, he gently moved Kevyn off his chest.

'You want a cup?'

Kevyn hesitated, unsure of what had changed. 'That's okay.' She pulled his discarded shirt over her head. 'I'll go.'

Trying to understand his strange tone and distant look, Kevyn shuffled into the kitchen. She spooned dark granules into the filter and thought about how little she knew of Sam. He was good-looking, and a lot more exciting than any man she'd ever known, but was that really enough to jump in a car and drive off with him? He turned cold with every mention of her father and now again this morning.

She didn't know much about what a widower went through. Maybe he woke every morning and ran through his life with his wife. Maybe he missed her so much that he felt he was betraying her with Kevyn. Maybe he felt he was moving too fast now. The maybes were endless.

Kevyn returned to the bedroom with two steaming cups of coffee. She stopped in the doorway to watch Sam.

Sitting on the side of the bed, his elbows rested on his knees as he rubbed his left ring finger.

The surf t-shirt of Sam's Kevyn wore smelled of musk, and a man who was truly invading all her senses. She was thrilled to have Sam erase the memory of past relationships, but at that moment Kevyn wasn't so sure she should be erasing Sam's.

She placed the coffee on the small rattan table and knelt on the bed behind him. She placed her hands on his shoulders and began to massage his muscles.

'Sorry,' he whispered, removing her hand from his skin. 'I just need a minute.'

'Sam, what happened to Beth?' Kevyn sat back on her heels. 'You can talk to me, if you'd like.'

Sam shook his head. '*I* happened to Beth.'

Kevyn returned her hand to his shoulder.

'I was the one who wanted the boat. I was the one who wanted to buy the store. I was the one who wanted to go diving all the time. I wasn't there when she needed me.' Sam resumed rubbing his finger where his wedding ring had once been. 'I got up early one morning and left her alone on the boat. Two guys climbed aboard.' Sam choked on a sob.

Kevyn swallowed, not wanting to hear what came next.

'They caught the guys.' Sam stared at his hands as if his memories were embedded in his palms. 'They were two kids...down from Rhode Island for spring break. They'd been out drinking all night. They were used to breaking into vacant summer homes.' Sam pushed at his finger to crack the knuckle then went back to rubbing the invisible ring. 'During the trial one kid said they were surprised to find Beth there and didn't know what to do. They were just looking for some booze and cash.'

Kevyn squeezed his shoulder, unsure of what to say.

'They panicked when they found her. They tied her up and taped her mouth shut.' He paused. 'With a roll of blue tape I had for varnishing the cap rails.' His tone turned desperate, 'They didn't know what they were doing. They taped both her mouth *and* her nose.'

'Oh, Sam.' Kevyn squeezed again.

'She suffocated while they ran away,' Sam whispered the words like it was a secret he kept from the world.

Kevyn sat behind him on the bed holding Sam tight and wishing there was something she could say.

'I should have been there.'

Even though he couldn't see it, Kevyn shook her head. 'You can't blame yourself.'

'If I'd been there they wouldn't have come onboard.'

Kevyn leaned over Sam's shoulder, cupped his chin and made him turn to look at her. 'You don't know that.'

He shook her off and stood up. 'They got fourteen dollars. That's what her life was worth, the fourteen dollars they found in her purse.' With that, he walked into the bathroom and slammed the door.

Kevyn felt like an anchor had dragged her to the bottom of the ocean as she sat, staring at the coffee that'd now turned cold.

The sun was up and over the trees in the yard by the time Sam reappeared. Kevyn had spent the morning on the porch, unsure of what to say or do. They both had baggage, although hers they were able to confront. Sam placed a fresh cup of coffee on the side table and sat down in the rocking chair beside her. 'I'm sorry.' He cupped the mug in his hands. 'I thought I was getting over all this.'

'It doesn't sound like something you ever get over.' Kevyn prayed she spoke the words Sam needed to hear. 'Maybe, with time, you can get past it, but it's never over.'

Sam nodded.

'I don't want to make things harder for you.' It was now Kevyn's turn to stare at her hands. 'I'd understand if you want to go home now.'

'I don't want to go home.' Sam turned to Kevyn. 'In fact, I think leaving might have been just what I needed to do.'

Kevyn reached up and ran the back of her hand down Sam's cheek. 'I know just how you feel.'

Three hours later, Kevyn and Sam walked hand in hand down the street, past cottages identical to the one they'd rented. Pastel, wood-framed, gingerbread houses with widow's walks were nestled behind ancient gumbo-limbo trees. Kevyn ran her hand along the white picket fences of the yards they passed and tried to count how many wooden porch swings she saw.

'Tell me again who this guy was?' Kevyn asked.

'Mel Fisher was the grandfather of treasure hunting here in Florida. In the seventies, he started looking for the *Atocha*, a Spanish ship that sank in the Marquesas.' Sam's earlier dark mood had passed; the memories once again buried deep. 'There were actually two ships – the *Atocha* and the *Santa Margarita* – that sank in a hurricane. There were a few survivors who reported the location, but before the Spanish could pull together a crew to rescue the gold, another hurricane blew through the area.' Sam sounded like his old self when he talked of sailing ships and unknown treasure. 'The second storm broke the ship apart and scattered its remains across the floor of the ocean, covering them in the sand. Both ships were lost.'

'Let me guess. My father found one of them.'

Sam shook his head. 'When wreck-diving became popular everyone started studying half-forgotten treasure lore. Guys like your father began traveling to the Caribbean to check out the places made famous by pirate stories. Mel was one of the successful ones.' They turned a corner onto Caroline Street. 'It took him the better part of fifteen years and every penny he had, but in the end he found both ships and recovered more than four-fifty million dollars worth of treasure.'

'And *he* knew Alex?'

'I'd imagine so. Mel died about twenty years ago, but his museum's still open. I know Alex spent a lot of time here with the woman who runs it.'

They turned onto Green Street. The three-story grey stone building with tall white-framed windows on either side of the door looked more like a courthouse than a museum. Old-fashioned cast iron cannons flanked the steps leading to the glass doors of the entrance. Banners that hung from the second story announcing an upcoming exhibition flapped in the breeze like the sails on *Wander*.

Upon entering the gift shop, they were met with a blast of air-conditioning, a welcome respite from the heat of the day. A college girl worked the till. She looked much too young to hold many answers, and Kevyn was just about to ask for her superior when Sam spoke up.

'Hey, Mandy.'

'Sam! We haven't seen you in a while,' the blonde practically purred. 'You've been avoiding us.'

What is it about Sam that turns women into jelly? Herself included, Kevyn thought. She hoped she didn't look as silly as the women who constantly hit on him.

'Shop's keeping me busy.' He shrugged. 'Not much time for road trips these days. Is Trista around?'

'She's in the office. I'll get her.' Flashing him a smile that shone brighter than a mast light, the young girl disappeared.

'Guess you've been here before,' Kevyn said.

'I used to intern here. This is one of the biggest museums in the southeast for nautical archaeology.' Sam steered her to the bench inside the main door. 'I haven't been back much lately, but Key West has a way of getting into your bones.'

Kevyn wondered what else had gotten into his bones.

A woman who looked to be in her early forties came out of the back room wearing a tailored beige suit. Her auburn hair was sculpted in a style that framed her angular face and fell neatly to her shoulders.

Staring at Sam over a pair of winged librarian glasses, she wore a serious, yet faintly amused, smile on her lips.

'Sam, I didn't know you'd be here today.' She leaned in and kissed his cheek. She shifted her weight away, expertly balancing on her heel. 'I thought you'd be busy getting the store back on its feet.'

Sam glanced at Kevyn before waving away the comment. 'Shop's going to be fine. Just a slight glitch.'

The woman smiled as Kevyn wondered what they were talking about. 'To what do I owe this pleasure, then?'

'Trista, this is Kevyn Morgan. She's looking for Alex.'

The woman's jaw clenched and her eyes narrowed. Swiftly she removed her glasses and stared directly at Kevyn. 'Alex Morgan is your father.' It was more of a statement than a question. Her attire and demeanor were pure business, but the color of her skin indicated she spent at least a little time in the sun enjoying life in the Keys.

'Yes, ma'am. Do you know him?'

Trista glanced at Sam, holding his eye a beat longer than normal. 'Alex and I,' she paused. '…know each other.'

'Have you seen him lately?' Kevyn's voice sounded pleading in her own ears compared to the elegance this woman exuded. She wondered when it was that she actually started *wanting* to find Alex.

'About a year and a half ago, now. He was here looking for a place to stay for a time.' Trista shifted her weight again, leaning on her left hip. 'He played around in our archives for a bit, until one day he just took off. No good-bye, no explanation.'

'Do you know where he went?'

Trista's reddish-brown hair glided across her shoulders when she shook her head. She reached up and flicked the strands back. No ring adorned her fingers, and no bright polish gleamed on her nails – just a simple elegant manicure to match the rest of the well-put-together picture. 'My guess is he's in the Virgin Islands. He mentioned a ship that was supposed to have sunk off the reef in Anegada.'

Sam's head snapped up. 'Can you find out for sure?'

'I can check his log-ins on the computer,' Trista offered. 'Come on back. I'll show you around.' She glanced over her shoulder at Sam. 'You've seen this before. Why don't you go get a coffee and we'll catch up with you when we're done?' She left no room for arguing.

Sam paused.

'I'll tell you what we find.' Kevyn placed her hand on Sam's arm.

Sam nodded and kissed her on the cheek. 'I'll be at the coffeehouse down the street.'

Trista punched in an entry code on the pad by the door and directed Kevyn to a chair in her office. It was exactly what Kevyn expected from a museum. Piles of antique looking parchments were stacked on a side hutch. Coffee table picture books focusing on sea life and ancient civilizations lined the bookshelves in the corner. Newspaper clippings and pictures from the discovery of the *Atocha* covered one whole wall.

Trista walked around the oak desk and set her glasses beside the computer screen. A single picture frame with a little boy playing on a tire swing decorated the desk, almost buried under piles of manila folders and papers. 'So, Alex disappeared again, did he? When was the last time you saw him?'

'Actually, I've never met him. He left when I was just a baby.'

Trista didn't flinch at this piece of information. 'Your father has a habit of coming in and out of people's lives. He never stays long, and you're always left wondering if he was ever really there at all.'

'Well, he hasn't *ever* come into my life.' Saying the words out loud made Kevyn feel exhausted and discouraged all at the same time. 'I came down from Savannah to find him, but so far I've run into dead ends everywhere I turn. No one seems to know where he is.'

'Well, let's see what we can come up with.' Trista peered at her computer screen. 'Alex was here for three months in the spring. He was in this office almost every day working on research. I'm sure we can find a paper trail of what he was looking for.' Trista punched at her keyboard and nodded at the screen. 'Says here that it was the *La Victoria* he was researching.'

'*La Victoria* sank in the Virgin Islands? Is that where I should look for him?' Kevyn wanted someone else to confirm that her search was headed in the right direction, and this woman exuded the wealth of confidence to do just that.

'I'm not saying that's where he is now,' Trista cautioned. 'Alex gets interested in something and devotes all his time to it, but he just as easily gets sidetracked and runs off to work another project that interests him more. That's why he was never a threat to Mel. Mel knew he would never stick around long enough to see it through.'

'That seems to be what I'm hearing from everyone.'

Trista narrowed her eyes. 'Do you know anything about Alex?'

'I know he left my mother and me over thirty years ago. I know he travels a lot hunting treasure chests, and I know he sails. Other than that, I'm still trying to sort out what's true and what's part of the lie I've been fed since I was a little girl.'

'Your father and I have known each other for a number of years.' Trista clasped her hands in front of her. 'He's a hard man to get close to.

Hunting treasure is a lonely profession, and he spends his days on the bottom of the ocean floor cut off from other people, or buried deep in a book and lost in his own world. But when he gets to talking about his work…' She shook her head and whistled. 'He lights up like a kid at Christmas. Alex becomes larger than life when he's telling tales of deep-sea adventures and lost treasure.' Trista's voice revealed some of the excitement she must've felt for the man who delivered the curator a real slice of history for her museum. 'Your father's stories ignite a forgotten passion in people. Here in Key West, he's likened to Hemingway…a true throwback to another era.'

'It sounds like he's your hero.'

Trista snorted. 'Not hero by any means, but I do understand where he's coming from. He's kind of like the ocean. You can't harness or tame him.'

'Right now, I'd just be happy to find him.'

Trista shifted her focus back to the computer and her voice returned to business, '*La Victoria* sank in 1738 with a reputed $1,750,000 worth of treasure on board.' She looked up from her screen. 'Phew, that'll be a lot of money by now.'

'I guess that's where I'll head then.'

'I have a crew in St. John's, a few islands southwest of Anegada, working another site. I'll call down and ask if they've seen or heard anything about him.'

'That would be fantastic! I wasn't sure where to go from here.'

'Let me make some calls and I'll get back to you.' Trista stood up and smoothed her skirt, signaling that the meeting was over. She walked Kevyn to the door. 'Whatever I *do* find out doesn't change the fact that Alex is a fool. He never should have left, and he never should be doing what he's doing now.'

*****

Chapter Ten

Kevyn walked out the glass doors of the museum into the heat of the day wondering what it was her father was doing. Trista's phone had rung before Kevyn got the chance to ask. It must have been something important because Trista had abruptly said goodbye and whisked her out of the room before she returned to the call. Did this woman know more about Alex's business than she was letting on?

The air felt warm and damp at the same time, hanging thick like the steam iron she sometimes used to strip varnish. She walked down the street to meet Sam, with a desire to meet her father growing inside her. She may not have found Alex yet, but she was starting to get an idea of who he was. The image wasn't that far off from the man she created in her mind all those years ago.

Between what Trista and Pete told her, he sounded like an adventurer. She imagined his life as exciting – a continuous game of hide and seek. He was an underwater detective, searching for the past. His world was filled with stories of a forgotten era – a time of pirates, exploration and adventures on the high seas. A thrill ran through her and, for a minute, Kevyn was convinced that he was someone she would want to get to know.

And then it hit her. Once again, the thought that he didn't want to know her flooded her mind. For the past two weeks since she'd found out he was alive, the idea that he'd known she was out there this whole time and hadn't even tried to contact her played with her emotions. One minute she was excited to go find him, the next she was devastated that he'd never come see her.

If he was so great, how could he have been gone all these years? How could he not even have wondered what she looked like? What she did? Who she was? She'd asked herself those questions about him from the time she was a child. Even when she'd thought he'd died, Kevyn had still laid in her bed, listening to her mother drinking and crying in the next room, and wished that he'd come back for her.

And now, it turned out, he could have. He could've shown up at any time in her thirty years, walked right up to her and said, 'Hello Kevyn. I'm your father and that's my boat that you live on. We are a lot alike, you and I.' But he hadn't.

The excitement she'd felt just moments ago blew out of her body like a tree branch in a hurricane, and she crumpled to a bench on the side of the street. Pulling her knees up to her chest, she hugged herself tightly. What was she doing? She was chasing after a man who'd abandoned her.

It was in this position Sam found her half an hour later. She stared blankly at the sidewalk when he approached. He sat down beside her and wrapped his arm around her shoulders, and she leaned into his body.

'I'm sorry.' Sam stroked Kevyn's hair. 'Trista told you?'

'Told me what?' Kevyn sniffled. 'She hasn't seen him. All she knows is what he was looking for a year and a half ago. Not much to go on.'

Sam twisted on the bench to look at Kevyn. His forehead scrunched in confusion. He opened his mouth to say something but shut it again.

'What?' Kevyn pleaded.

Sam shook his head. 'Did she say what he was looking for?'

Kevyn wiped the tears under her eyes. 'A boat called *La Victoria.*'

Sam's eyes widened and he grabbed her wrist. 'Has he found it?'

'She doesn't know.' Kevyn pulled her arm away and rubbed where his grip had tightened on her and wondered why he was acting so strange. 'What's wrong?'

Sam's cell phone rang. Holding up a finger, he fished it out of his pocket.

Kevyn heard Trista's muffled voice on the line.

'Okay, come for dinner,' Sam said. 'We'll talk then.'

Sam and Kevyn returned to the cottage with groceries and two pounds of filleted mahi-mahi from a fisherman on the dock. Kevyn placed a tin of back-fin crabmeat in the refrigerator.

She'd had all afternoon to think about what was happening in her life. Part of her was intrigued and thrilled to be searching for her father, while another part was terrified at what she'd eventually find. The third part was simply confused. Some of the pieces of the puzzle didn't quite fit together—Sam being one of them. She'd just met him and here he was helping her find a man he didn't even like. Was he showing interest in her, or was there a secret that he just wouldn't reveal?

'Are you sure you want to be here?' Kevyn pulled peppers and cheese from her cloth grocery bag. 'What Trista said about the store today, can you afford to be away?'

Sam buried his head in the fridge, putting the food away. 'The shop is just going through a slow period. It'll be alright soon.' He didn't even look her in the eye.

Trista arrived at seven. Gone was the studious career woman attire; in its place was a Polynesian-flowered summer skirt and sage green t-shirt. She had pinned her hair back from her face, making her look young and carefree. And she carried with her a photo album tucked under her arm and a bottle of Bombay Sapphire in her hand.

Again, she leaned in and kissed Sam on the cheek, but this time she gave Kevyn a hug as well. 'Thanks for inviting me. I rarely get to know new people. Tourists are coming in and out of the museum all day long, but none stay more than an hour or so.'

Sam poured Trista a glass of wine. 'You said you had news on where Alex is?'

'I called our archaeologists in St. John's. He thinks Alex has been working out of Anegada.'

'He's there now?' Kevyn asked.

'Len said he saw him a month ago and hasn't heard that he left.' Trista walked over to the bowl of crab dip and picked up a sliver of red pepper. Biting into it, she added, 'Problem is, salvaging at this point – before a discovery is made – is a bit of a game between hunters. Alex and Len know each other but are basically competition. If they did see each other, Alex wouldn't want to reveal his theory of where *La Victoria* is until he can claim it as his own, so he may try to hide or avoid Len all together. I could ask Len to head over to Anegada and take a look if you're worried, but I doubt Alex will talk to him.'

Sam nodded. 'These guys play a lot of games to throw one another off the trail of treasure. I know of one operation that moves their boat every three hours to new dive sites just so no one will suspect which site is the hot dive.'

Kevyn thought for a moment. Would her father hide from *her*, as well?

'That's okay. I just needed an island destination to head to. I guess I could sail to St. John and talk to Len myself.' Kevyn let her words trail off as she looked out the window over the bougainvillea, trying to sort out this new bit of information. 'It seems silly to check up on someone who obviously wants to stay lost.' She twirled the end of her ponytail around her index finger, creating one large ringlet. 'Maybe I should just let him be.'

Trista began to speak but she paused, glancing up at Sam instead. A look passed between the two that Kevyn couldn't read. She was about to say more when Sam stood and walked across the room. Moving behind Kevyn, he placed one arm around the top of her chest and pulled her close.

'Hey, this is good news.' Sam planted a kiss behind her ear. 'You know where to head.'

Kevyn turned to look at him, and smiled. The man she had just met was being more supportive and caring than her father had ever been. She should stop wondering why he'd come along to help her. He was a nice guy--that was all.

'Maybe I should go.' Trista reached for her purse. 'You don't need me here.'

'No, stay.' Kevyn snapped out of her daydream. 'You seem to know Alex better than anyone, especially me. I'd love it if you could tell me more about him.'

It was Trista's turn to get a hazy look in her eye. 'I'm not sure how much I can help, but I'll tell you what I know.'

'I'll start dinner and let you two talk,' Sam said, exchanging yet another look with Trista that Kevyn couldn't read.

Trista nodded as Sam poured Kevyn a glass of zinfandel and gently steered her to the patio. He placed the vegetables and dip on the table and retreated through the French doors to the kitchen.

'You've found a *real* treasure with that one.' Trista motioned at Sam as she took a seat at the wrought-iron table. 'I don't think I've ever had a man make me dinner before.'

Kevyn watched Sam through the glass doors. 'Athens, my cat, and I, have eaten alone for so long now I can't remember the last time I've even seen a man in the kitchen.'

Early in her twenties Kevyn had tried her hand at being married. She'd really just picked him because she thought she was lonely. It'd been after living on *Wander* for a few years that Dan had come along and made her wonder what it would be like to be a couple. Turned out, she liked being alone on her boat far more. She gave it six months before she packed up her two duffle bags and patiently waited for him to come home. Sitting on the bed they shared, she looked around the small house they'd rented with its peeling wallpaper and a stove that wouldn't light, and knew it would never feel like a home. So she'd gotten up, written Dan a note and walked out the door. She'd felt guilty ever since that she'd just walked away. With the resent revelation that Alex had done the same thing she wondered if that was a family trait.

'I know what you mean. It's always me in the kitchen and Kyle waiting at the table.'

'Kyle's your husband?' Kevyn hadn't noticed a wedding ring, but these days that wasn't the best indication of a person's relationship status.

'Son.' Trista held the deep-bowled crystal glass up to her nose. She bent her head forward, placing the top of the glass practically on her forehead, and breathed in deeply before taking a sip.

It was the same ritual Sam had performed and Kevyn wondered if he'd learned it from her.

'Kyle's five. It's just him and me, so I do all the cooking and he does all the eating.'

Kevyn smiled. 'It must be hard to juggle a career and a child at the same time.'

'It's a little more laid back here in the Keys. I can be flexible at the museum and a neighbor watches Kyle after school. It's not like I'm running MoMA or anything.' Trista shrugged and changed the subject. 'What about you? Today you said you didn't even know Alex. What brought you here looking for him?'

'I guess it started with my grandfather's request. I owe him so much. I just wanted to be able to do something for him.' The breeze rustled through the palm fronds in the yard reminding Kevyn of the grasses in the river by her grandfather's house. 'Also, it's probably to spite my mother. She and I aren't close; the more she fought against me searching for him the more I wanted to find him.'

The scent of jasmine filled Kevyn's senses as she drew in a deep breath. When Sam had asked the same question, she'd answered with the facts. With Trista, she elaborated, 'I haven't been living much of a life. I'm thirty, and I don't know who I am.'

'And you think Alex is going to hold the answers for you?' Skepticism dripped from her words.

'No, the one thing I've learned about my father is that he's more screwed up than I am.' Kevyn sipped her wine. 'A month ago I thought I was one person, and within an afternoon I found out I'm someone else completely. This is the new Kevyn Morgan…the one with a father and the one who can sail down to Florida, meet a guy and go away for the weekend with him without a second thought.'

'The search for Alex is giving you a second chance at life.'

'Something like that.'

Sam came out the doors to light the barbecue. Both women rose and helped him carry plates and platters to the table as he waited for the temperature to rise on the grill.

The women returned to the table on the opposite side of the yard, well out of Sam's earshot. 'Maybe you're giving Sam a second shot at life, too.'

Her statement startled Kevyn. 'You know about Beth?' That must've been the source of all the strange looks traveling back and forth between Trista and Sam.

'Sam spent a lot of time down here after it happened.'

Kevyn watched him test the heat of the grill with his hands and gently place the fillets of mahi on the bars. Grinding sea salt on top of the fish, he then reached for the fish whip when it was time to turn the fillets.

'I can't even imagine what he went through,' Kevyn whispered.

Trista shifted her gaze from Sam to the frangipani tree flowering in the corner of the yard. 'Everyone goes through things in life. You just have to pray that the people around you are strong enough to pick up the pieces when something terrible happens to someone you love.'

Kevyn thought about Trista's words. *Did Sam have people around him to pick up the pieces?*

Within minutes, Sam crossed the yard and joined them at the table, carrying three steak-sized pieces of fish adorned with the diamond-shaped cross of the grill. He picked up a small bowl and spooned a sauce of green onions, cilantro and garlic over the fillets.

'*Bon appétit.*' He raised his glass.

There was silence for the next ten minutes as everyone devoured the fish.

'This is...' Trista stared at her plate and frowned. 'It's...' She seemed to be searching for the right word.

Sam laid a hand on hers and smiled. 'It's mahi from the docks.' It was a tender gesture that filled the awkward moment of Trista's blunder.

Trista returned Sam's smile. 'I was *going* to say, delicious.'

Kevyn watched the exchange. She was starting to wonder if Sam had a history with this woman that went much deeper than friendship.

'Sam, why don't you grab a beer down at Sloppy's while I help Kevyn with the dishes?' Unlike her earlier direction of him waiting at the coffee shop, this was more of a suggestion than a command.

Trista's earlier stumble with what she wanted to say had passed. Not for the first time, Kevyn marveled that the woman was so confident and direct. Kevyn knew she could never be that bold.

'You cooked. We'll clean.' Kevyn grabbed the empty fish platter from his hands, wondering if Trista was going to tell her what had happened between her and Sam in the past. Maybe she was the one who got him through the horror of what happened to Beth?

For the second time that day, Sam left them alone to talk.

86

Trista began flitting around the kitchen, moving dishes from one pile to the next. She wasn't being very productive and looked completely out of place. Finally, she gave up and grabbed the bottle of Bombay she'd brought along.

'Come on, you'll need this.' She led Kevyn back to the table. Pouring two long shots, she looked deep into the bottom of the glass before she drained the liquid in one gulp.

'Alex spoke of you once.' Trista poured another gin over her barely melted ice cubes. 'He said he had a daughter up north. I went so far as to look you up on the Internet. Read all about your restoration business.'

Kevyn remembered the article in the *Savannah Herald*. A reporter had come to interview her in her shed. They spoke all about how she combed estate sales and drove around searching the curbs on garbage day for any neglected pieces. It had been a series about people from Savannah who were preserving the past. It now struck Kevyn as ironic that there wasn't a piece on her father, too.

'Kevyn, I told you I had a son.' She opened up the photo album and tapped her perfectly manicured nail on his picture. In it, a dark-haired, brown-eyed little boy sat in the grass playing with a toy truck. 'I named him Kyle as a tribute to your father's boat, the *K Sea*.'

Kevyn thought it odd that a successful, confident woman like Trista would do something as schoolgirl-ish as that. 'Isn't a boat usually named after a person?'

'It was.' Trista swallowed another mouthful of gin. 'It was only after Kyle was born that I realized the boat was named after you… Kyle's sister.'

Kevyn snapped her head up from the picture. *What did she just say?* 'He's Alex's son?'

'Yes.' Trista nodded.

'I have a brother?' She looked at the picture again. The smiling little boy did have the same color chestnut hair she did, and their eyes were the same color green. The picture Kevyn carried of Alex was taken too long ago to make out the color of his eyes, but her grandfather had told her they were the same color as hers.

'Yes.' Trista lowered her eyes, studying the drink in front of her. 'Kyle is your brother.'

'Does Alex know?'

Trista rolled the ice cubes around in the liquid, remaining silent.

'He abandoned *another* child?' Kevyn's thoughts reeled with this new information. Her family was growing at an alarmingly fast pace.

'I didn't tell Alex.' Trista's voice, raspy from the gin, sounded like Lauren Bacall.

'You didn't tell him?' Kevyn felt like a parrot, repeating everything back to the speaker.

'I knew he already had a family out there somewhere that haunted him and that he had demons. I didn't think he could handle any more. He's been here and spent time with Kyle, but he never asked and I... never told.'

'What about Kyle? Doesn't he deserve to know his father?' Why did all these people think they had to shelter kids from the truth?

'Kyle needs stability in his life, now more than ever, and your father couldn't provide that. For the time being, I can. I would rather he not be disappointed so early in life. He's going to learn soon enough what life is really like.' Trista raised the glass to her lips. She paused momentarily, holding the glass inches from her mouth then placed it back on the table, untouched.

'Do you really want his first lesson in the harshness of life to be that his mother lied to him for all of it?' Kevyn slammed her own glass down on the table.

For a second it looked like Trista had been slapped. She winced and drew in a short breath. 'I don't expect you to understand, Kevyn. You don't have kids but when you do you'll do anything to protect them from pain.'

'I may not have a child of my own but I was in the same situation of being lied to about my father. It didn't stop me from missing him or feeling sad.'

'You're right, but I've never lied to my son. I just haven't found a way to tell him Alex is his father. He's only five year old and too young to comprehend why his father isn't around. Maybe after you've met Alex you'll understand.' Trista stared at the glass in her hand. 'Either way, I'd like *you* to be a part of Kyle's life.'

Kevyn's sarcastic tongue lashed out, caustic as her varnish stripper. 'As a sister? Or do you want me to lie to him, too?'

Trista sucked in a deep breath. 'As a sister, if you'd like. I don't want to keep Kyle from his family any longer.' She stood up to leave. 'Why don't you come by after school tomorrow and spend some time with him? I'll leave the address on the counter.'

Sam returned to the cottage shortly after Trista left.

Kevyn had moved from the table to a stand of date palms in the corner of the yard. Delicate orchids of varying colors wound their roots around the trunks, clinging to the strength of the tree for support.

Sam laid a hand on her shoulder and squeezed.

'You knew, didn't you?' She recoiled from his touch.

'I was here when Trista found out she was pregnant.' His voice came out like a whisper.

'That's why you hate Alex.'

'I don't hate him for that.' Sam grasped Kevyn's hand and held on tight, not giving her the option to pull away. 'I just saw how much Trista has struggled over the years. I'm smart enough to know that it's Trista's responsibility to tell him, but I can't help but wonder why he hasn't put two and two together.'

'Well, he put them together with me and *still* left.' Kevyn ran her free hand over the ridges of the tree trunk beside her, stopping when she came to the lemon yellow flower attached to the rough bark. Her voice was as soft as the petals when she spoke, 'Maybe Trista's right. Maybe she's better off without him knowing.'

'And that's her choice,' Sam agreed. 'But it seems like Alex is skating through life without a care in the world when he has two very *real* cares right here.'

Kevyn didn't know what to say. He was right. Alex did have responsibilities whether he liked it or not. This was no longer just about her. There was someone else out there Alex was letting down.

Sam retreated to the cottage, leaving Kevyn lost in thought. She stood staring at the orchids long into the night.

Kevyn slid out of Sam's car and smoothed the wrinkles from the front of her skirt. She'd fretted all afternoon about what to wear and what to say, feeling like a teenager attending her very first dance.

Sam placed his hand on the small of her back and guided her up the stone walkway. She twisted the handle of the bag she carried into a tight knot and hesitated at the door. Sam reached out and rang the bell.

A dark haired boy with sun-browned skin opened the door. In his hands was a toy monkey; the fur on one side was worn thin and bits of stuffing peeked through the threadbare material. Clutching the well-loved stuffed animal to his chest, the boy cocked his head to one side. 'You aren't little.'

'No, I'm not.' Laughter bubbled out of Kevyn. She bent her knees and squatted to be the same height as her brother. 'I'm Kevyn. You must be Kyle.'

'Mommy said a friend was coming to play.'

'Well, I hope we'll be friends.' Kevyn held out a bag for the little boy. He ripped it open to find an antique toy fire engine. It was half the size he was, with an expandable ladder that would reach over his head.

His green eyes widened. 'Cool! Come on, we'll play in my sandbox!' He grabbed Kevyn's hand and pulled her into the house.

'I'll be in the kitchen.' Sam stepped inside and closed the front door behind them.

'Mom's in there. She's got cookies if you're good,' Kyle yelled back over his shoulder as he led Kevyn to the sliding glass doors on the other side of the living room.

Kevyn caught sight of Trista standing behind the counter in the kitchen. She waved and Trista nodded hello, but there was no time to exchange greetings as Kyle hurried her through the house.

The backyard was a mix of kid's playground and adult courtyard. A tire swing hung from a banyan tree that dominated the area. A slide, the same color of red as the toy fire truck cradled in Kyle's grip, ran from a low hanging branch to a pile of sand below. Primary colored lengths of wood were nailed to the trunk, allowing access to a fort built in the tree's center. Abandoned toy cars and trucks were half-buried in the sand and scattered over the grass.

On the opposite side, a more adult play-land existed. A Jacuzzi ran quietly under a canvas sail awning, and the teak bar that ran along the fence line offered a pitcher of lemonade and oatmeal cookies for the new guest in the yard. Spikes of sunburst palm trees lined the far side, secluding the space from the neighbors and casting shade over the deck.

Kevyn suddenly wished that she had grown up with all this instead of crammed in the single apartments where she and Brianna had lived. She'd always loved being outside at Grandfather's, but she was never there enough. Here, she and Brianna could have played together and bonded like a mother and daughter should. Growing up in a house like this, she might have smiled a little more as a child, which was just what Kyle was doing now.

He plunked himself down right in the middle of the sand and drove the fire truck with one chubby fist. 'Rrrrrr,' he hummed as he ran the truck over the upturned cars.

'You should turn on the siren so those cars get out of your way.'

'Yeah, good idea.' He turned the fire engine around and took a big breath, puffing out his cheeks like a saxophone player. 'Whirer, whirer, whirer.' Kevyn reached out to move the cars in his path. She watched his every move. Did he look like Alex? She had no way of knowing if the cowlick above his right ear had been passed from father to son.

'The school's on fire. We have to get there and put it out!' he squealed, oblivious to her intense study.

'Okay, okay,' Kevyn laughed and Kyle joined her. His was a laugh that started in his toes. Innocent joy bubbled out of him.

She was envious. Everything was still so exciting for Kyle; he hadn't yet been disappointed. The dark side of people was still a mystery to him, and he hadn't had to be responsible and clean up the empty vodka bottles at an early age. Kyle hadn't felt lost and alone, with everyone in his life keeping a secret from him. She was glad Kyle and Trista lived like this and wished she hadn't been so hard on her the night before. She was obviously doing a fantastic job of raising Kyle. Kevyn swallowed down a sob and pushed more toy cars out of his way.

They played outside for an hour while Trista watched through the window. Kevyn saw the worried look on her face and sent her a smile to assure her that all was going well.

'How about going inside and showing Mommy your fire engine?' Kevyn asked after half an hour of rescuing G.I. Joes from a burning building.

'Yeah, then I'll show you my room.'

It took another hour for Kyle to show Kevyn all his toys. He pulled out every plastic dinosaur he had and named each one. Grabbing his model airplane, he buzzed around the room in a circle before pulling books off a shelf and explaining what they were about. Finally, he resurrected a plastic boat from his toy chest and handed it to her.

'This is where my daddy is,' he said, as if that was the most normal statement in the world.

Kevyn's head shot up from the toy train she was playing with. She thought Kyle didn't know about Alex. 'Have you seen him?'

'No, he lives on the boat. He's sailing around the world and fighting sea monsters. He has a hook for an arm.'

Kevyn searched the little boy's face for any sign of sadness, but found none. It was the innocent statement of a five-year-old. 'Well, he must be very adventurous and heroic.'

'Yeah, I'm going to go help him fight the pirates when I'm older.'

'He'd be lucky to have your help.' Kyle's smile revealed his first missing tooth. She had already missed so many milestones in his short life that Kevyn didn't want to miss any more.

By the time Trista stuck her head in the door to announce that it was time for dinner, Kyle was deep into pointing out all the fish in his fish tank. 'This one is Bubbles, that's Fish Sticks, the blue one is Float, and this here is Squiggles.'

'Come on, Kyle. You'll have plenty of time to show Miss Kevyn all this stuff later.' Trista rubbed Kyle's shaggy hair. She turned to Kevyn. 'I hope you don't mind pizza. It's this little man's favorite.'

'No mushrooms, Mom. I hate mushrooms.' This was the life-and-death statement only a five-year-old could utter.

Kevyn winked at Kyle. 'I agree! I don't like mushrooms, either!' She turned to Trista. 'As long as you don't mind us staying.'

Trista began to say something, but Kyle cut her off. 'Yeah, stay! Then after dinner we can watch the movie about when I was a dolphin.'

Trista laughed. 'I took him to swim with the dolphins last summer and now he thinks he is one.' She started out the door after Kyle's quickly moving figure.

Kevyn grabbed her arm. 'Thanks for this.' She didn't know what else to say.

'No, thank you.' Trista checked down the hall to make sure Kyle was in the kitchen and turned back. 'A lot of what you said last night made sense.'

Kevyn watched Kyle pull his chair over to the counter to get at the pizza, completely oblivious to their conversation.

'Kyle and I will have a long talk tonight,' Trista said.

'He's a great kid.'

'Yes, he is.' Trista smiled.

'He has some imagination. Do you know he thinks Alex is off fighting pirates?'

Trista sighed. 'I've never lied to him about his father. I told him that Alex is on a boat. With the museum and all he sees here in Key West about pirate lore, he's come up with this magical flying boat that Alex sails on.'

'He's not that much different from me.' Kevyn took a last look around his room and pulled the door shut. 'When I was his age, I thought my father lived in the clouds.'

'I guess you believe what you have to until you can understand. For Kyle, it's not that his father abandoned him, it's that his father doesn't know he's a father. I'm not sure how to explain that.' Trista's brow furrowed in confusion.

'You'll figure it out.'

'He's just so young.'

'He won't be too young forever.'

'I know. But I just don't want to have him disappointed. If Alex knew and ignored him like he did you, I couldn't stand it.'

Kevyn swallowed the mixture of pain and jealousy that was welling in her throat. 'Look, I'm the last person to understand my father, but maybe he's changed. Maybe he's *ready* to be a father now.'

'I don't know, Kevyn. I hope you're right.' Trista offered her a sad smile. 'And I hope you find what you're looking for.'

Kevyn nodded. 'Who knows? Maybe I'll find it for Kyle, too.'

'Maybe...' Trista's voice trailed off. She gnawed on her bottom lip. 'If you find him, ask him to come visit. It's time I faced up to this.'

'Come ON, Mom!' Kyle urgently called from the kitchen. 'PIZZA!' It didn't take long for it to disappear.

Kevyn rode home in silence. Sam pulled into the driveway of the rented cottage and turned off the ignition. He had his hand on the door and was about to get out of the car when Kevyn finally spoke. 'I'm going to Anegada to find Alex. He has to know he has another child. Kyle can't grow up without a father like I did.'

Sam's face was set in stone. A hardness filled his eyes like it had that first day they'd met. 'I'm going to sail on Thursday.'

She hadn't known her plan until she said it out loud.

'You shouldn't do this alone.' Sam stared over the steering wheel, gripping it tight in his fists. 'I want to come with you.'

'I can't ask you to do that.' Kevyn wasn't totally surprised by the offer. Sam was quickly proving to be the most responsible person in her life, but the hardness that steeled his voice made her wonder why he was offering. 'I'll be fine.'

'No. You won't. It's a big ocean and you've only seen a small part.'

Kevyn felt her temperature rising. *Was he saying she couldn't handle it? Did he think she needed rescuing again?* 'I've gotten this far. Besides, you don't even like Alex. Why would you want to help find him?'

'I don't like Alex, but I do like you.'

Kevyn's next argument was already formed and on her tongue, when Sam's words stopped her. Was she fighting him on this because he insulted her ability, or because she was afraid to share her space with someone again? She immediately softened her tone. 'I like you, too. And I'd love to get to know you better. But I have to go find my father first.'

'I know, but I can't stand the idea of you being out there alone.' Sam twisted in his seat to face her.

'Just because something happened to Beth doesn't mean it will happen to me.'

Sam winced at the sound of her name. 'I know. But, I'd like to help.' A little boy look replaced the hardened look. 'Let me come with you.'

'I don't want you to feel obligated.'

'*Obligated?* Are you kidding? Sailing around the Caribbean with a beautiful woman? That's not an obligation, that's a privilege.' Sam laughed. 'Besides, you'll be in a bikini all day long. How could I *not* want to go?'

*****

93

Chapter Eleven

The following afternoon Kevyn walked over to Trista's to tell her they were leaving and say goodbye to Kyle. She knew he wouldn't be home from school, but she wanted a few minutes alone with Trista to talk more about Alex.

She thought about how much her life had changed in the past few days as she turned down the quiet tree-lined street. Trista's golden yellow cottage was at the end, tucked away behind a white picket fence decorated with bright pink bougainvillea blooms—it was a colorful view.

Kevyn walked up the stairs. A wicker basket piled high with toys sat beside the porch swing. She knocked on the door and waited. A few moments went by without Trista answering so Kevyn knocked again. Just as she was about to leave, the heavy wooden door swung open.

'Kevyn, you startled me. Excuse me, I was just having a nap.' Trista stood there in a pair of checkered flannel boxers and a white ribbed tank top. Her eyes looked sunken; lost in the huge dark circles beneath them. Her perfectly groomed hair was matted on one side and straggly. She looked nothing like the poised and powerful woman Kevyn had met at the museum just the other day. 'Come in. I'll put on some coffee.'

Kevyn shook her head. 'I don't want to bother you. I just came to say goodbye to Kyle.'

'He'll be home from school soon.' Trista led Kevyn into the kitchen. Halfway down the hall, she stumbled. Kevyn reached out to grab her arm and scanned the floor for the likely scattered toy that'd tripped her. But nothing was there. Trista waved off Kevyn's hand and ignored her concern. 'You're leaving then?'

'Yes, Sam and I are going back to Lauderdale and sailing for the Virgin Islands as soon as I can check the weather and provision the boat. It's a long trip, over a thousand miles, so it'll take the better part of a week to get there. But with Sam along it should be smooth sailing.' Kevyn rambled on, taken aback by Trista's appearance.

Pouring the water into the coffee maker, Trista seemed oblivious to the world around her as she reached above the counter to retrieve two mugs. Kevyn couldn't help but notice that her hands shook as she set the cups in front of her. One mug teetered on its rim for a second and rolled off the counter, smashing into pieces on the hardwood floor. Tears welled up in Trista's eyes as she brushed a stray hair from her forehead with the back of her hand.

'Trista, are you okay? No offense, but you don't look so good.'

Trista's smile was weak. 'It's alright. It'll pass.'

She retrieved a dustpan from the closet and began cleaning up. 'What will pass?'

Trista took a deep breath. 'I have Huntington's disease.'

Kevyn gasped. She didn't know a lot about the disease, but she knew it wasn't good.

'I'm fine,' Trista added quickly. 'It's just the early stages, but every now and then I get hit with a wallop of low energy. It's nothing to worry about yet. I just need some time to rest.'

'You've gone through this before?'

'The symptoms started showing up a few months ago.' She pulled another mug down from the cupboard. 'It doesn't last long, but it takes it out of me physically. Yesterday I felt fine, but it was an emotional day and it drained me. I just need a day to catch up.'

'What about Kyle? How can you take care of him when you're like this? Do you have someone I can call?' Kevyn was immediately worried.

'When the time comes, I'll have a caregiver in the house. It'll get worse and I'll need help, but so far it's been good – real good. Right now, it's just Kyle and me.' She poured the rich, black coffee. 'Your father is the closest thing to family Kyle and I have and, well… you know how close that is.'

Kevyn swallowed the wave of anger at her father. 'How bad is it?'

'Eventually, it will kill me.' The confident Trista was back. She sounded clinical and in control, like she'd done all the research and accepted its results. 'But that could be years from now. It's degenerative, but I have more good days than bad and even long stretches where I'm perfectly normal.' Trista shook her head. 'It's not worth worrying Kyle about or anyone else, for that matter. Most days I'm one hundred percent, and I have a woman down the street who looks after Kyle when I'm not. I'll take Kyle there when he comes home.'

'Is he…is *he* okay?' Kevyn felt her heart beating out of her chest.

'It's hereditary, if that's what you mean. He has a fifty percent chance of developing the disease.' With this information, Trista's voice broke. 'I didn't know I had it when I got pregnant.' A small sob escaped her lips and her shaky hand flew to her mouth to cover it. 'I'd never do this to him on purpose.'

Kevyn sat down, completely stunned. 'Does he know?'

'No. And I don't want him to,' she stated firmly. '*This* he is definitely too young to learn about. If he does have it, it won't show up until he's in his late thirties or forties, and by then there may be a cure. There's a lot of living for him to do before then.'

'Won't he know that you have it?' Kevyn prodded.

Trista looked down at her boxers as if wanting nothing more than to sail from the room — far away into a world that was free of worry and regret. 'Not yet. I'm tired a lot and have trouble making the words I want come out sometimes, but he's too young to realize what's going on.' A small smile formed on her lips. 'He just thinks I'm funny.'

'Why don't you let me help? I could spend the afternoon with Kyle and let you rest. In fact, I could stay and help out around here. I don't need to leave.'

'That's sweet, and I'll take you up on that offer this afternoon, but you do need to find Alex. You would be more of a help to me if you found him and brought him back here to formally meet Kyle as his son.' She looked down at the pieces of broken pottery in the dustpan. 'Kyle is going to need a parent in his life if this disease progresses rapidly.'

Kevyn felt her body tremble with tears. She didn't know what to say.

'I meant what I said yesterday.' Trista straightened her spine, her resolve set. 'It's time they know each other. It's time for *all* of you to know each other.'

Kevyn spent the afternoon playing with Kyle in the park. She brought a Frisbee, which Kyle could throw better than she could, and a kite to fly. He ran up and down the length of the park trailing the string behind him, hoping to catch the right amount of wind to hoist the rainbow-colored wings in the air. The kite lurched up and sharply down, burying its nose in the grass. Kevyn watched Kyle trip over the string and roll in the grass, laughing with his entire body. Life seemed so simple for him. She wasn't sure, even at his age, if it was ever that simple for her.

The backpack that Trista had sent with them was full of Kyle's cars and trucks. Kevyn watched Kyle play with a canary yellow tow truck, lost in the world he made up in his head. She knew that world he retreated into; she'd learned long ago how to entertain herself without having someone to talk to, laugh with, or share a secret. It was a lonely enough world already without having two parents to lay your trust in. If Trista weren't around, Kyle's world would become a whole lot lonelier.

The day was another scorcher, and it wasn't long before they were ready to head home and jump in the pool to cool off. Kyle swam to the side of the pool to grab his plastic sailboat. He floated it on top of the water, running it in circles like he had his cars.

Cupping her hands together, Kevyn splashed a little water at the boat. 'Look out for waves.'

'She's taking on water!' Kyle screamed as he pulled the stern of the boat below the surface. 'She's going down. Ahh!' The screaming turned to giggles as he sank the toy boat.

'You know, I have a sailboat that I live on with my cat, Athens.'

Kyle's eyes grew wide. '*Really?* Cool!'

'In fact, I'm going on a sailing trip down to the islands to look for someone, but when I'm done maybe I could come back here and you and I could go sailing together?'

'Yeah, I love boats. I'm going to live on one someday, when I go help dad.' Kyle didn't even flinch when he announced his plans. To him, it was just a statement like any other. 'Hey, maybe you'll see my dad.'

Kevyn's throat tightened. 'Yeah…maybe I will.'

'You knew about her Huntington's?' Kevyn asked Sam when she returned to the cabin that evening. She'd walked the long way back from Trista's, trying to come to grips with what she'd learned.

'She got her blood work done and found out she carried the gene while I was down here after Beth was killed.'

'She's going to need help,' Kevyn said.

Sam nodded. 'Kyle's only five.' Kevyn's voice caught in her throat, 'He's too young to deal with this.'

'There's never a good time to deal with this.' Sam put his arm around her shoulder. 'Kyle's going to need you. Trista may live a long time, but eventually it'll kill her.'

Kevyn let out a sob for the woman she'd just met and the brother she barely knew. 'It's going to be hell getting to that point.'

Sam stroked her hair. 'No matter what age Kyle is when she starts deteriorating, he's going to need family he can lean on.'

Kevyn began to understand the choice Brianna had made all those years ago. It made far more sense now. She'd give anything to keep the bitter truth far away from Kyle's innocent ears.

Kevyn and Sam returned to Lauderdale the next day to prepare *Wander* for their trip. Sam helped change filters and tighten belts; he checked the engine and changed its oil. The watermaker needed some serious attention, as it had developed a slow leak on her journey from Savannah.

Kevyn filled her days with grocery shopping for the Caribbean and researching Huntington's. Everything she learned saddened and enraged her even more. No matter how much she read there was simply no cure.

On the last day, Kevyn treated Sam to a night out. It would be their last chance to drink cold beer and stand on a solid floor for a while. The Trove was quiet when they arrived, but Kevyn hesitated at the door when she saw Lemon leaning on the bar hunched over a beer. His face glowed a shiny red color, highlighting the roadmap of veins on his nose. This was obviously a regular occurrence for him.

He was concentrating on the bottle cradled in his hands and didn't see Sam and Kevyn at first. She avoided looking at him directly. Steering Sam to the opposite end of the bar, she turned her body away from Lemon and hoped he didn't notice her.

The bartender who talked to Kevyn the week before was on duty. 'Hey, I saw your boat was still in town. I wondered if you'd be in again.'

'Only one more night, then *Wander* sets sail for the Virgins. So we're here to celebrate our last night on land.' Kevyn held up the Corona he had placed in front of her in salute.

'A goodbye drink, then.' The bartender pulled out another bottle for Sam, popped its top and grabbed his own plastic cup. Holding it up, he said in a loud voice, 'Bon Voyage!'

Lemon looked up and struggled to focus on the commotion. 'You goin' somewheres, Strider?'

Kevyn stiffened and prayed he wouldn't come over to talk.

'We're headed to Anegada to look for Alex. You heard anything from him?' Sam spoke easily to the drunken fool, like they were old friends. Kevyn bit her lip and restrained herself from cutting in. She hated Lemon knowing anything about her plans, but any information he may have on Alex was help she sorely needed right now.

'Alex, Alex, Alex. That man don't deserve being looked for. I told the pretty little lady I ain't heard from him.' Lemon tipped the rest of his beer down his throat. 'If he's in them islands, he better stay there. He shows his face 'round here again, and it'll be the last thing he does.'

Sam placed his hand on Kevyn's knee and gave her a squeeze of support. 'I'm surprised you're goin' after him, Strider. After all he jerked you over for.' Lemon's hazy eyes focused on Kevyn, offering her a smarmy smile. 'Maybe, not so surprising, really.'

Kevyn shuddered and tried to ignore him.

Sam changed the subject. 'How's Carly doing in her new school?'

'Hmm, how should I know? She ain't talked to me since she left. I ain't good enough now to be her father.' Lemon signaled for another beer.

'Last one, Lemon,' the bartender warned.

'Yeah, yeah. I'm just leaving anyway. Conversation turned sour 'round here.' Lemon drained his last bottle. The bags under his eyes reminded Kevyn of the cartoon dog who always walked around with a droopy face. It looked like nicotine had stained the whites of his eyes, and his greasy grey hair hung in a mess of vile curls. 'Anegada, huh? You find him you tell him I ain't forgotten.' Lemon limped out to the street and stumbled into the darkness.

As soon as he was out of sight, Kevyn let out the breath she hadn't realized she was holding. 'That man makes my skin crawl.'

'Lemon's been screwed over in this life.' Sam took a swig of beer. The lime lodged in the neck of the bottle. 'There was a time when he was alright, but something happened. Showed up after a night of hard drinking with a broken leg and three broken fingers; some guys worked him over pretty good.' Sam looked out the door and watched Lemon stumble across the street. 'His wife couldn't handle it. She took Carly and moved to Wyoming. For all his bravado, he's never gotten over it.'

'What did he mean by Alex jerking you around?'

Sam waved a hand dismissively. 'Man was drunk.' He shifted his stance uncomfortably from one foot to the other.

'Is he always here?' Kevyn was still not convinced Lemon was harmless.

'Most nights. But this is the last we'll run into him. We'll see nothing but blue water for the next week or so.' Sam pulled Kevyn's barstool closer and playfully bit her ear. 'Are you ready to be locked in thirty feet of space with me, confined to one room…with no escape?'

'You make it sound like prison.'

'A prison cell with the chance of drowning,' Sam quoted Mark Twain.

'Well, when you put it that way…' Kevyn played with the Corona bottle on the bar. Prison was kind of how she felt about her short-lived marriage. Did she really want to jump into another relationship? 'Are we going to be able to do this?'

This was it: the first time Kevyn shared her space with someone else it had ended in divorce. Now, here she was about to spend two weeks crammed into a thirty-two foot sailboat with a man she'd just met. She envisioned another short-lived relationship. What was she thinking? To call her nervous would be an understatement; downright petrified would be more like it. It'd been a long time since she'd spent this much time with a man. They would really get to know one another; it would be a long few weeks if they didn't like what they discovered.

'Sure, lots of people sail to the Caribbean.' Sam laughed. 'I'm not guaranteeing we'll find Alex, but we *will* find the islands.'

Kevyn forced a smile and hoped her fears of sailing off into the sunset with Sam were just jumpy nerves. 'Well, it's a start.' She raised her beer bottle for a toast. 'Here's to smooth sailing.'

Kevyn took a swig of her Corona in an attempt to drown the butterflies fluttering in her stomach.

*****

Chapter Twelve

Wander motored due east from Lauderdale early the next morning.

Sam took the first shift of sailing and directed the boat out of the river and into the ocean as Kevyn stood on the bow, holding the rigging in her right hand and watching the open sea ahead of her. Sam called for her to raise the sails and she jumped back into the cockpit to handle the lines. Adjusting the tension on the jib until it stopped fluttering, she then took a seat opposite Sam to evenly distribute the weight.

Sam rested one arm on the tiller. Every now and then he looked up at the sails, but his concentration was on the path ahead.

For the first few hours, as they crossed the Gulf Stream, both Kevyn and Sam stayed on deck to adjust sails and stand watch. The winds blew from the northeast at ten to fifteen knots with three to five foot seas. It certainly wasn't the fierce storm Kevyn had sailed through, but it was enough to keep them both busy and vigilant. By late afternoon they'd entered the Northwest Providence channel and were protected by Grand Bahamas to the north and Andros to the south. The seas calmed, and *Wander* began to relax.

Kevyn went below to fix dinner. She bent her knees to steady herself from the motion of the sailboat as she reached into the tiny refrigerator and pulled out a roast chicken she'd bought at a market in Lauderdale. Leaning her hips against the small counter, she tore the chicken apart and stewed it with onions and poblano peppers on one of the two burners offered by her gimbaled stove. She added a can of white beans and cumin to create a white chili that she spooned over brown rice, and brought a plate up to Sam.

'Wow! This beats Ramen noodles. When Beth and I sailed we usually just ate sandwiches.' With the mention of Beth's name, Sam's eyes drifted out over the ocean. He seemed lost in thought and unaware of Kevyn standing in the companionway holding his plate out to him.

Her heart ached for him. Should she say something? Leave him to his thoughts? Figuring out if Athens wanted to be rubbed behind his ears or down his tail was as complicated a relationship dilemma had been for her lately, so dealing with a widower and Sam's baggage was more than she knew how to handle.

She took a deep breath and handed him the plate. 'You help me sail, I help you eat. Besides, I have a lot to compete with. You've been doing all the cooking. I don't want you thinking I'm completely helpless.'

Sam snapped back into the present and scooped up a forkful of stew. 'Hardly helpless. Look where you are.'

She snuggled onto the bench beside him and elbowed him in the ribs. 'Yeah, in a boat that you didn't think I could handle alone. You thought I was drowning in a kayak.'

Sam bowed his head. 'I stand corrected.' He finished eating quickly and grabbed both of their empty plates. 'In fact, you obviously don't need me here, so I'm going to try to sleep. I'll be back for the midnight shift.' He shut the door to the cabin behind him and went below.

She lifted the binoculars to her face and scanned the horizon for boats. The day melted to dusk setting the world aglow with a golden light that sparkled off the rippling water making it hard to spot another vessel. She adjusted the main sail and took over the cruising. It was nice to have Sam onboard but she was used to being alone on *Wander*.

Athens slunk out the cat door and snuggled onto the seat beside her; even he seemed to feel it strange with someone else onboard.

Kevyn reached down and rubbed his belly until he purred. Athens wasn't her idea. She never wanted to be the crazy cat lady living alone with her books and antiques. But one day in the shipyard, the calico had jumped aboard and curled into the aft seating to catch the late day sun. He never left. Secretly, Kevyn welcomed the company. She thought maybe Billy had planted the cat on her boat for companionship. Either way, Athens had come into her life after she'd left Dan, and it had been just the two of them ever since. She wondered if Sam had any comfort like that after Beth died.

Sailing on through the darkness, Kevyn wondered if there was room enough on *Wander* for herself, Sam, Athens and, the weight of both their pasts.

Kevyn and Sam fell into an easy routine sailing together. After dinner each night, she'd pull out her violin and run her bow across the strings. She started with the Dylan songs she knew and progressed to The Eagles, with some Clapton thrown in for good measure. She'd lived alone on *Wander* so long that she had lots of time to practice, but this was the first time she had an audience.

On the second night of their sail through the Bahamian islands, Sam filled Kevyn in on more of the missing story of her father's life.

'Alex once told me that he searched for the *Maravilla* just north of here in Little Bahamas Channel.' Sam was calm, setting up the boat to tack. The melancholy of the previous day seemed to have floated away on the waves. 'You know, he was a real pioneer in the industry.' Sam sounded a bit impressed with his words, instead of the usual anger that lit his tone whenever Alex's name was spoken. 'He worked as a diver for Bob Marx in the late sixties searching for the *Maravilla*.'

'Late sixties? That was before he went to war and met my mother.' Instinctively, Kevyn switched sides as Sam tacked to have her back against the wind. They moved without speaking, like a dance they'd performed a thousand times before. When they settled onto the bench, Sam's thigh pressed against hers.

Sam shrugged. 'Must have been. He didn't stay long enough to reap any of the rewards, though. Marx searched for that ship for twelve years before he found it.' Sam shifted back on the bench away from Kevyn. 'Funny thing is, he'd actually found it on the first day he looked, twelve years earlier, but when he dove to investigate he found a sunken sailboat from the forties sitting right on top, hiding the galleon. He dismissed it as a recent wreck and moved on. Had he just dug a little deeper, he would have hit gold his very first day.'

'So why did he go back?'

'Just dumb luck actually.' Sam pushed the tiller slightly away to adjust course. 'Marx anchored in that same spot twelve years later, and when he pulled up the anchor, he brought up two ballast stones from the galleon. Sometimes that's all it takes. All that fancy equipment, years of searching, tons of money spent and he found it with simple luck.'

'But Alex was gone by then?' Kevyn pressed further.

'Yeah, Marx didn't find the *Maravilla* until '72. Your dad and many others had come and gone by then.' He draped one arm on the tiller and the other around the back of the bench. 'Treasure hunting's a tedious job, day in and day out searching through sand.' He sighed, leaning his head on his arm. 'And you can only do it part of the year here. Hurricane season is way too rough to see clearly. There are many days, years, for that matter, when you come up with nothing. It takes its toll on a person after awhile.'

'From everything I've heard, my father doesn't have the patience to stick with a search for twelve years.' Kevyn watched the stars above grow brighter as the night deepened. 'Doesn't seem to have the patience to stick with anything.'

'Not many have that kind of patience, or backing. It costs about a hundred thousand a month to run a salvage operation, depending on the scope of it. Seems to me your father is a much better researcher and adventurer than money gatherer.' The now familiar anger for her father flashed in his eyes. 'Alex isn't good with money.'

'Does he owe you money?' Kevyn hoped Sam would elaborate on what made him so mad…but he didn't.

'Not quite.' The anger washed from Sam's face as he continued his tale, completely ignoring her question. 'To launch a big hunt you basically need a fulltime money manager looking for investors and handling the logistics of the funding. Alex is a storyteller. He can get anyone and everyone excited enough about the possibilities that they turn out their pockets, but he's too busy running everything to put the effort into the accounting side of things.'

'You mean he keeps moving because he runs out of money?' The night had turned chilly. Kevyn moved closer to Sam.

'These days, yes, I'd imagine so.' Sam wrapped his arm around her shoulder. 'The maverick days of treasure hunting are over. When your dad first started, he could just go out and dig in the sand, but now there are regulations. He has to apply for a lease to search, file a claim once he finds anything, and apply for salvage rights. He's supposed to have a full-time underwater archeologist on board to make sure they're recording the history properly – the list goes on. It's no longer a case of diving into tropical waters and coming up with a handful of gold coins.'

'It's not finder's keepers?'

Sam shook his head 'When a salvager gains rights to a wreck they basically agree with the government to keep a percentage of what they find. The rest goes to the government for museums and such. There's always a dispute and questions about what's found in international waters and who deserves what. Quite often Spain gets involved and fights for their stake, as it was their gold to begin with. It can get really ugly, really fast. Many operations have lost their leases halfway through a recovery over fights with the government.'

'Everybody wants a bigger piece of the pie,' Kevyn interjected.

'Something like that. It's called Treasure Fever. Once you hold a small piece of it, you want more. Human nature, I guess.' Sam shifted on the bench. He avoided looking at Kevyn and fiddled with the tiller. 'These guys don't always follow a code of ethics.'

'What do you mean?'

He looked up at the sails and sighed. 'Kevyn, you should be aware that over the years there has been talk about Alex, stories and rumors mainly, nothing confirmed.' Trimming the main sail, he headed *Wander* closer to the wind.

'What about?'

'Well, you know Lemon hates him for some deal gone wrong, but there has been talk of his not claiming all his finds.'

'He's *hiding* treasure?' Kevyn felt a chill run through her at the thought of her father being a thief as well as a possible drug runner.

'It's more than that. It isn't just the money. It's the historical record that they're pillaging. Historians don't have the know-how to launch these salvage operations, so they have to rely on independent salvagers to do the work. But some of these guys don't care as much about the history as they do the gold, so they tear through the site. They don't document properly or hand over everything to the researchers. They're basically just taking the loot, like an underwater grave robber.'

'And you think Alex is one of these guys?'

'I think there's a whole shifty underground that Alex's name has been linked to.' Sam avoided looking Kevyn in the eye. 'It doesn't mean he's guilty...but there's talk.'

'I thought you just said they were required to have archeologists on board with them?'

'That's based on the assumption that they apply for a claim and go through the proper channels. It's a big ocean out here, and you can't police it all.'

'Is that why he's so hard to find?'

'Maybe. I'm not saying he's one of those guys. I don't know him that well.'

'That makes two of us,' she muttered.

Kevyn didn't know anything about Alex. After all, he had been gone thirty years. He led a life that included *maybe* being a drug smuggler, *maybe* being a shipwreck destroyer, and *definitely* being the father who abandoned her. Another definite was the fact that he had been in the war and was possibly responsible for the deaths of a number of sailors, as well as an innocent little girl. Now living in the Caribbean, he owned at least two different boats that she knew about. One had sunk. But what did she know of him as a person? Was he a pillager? A criminal? Every story she'd heard had made the pieces of his life flake away, like paint on an old armoire left in a sweltering attic of a southern home.

For years, she had gone to sleep every night wondering what he'd been like, what he had thought about, and whether he loved her. As a child, she'd laid in her bed listening to the freezer open as her mother reached for the next bottle of vodka. She'd hear ice clink in the glass before the door shut again. Then, she'd pull the blanket up around her shoulders and imagine Alex flying through the clouds in an old ship. She saw him as captain with her as first mate, standing by his side. The clouds were always fluffy and white, and the sky was always a robin's-egg blue. She was always eight years old in her fantasy, wearing a peach-colored dress with elephants embroidered on the front. They lined up single file with the first of their trunks hooked through the next one's tail. Alex always had his hand on her shoulder and would look down at her, always smiling.

Now the question was, did she really want to replace that fantasy with what was shaping up to be a horrifying reality?

The sun hung low in the afternoon sky on the third day of the voyage. It had dropped in altitude significantly in the past twenty minutes that Kevyn had stared at it.

Sam draped one arm over the tiller with the other over the gunwale. His legs were stretched out in front of him as he stared out to sea. With his sunglasses on, Kevyn could barely tell if he was sailing the boat or taking a nap. He hadn't shaved since *Wander* had left the dock, and the dirty blond stubble added a rugged look to accompany his wind-blown hair. At that moment, he looked sexier than anyone ever had in Kevyn's eyes. Reaching up, she rubbed the stubble on his face and wondered if they would share more days like this.

Sailing with him was easy. When Sam called for a change of sail later the next day, Kevyn reached up from her post on the opposite cushion to un-cleat the main sheet. 'Ready!'

'Hard a-lee!' Kevyn followed his command by letting out the sheet, watching as the wind grabbed the material and mushroomed in the breeze. They worked efficiently throughout the day at the sail changes watching *Wander* slice through the water.

Days passed quickly with their routine. It wasn't until noon on the fifth day that the pattern changed. Sam had just finished tacking when a loud crack split the air. Kevyn looked up from the book she was reading.

Sam bent over the tiller and wiggled it with his right hand. It bent at an unnatural angle. 'Shit.'

'What's wrong?' Kevyn pushed her sunglass to the top of her head and leaned in closer.

'I think we've cracked the tiller.' Kevyn laid the book aside and stood up. She knew there would be minor problems along the way and had come prepared for any number of disaster scenarios. She studied the wooden tiller. The rich-colored mahogany wood was the same she'd worked with many times while restoring furniture. At SCAD in Savannah, her teacher had taught her how to brace the wood and hold it with a vice while the wood glue set. She needed to jury-rig something similar for this long shaft of wood. Thinking for a moment of what she had on hand, she rummaged through her tool kit below and returned with two long wrenches. Placing one on either side of the wooden shaft, she wound duct tape along the whole length of the contraption. 'That should help, but we can't do too many more miles like this.' The memory of the storm was still strong in her mind. Having Sam aboard was a comfort but faulty equipment was a problem whether he was there to help or not.

Sam brought up the charts of the area. He studied them for a moment and pointed to one of the islands south of the Bahamas. 'Turks and Caicos is our best option. There's a marine store on Provo.'

'Hopefully they have what we need.' Kevyn chewed the side of her lip, worrying about any delay in their progress.

'Shouldn't be more than a day if they have the right parts in stock.'

'Great! I want to get to St. John's and talk to Len as soon as possible. Hopefully he'll help us find Alex and we can take him home with us.' She smiled as bright as the sun overhead.

The excitement of finding Alex was building inside of Kevyn the closer they got to the islands. She still wasn't sure what she would say to him, but she now knew she wanted to find him. It was more than just a duty to Grandfather or Trista, now it was a challenge. Like her restoration business back home, where she'd search for somebody's forgotten treasure, research its history, and then gently bring it back to life – in her mind, Alex was becoming the next project to restore. She had found out his history, had come searching for him, and hoped to one day make their relationship shine.

Sam looked up from the tiller and studied Kevyn. 'Is that what you think is going to happen?'

Kevyn's smile faded fast. 'No. Yes. I mean… maybe,' she stumbled.

'Oh, Kevyn.' Sam reached out for her hand. His eyes were tender but filled with intense worry.

Kevyn turned away. 'I know. It's silly.' She stared out over the endless blue. 'It's just that somewhere between learning I still have a father and finding out about a brother I never even knew about, I started to hope that maybe I could have a complete family one day.'

Sam squeezed her hand. 'I know all about wanting to find connections. Life can be lonely and cruel.'

Kevyn shook off the moment and forced a smile. 'Anyway, a trip ashore will give me time to explore a new island.'

'A guy I know from college used to live on Provo.' Sam thought for a moment. 'He's a treasure salvor, too.'

'Another one?' It stunned Kevyn how big this network of hunters was. It seemed like everywhere she turned since her arrival in Lauderdale she'd run smack dab into someone involved with the treasure-seeking world. 'Do you think he knows my father?'

'It wouldn't surprise me.' Sam shrugged. 'It's a small world. He'll have heard of him, at least.'

'Let's go find him.' Kevyn felt her excitement heat up. This search for her father was becoming addictive.

'I don't know.' Sam was skeptical. 'We're not what you'd call friends.'

'Aw, come on,' she pleaded. 'He might know something about Alex.'

Sam seemed to mull this over for a moment. 'Okay. I'll see if I can find him. I haven't spoken to him in years.'

'Great. I want to get to shore and call Kyle anyway.'

Sam trimmed the sails and *Wander* heeled slightly, heading as close to the wind as possible. They raced across the banks toward the cluster of islands; short white cliffs and green scruff on the low island soon came into view.

Kevyn squinted from the blinding sun as she tried to read the colors of the surrounding water to determine depth. She knelt on the bow looking out for coral heads as they cut through the reef and into the bay, but it was a formality. She trusted Sam knew what he was doing.

Flying fish soared as *Wander* plowed through their school. Kevyn studied the channel on their way to the Provo anchorage when the water to the right of the bow parted and a lone dolphin exploded from the turquoise pool. Arching his back like the hook of an umbrella, his large grey body contorted to re-enter the water. He looked sleek as he swam like a torpedo in front of *Wander's* bow. And within seconds, he launched his body gracefully out of the water again. Kevyn squealed like Kyle had when they'd played in the pool.

She held on to the lifelines and leaned out over the water in order to watch her new companion, as she beat her hands on *Wander's* hull like a set of drums every time the dolphin re-surfaced. She swung her head back to make sure Sam could see as well. 'Don't hit him!'

Sam laughed. 'Hang on!' He adjusted the sheets and heeled *Wander* even farther, dipping Kevyn closer to the water in order to play with the dolphin.

Again and again he leapt out of the water and through the ripples that danced on the surface. Kevyn cheered every acrobatic flight he made. But as suddenly as he'd appeared, the dolphin veered to the right and shot off over the shallow water to go play somewhere else. He didn't have a care in the world, it seemed. Kevyn wondered if her life would ever be like that. Would she ever feel so carefree?

Kevyn twirled around to Sam. 'Did you see that?' She felt like a child in an amusement park.

Sam let out the sheet a little to right the hull and evened out *Wander's* decks. 'Ready to join civilization again?' He pointed to the bay in front of them.

'Just long enough for a repair.' Now that *Wander* was sailing south she hated to slow her progress. 'I want to keep moving.'

*****

Chapter Thirteen

Once anchored, Sam unlashed the eight-foot rubber dingy from its secured spot on the bow and launched it in the water. After assembly was complete, he pulled the cord and the motor sprung to life.

Kevyn grabbed her passport and wallet and locked *Wander*, leaving Athens curled on the bench in the same position he had been since they arrived. She was still bubbling with excitement over the encounter with the dolphin when they approached the woman at the immigration desk.

'Sounds like you've had a good morning already.' The woman chuckled while looking over their passports. She typed their numbers into her computer and stamped each passport.

Kevyn flipped hers open and inspected the stamp. The blue ink looked so fresh sitting beside the faded one from the Dominican Republic. Years ago, she and Dan had flown to Puerto Plata for a seven-day, all-inclusive honeymoon. That faded memory was the one and only stamp in Kevyn's passport until now, and she was secretly thrilled. She tucked it into her back pocket, proud to have collected another stamp.

'Enjoy the island.' The woman tipped her head before turning her attention to the next traveler in line.

Sam had gone through immigration ahead of Kevyn and was already outside on his cell phone when she walked through the doors. He looked up and smiled at her, raising his index finger. 'Okay, we'll see you this afternoon.'

'You found him?'

'Yeah, he's still here.' Sam returned the phone to his dry bag. 'Digger came down here during college and worked the Molasses Reef excavation as part of his Nautical Archaeology degree. I guess he liked it and stayed.'

The heat sizzled Kevyn's skin, warming her whole body. Even with her sunglasses on she had to squint. Walking across the dirt path, she took shelter in the shade of a nutmeg tree. Its dark green waxy leaves shielded some of the fierce rays.

She thought about how much Kyle would love it. The tree was the perfect shape for climbing, with branches spreading wide and low to the ground. The teal water glittered like white icicle lights on a Christmas tree, and a windsurfer glided across the bay, propelled by the warm breeze. 'What's not to love?'

Sam rented a scooter and Kevyn wrapped her arms around him. She didn't need to hold on so tight, but she liked the feel of her arms around his waist. She curled along his spine and rested her head on his shoulders as they puttered down the road.

For an island, the roads were in great shape – paved and smooth. The resorts they passed were brand new. No litter decorated the side of the road, and there were no run-down shanty houses in sight. The picture postcard beaches reminded Kevyn of a *Stepford* community.

It didn't take them long to locate a new tiller and round up the few odds and ends they needed to continue their journey. Kevyn stopped for some new reading material, and Sam picked up a copy of the *Daily Telegraph* to find out what had happened in the world since they'd been gone.

It'd only been a few weeks since she left Georgia, but to Kevyn it felt like she was a million nautical miles from home. Her mother's drinking was on another landmass entirely now. Her own taciturn self, the one who kept her head down while scraping and varnishing other people's lost treasures, had also been left behind. Her best friend, an eighty-two-year-old man who never left his front porch, was far away. Here, she was traveling with someone who was more interesting than all of the people she'd known in her life put together, and Kevyn had no urge to read the newspaper and risk being pulled back into the real world.

By the time they returned to Turtle Cove Marina, Kevyn had seen enough of the island. It was a little too perfect and not at all what she envisioned a Caribbean island to be. Sam hung their helmets over the handlebars of the scooter, placed a hand on her lower back and followed her up the path to the bar.

'There he is.' Sam guided Kevyn to the far side of the u-shaped bar where a man in a black shiny shirt and tight black pants held court with a number of islanders. These men were darker than any men Kevyn had seen before. Heavy gold-link chains hung around each of their thick necks and fancy gold watches circled their wrists. Diamonds the size of pencil erasers hung from their ears. Each one could easily have played defense for the Falcons. Two of the men were enormous; their chests were so muscular that they couldn't hold their huge arms straight at their sides. Instead, they hung at 45-degree angles, like the inside of a peace symbol. The third was just as large; not fat, but built thick with power.

'Sam, you made it!' The much smaller, but equally fit man, locked hands with Sam and pulled him into a masculine sort of hug. His shirt hung open to expose his deeply tanned torso, and the sleeves barely covered his tattoo of a Great White on the prowl. 'What brought you to the islands?'

Sam turned to introduce her. 'Digger, this is Kevyn Morgan.'

She held out her hand to shake. The tropical sun shone off the top of his shaved head as he bent to kiss her knuckles. 'Walter Maddock, at your service.' His steel gray eyes looked her up and down, lingering just a moment too long on the cut of her neckline. A shudder ran down her back.

'This is my crew.' Digger waved a hand at the group of men and each one grunted their hello. Digger turned and bumped fists with them, telling them to meet him at the docks at sunset.

'You night diving?' Sam asked after the men had shuffled off.

'Just loading some cargo. I'm sending some stuff back home.' Digger slapped Sam on the shoulder. 'So, what brings you here? I thought you set up shop in Florida.'

'Shop's still there. I'm just helping Kevyn sail down to the Virgins to look for her father.'

Kevyn's throat clenched.

'We stopped in to repair a broken tiller.' Sam signaled for a round of drinks unaware of Kevyn's shocked expression. Just helping, he'd said. Was that why he had joined her? She'd thought whatever had been going on between them was more than that.

'Sailboat, huh? How big's your boat?' Digger asked.

'Thirty-two feet. An old classic sloop.' Sam smiled at Kevyn, a gesture she did not return. 'Kept it in great condition.'

'Cozy. Not many lovebirds make it after a voyage together on a sailboat.' Digger signaled for the round of drinks to be delivered faster. 'No place to run if you have a fight. No place to hide.'

Kevyn was now unsure whether calling her and Sam lovebirds was the term to use. Lust, for sure, at least on her part. After his comment of just being there to help, love seemed way too strong a word.

'We're not a couple.' Sam avoided looking at Kevyn this time. 'As I said, I'm just helping her look for her father.'

Kevyn's jaw clenched tight and her lips pursed together. There it was again. Is that what's been going on in his head? Maybe they *were* still getting to know each other, but they sure were a lot farther into this relationship than him just lending her a hand...or, so she thought. She wasn't some damsel in distress who needed him.

'Sam will be flying home as soon as we reach Anegada.' She straightened her spine and ignored the look Sam shot her. She couldn't believe she'd been thinking about a future with him while he was just along to help her out.

Digger turned to Sam. 'You going down to meet her father? Kinda old fashioned isn't it?'

'Just the opposite actually. Sam's only here to introduce me to my father.' The words sounded silly when she spoke them.

Digger raised an eyebrow. 'You've never met your father?'

'No.' The drinks had arrived, and Kevyn concentrated on mixing her margarita with the colorful straw.

'And you have?' He turned his attention to Sam.

'Yeah, Alex is a regular seller in my shop.'

Digger shifted his beady eyes back to Kevyn. 'Alex? *Alex Morgan?*'

Kevyn looked up from her drink and nodded.

'Alex Morgan…the salvager?' he continued.

'I guess you know him, too?' Kevyn was truly amazed at how many people knew her father. Was she the only one he avoided? 'Maybe you know where he is?'

Digger shrugged in an, *I-am-so-cool* way. Between his manner, his dress, and his cronies, Kevyn felt like she was witnessing a rap video. 'Alex used to come by here every few months. He and I did some business together. Haven't seen him in a while.' He didn't elaborate.

'That seems to be the story everywhere we turn.'

'You're on your way to see him now?'

'We think he might be on a wreck in Anegada,' Kevyn said. 'We're stopping in St. John to talk to another salvager and then heading there to find him.'

'Anegada?' Digger twirled the straw through his fingers, not looking either of them in the eye. 'Last I heard, his boat sank. Guess he didn't go down with the ship.'

'You must know him better than I do. I only found that out recently.' The margarita was going to her head. She was telling this guy more than she normally would have felt comfortable saying.

Digger shrugged. 'It's called the drumbeat down here. News travels faster than tabloid gossip through these islands.' Digger thought for a moment. 'But I never heard he was still out there.'

Quickly changing the subject, Digger inquired about Sam's business and where he had been. The two had taken classes together at Texas A&M and had a few friends in common. Kevyn listened while they made small talk but soon found herself lost in her own thoughts. How could she have read the situation between her and Sam so wrong?

They ordered conch chowders and switched to the local Turks Head beer. The sun sank in the sky as they chatted. A cool breeze blew over Kevyn and she shivered.

Sam slid closer and put an arm around her bare shoulders. Shrugging him off, Kevyn moved farther down the bench.

After dinner Digger invited them down the dock to his boat, a sleek black and silver forty-foot speedboat resting at the far end of the marina. It was all nose. Three silver engines dominated the back transom.

'Whew, you find a treasure that I don't know about?' Sam whistled.

'Not bad, hu-uh?' Digger took the compliment and went on to impress his friend even more. 'The v-hull slices through the water. You just fly on this thing.' It was definitely hydrodynamic. The low sleek design screamed of speed; it looked more like a go-fast bobsled than a salvager's operation.

'Smooth ride?' Sam ran a hand over the exposed engines.

'Better be for half a mil.'

Sam shook his head. 'Nautical archaeology pays better here in the islands.'

Digger reached into the bar fridge in the cockpit and grabbed three more beers. 'To old friends.' He eyed Kevyn up and down. 'And new ones...*Miss* Kevyn Morgan.'

When they clinked the bottles, Kevyn avoided looking directly at Digger. She suddenly felt naked under his stare and was more uncomfortable than she'd been in a long time. Looking down the dock, Kevyn watched the three islanders from earlier approach and was glad for the excuse to leave.

'We should let you get to work.'

Digger frowned, but nodded when he saw his crew. 'Yeah, it's getting late. Maybe we can do this again tomorrow?'

'I was hoping to go for a dive tomorrow morning before we take off.' Sam held out his hand to Digger. 'But it was good to see you, man.'

'You, too.' Digger grasped Sam's elbow while they shook. 'You're off to find Alex, then?'

'Next stop is the Virgins.'

'Right, Anegada, you said.' Digger kissed Kevyn on the cheek, lingering a little too long. 'Good luck to you, Kevyn Morgan.'

She squirmed in his embrace. 'Yeah, see you around.' All she wanted was to get off the boat before she had to deal with his half-drunk friends, as well.

Kevyn hurried down the dock toward the tender, leaving Sam behind.

'Hey, wait up!' He jogged up behind her and grabbed her elbow.

Spinning around, she glared at him. 'What? You think I need help getting into the tender, too?'

'I think you misunderstood.'

'I didn't misunderstand,' Kevyn fumed. 'You said you were only here to find Alex. So when we find him you can go home. In fact, you can go now. I can get to Anegada on my own.'

'Kevyn, please.' He reached out for her, meeting her glare with a look of apology. 'I didn't mean that nothing was going on with us. I just don't like the thought of Digger knowing about my personal life.'

'What *is* going on with us?' Kevyn crossed her arms. 'Are you here for me or for Alex? Does he owe you money or something?'

Sam looked shocked. 'I'm here for you. I don't know what's going on, but I'm not leaving until I find out.' He wrapped his arms around her and lowered his lips to hers.

His kiss was tender and sincere and her anger washed away with the waves lapping against the dock.

Sam took a deep breath. 'But whatever *is* going on is between us, Digger doesn't need to know. I don't trust that guy.'

'I thought you were friends?' Kevyn's voice softened. Sam's kiss had a way of making her forget what she'd been thinking.

'Digger? No, we went to school together and worked some dives but we ran in different crowds.' Sam stepped back and watched the exchange between Digger and his men going on at the far end of the dock. 'He always had that *I've-got-something-going-on* quality about him. Still does by the looks of it.'

'What do you mean?' Kevyn asked, although she'd gotten the same exact feeling about the man.

'Back then, when he talked it was like he was daring you to ask what he was into, like he was proud of it. But he's changed over the years. He's calmer, in a way. Now, instead of being a kid trying to impress everyone with how cool he is, he's more in control. More of a commanding presence, like he's the boss.' Sam shook his head. 'That's not anything I want to get too close to.'

'Do you think my father's involved with him?'

Sam shrugged. 'I hope not.'

Digger's boat pulled away from the dock with Digger at the wheel. He planed across the water gaining speed, and it didn't take long for the boat to be out of sight.

Kevyn wondered why he hadn't bothered to turn on his running lights, and Sam just shook his head. 'That guy's trouble.'

The night bordered on pitch black as they worked their way down the opposite dock from where Digger had just been to retrieve their tender. A seventy-six foot Viking had come in from a day of fishing and the crew boasted an eighty-pound wahoo catch. Three men stood drinking beer and telling tales of the fight while a fourth cleaned the lean fish on a wooden table.

'Nice catch.' Sam whistled in appreciation.

'We's blessed today.' The scrawny man wiped a bloody hand on his cut-off shorts and held it up in a wave. 'Not every day the sea gives up its prizes.'

Kevyn watched the water below where three nurse and two bull sharks were circling.

The butcher picked up a long curved knife with one hand and held the head of the fish with the other. With one quick thrust he severed the head from the body. Blood pooled on the board as he tossed the head into the water.

The fin of the largest bull shark sliced out of the water as he opened his mouth revealing lines of shearing sharp teeth. He gulped down the wahoo head whole. It never stopped cruising.

Kevyn shuddered and stepped closer to Sam, squeezing his hand.

'Life in the islands.'

'Remind me never to get in the water if I'm oozing blood like that.' With her stomach roiling, Kevyn turned away and led Sam down the dock to the tender.

The next morning, Sam set up the dive equipment as Kevyn warmed tortillas and fried eggs to go along with the leftover salsa in the fridge. She hummed the chorus of Van Morrison's 'Into the Mystic' while she poured orange juice into two heavy plastic glasses, happy she and Sam had cleared the air the night before. Last night's rocking of the boat was not caused by rough weather, but rather by their lovemaking.

This morning, all seemed right with the two of them. They'd stayed in bed long after the sun rose, exploring each other like they had the island the day before. Eventually, their hunger broke the renewed bond. Kevyn reluctantly rolled out of the bunk to scramble up some breakfast.

It wasn't long before they were back in the water suspended in indigo, slowly floating past wide expanses of hard coral. The vibrant colors surprised and mesmerized Kevyn at every turn. Patches of bright yellow, fiery red and deep purple circled in front of her eyes. Teal colored parrotfish swam past their masks. The large black eyes of a red and silver fish followed their movement; it preened like a peacock extending a yellow dorsal fin like a fan. The visibility was crystal clear and Kevyn even caught a glimpse of the streaming tip of a turquoise triggerfish's tail as he darted out of sight.

It was so different from their first dive in Lauderdale.

Although Sam still held Kevyn's hand, this time it wasn't because she needed the support. This time she knew what all the gear did and how to use it.

While she chased a mosaic wrasse around the coral outcrop trying to memorize the exact color of blue and yellow, Sam pointed out a brown and tan trumpetfish trying to fool them into thinking he was a piece of coral. Schools of yellow snapper floated above. Sam reached out to fan the water in front of what looked to be Snuffelupagus's trunk and it retracted back to the coral it was hiding under.

Kevyn found herself wondering if Alex was somewhere out there diving. Perhaps they were sharing the same Caribbean seas right now… the closest they'd ever been. Only four hundred and fifty miles of salty blue water may be separating father from daughter.

They were just about out of time and at the turn-around point when Sam stopped and squeezed her hand. With his other hand, he pointed up.

An eagle ray soared between them and the boat. Numerous white spots on its dark upper surface came into view as it flapped its wings, flying through the water. Kevyn fluttered her arms to stay in place and watched as the peaceful creature glided above – completely unconcerned and oblivious to the divers below. She wanted to reach out and touch it, the ray was that close.

Back on the surface, Kevyn slipped out of her BC and treaded water with one hand while she pried one of the fins from her foot. The suction made it hard to be graceful.

'I'm starting to see how addictive the lifestyle down here can be.'

Sam slung one arm over the tube of the inflatable and placed his fins in the hold. He turned back to Kevyn and reached out to grab her fins. 'Am I luring you away from a life of sandpaper and plantation sales?'

'You could be.' Kevyn wiggled out of her BC and floated it over to Sam. 'What I mean is I understand why my father spends so much time in the ocean.' It was hard to make her point while treading water at the same time, so she swam over and grabbed the side of the inflatable to steady herself. 'The diving seems to be getting better and more interesting the farther we head south.'

Sam wrapped his free hand around her waist and pulled her close. Even in the warm water, her body shivered at his touch.

'Everything seems to be getting more interesting as we head south.' Sam's kiss floated on her lips.

Her heart soared like the eagle ray. The tropical lifestyle wasn't the only thing that was becoming addictive.

Sam left *Wander* at noon to return the scooter and buy a few last minute groceries. He'd been gone about an hour when Kevyn heard the rumble of an engine; it sounded nearby. She had been unsuccessfully trying to rearrange the cabin to find more room for Sam, but as the sound drew closer, she stuck her head out of the companionway.

Digger's speedboat rocketed across the calm bay at an alarming speed, creating a rooster tail of wake. Kevyn popped back into the cabin and grabbed a t-shirt of Sam's from the bunk to throw over her bikini.

'Aw, ain't this cozy.' Digger wore a smirk as the stern of his boat swung in line with *Wander's*. He'd already set his fenders over the side and lassoed his bow to a cleat like he was roping a calf. 'I thought Sam said you two weren't playing house?'

He stepped on board without asking permission and kept his eyes on Kevyn a beat longer than was comfortable. 'Nice boat.' He lowered his Oakleys and looked Kevyn up and down completely ignoring the sailboat. 'Very nice craftsmanship.'

'Sam's not here, Digger,' Kevyn announced, covering the unease in her voice with a hint of anger.

'My lucky day. Actually, I came to see you, Kevyn Morgan.' Digger pushed his rolled-up shirtsleeves farther up his forearms; his muscles flexed, making the shark tattoo swim.

Kevyn didn't know which creature was more dangerous, but right now she'd jump in with a school of sharks just to get away from the eerie feeling Digger brought to the deck of *Wander*.

His eyes flashed. 'I've got some things to tell you about dear old dad.'

'What about him?' Kevyn moved aside, allowing Digger to come further aboard. He stepped into the cockpit, standing a little too close for comfort causing Kevyn to back up until she was pressed against the cabin bulkhead.

'Alex used to stop by the island every couple of months. Usually in November, when he was headed down to the Caribbean, and again in July when he headed back.'

'He stayed on the island?'

'Sometimes on the island, sometimes on his boat.' Digger ran a hand up the main stay and peered down the topside to the bow.

'So, you knew him well?' she asked tentatively.

'Well enough. We worked a few gigs together. I'm busy with my… company.' His wink was nowhere near as knee-wobbling as when Sam did it. 'So I can't always get away. Alex was good enough to run some errands for me.' His smirk reminded her of the alligators back home.

'What kind of errands?' Kevyn pushed a little harder. He really wasn't giving her any new info.

'Oh, you know, this and that. Alex is always headed to some new place where I need things done.' His voice drifted off at the end of the statement. Digger was talking but he wasn't really concentrating on his words; he was too busy scanning the decks as if he'd dropped something.

'Digger, we talked about all this last night. Do you have any new news about Alex?' She put one hand on her hip and shifted her weight to her left leg.

'*New?* No, I just think it's funny that the *K Sea* sunk and Alex is still alive.' Digger raised one eyebrow. 'Seems suspicious.'

Kevyn had similar thoughts earlier but had no answers. 'Maybe he escaped by tender before it went down.'

'Seems real convenient, boat going down like that, untraceable location. He have an insurance policy he's trying to collect?'

Kevyn hadn't thought of that angle. Was her father running an insurance scam as well as drugs? Goosebumps popped out all over her skin. What else could he possibly be mixed up in?

'I don't know. The original call came from an insurance agent.'

'But no one knows if the boat is really sunk or not?' Digger leaned in toward Kevyn in the tiny space.

She tried to step away but found her knees pressed up against the starboard seating and unable to move. 'I guess not.' She chewed on the side of her lip. She really didn't have any concrete evidence at all where Alex or his boat really were. She'd started this hunt on the assumption that the phone call to Grandfather was legitimate, but she hadn't spoken to the agent herself. Maybe this was all a ruse?

'So, maybe you turn up in Anegada and find Alex and his boat sitting there with all the loot onboard.' Digger stepped even closer, pinning her in the corner of the seat and the cabin bulkhead.

She fought to remain calm and not let Digger know how uncomfortable she felt with him standing so close. 'I guess that could happen.' She didn't know what else to say. All she wished was that Sam would hurry up with the groceries. She didn't want to be alone with this guy for too long.

'Hey, do you have a Coke in there?' Digger swung his head in the direction of the cabin, changing subjects faster than his speedboat could go.

There was definitely no way she was going to let him down there and end up getting stuck inside with him.

'Yeah, just a minute. Wait here,' she said forcefully.

She ducked into the companionway, closing the hatch behind her to guarantee he wouldn't follow. She ran her hands through her hair and sighed. *Great! Now I have to wait for him to finish a drink.* Looking through her solo cupboard for the smallest glass she could possibly find, she came up with a plastic cup decorated with a shamrock on it, a souvenir from Savannah's St. Patrick's Day celebration years ago.

Her hand trembled while pouring.

She could hear him scuffling around above her and wondered what the hell was doing. She thought about adding ice from the chest to allow less liquid and speeding his drink time, but decided against using their last precious few cubes for someone like Digger.

Taking a deep breath, Kevyn opened the hatchway. 'Here you go…'

Digger wasn't in the cockpit. She looked in his boat, hoping he was already there ready to go, but it was empty.

'Thanks, doll.' Digger jumped down from the top deck.

'What are you doing up there?' She didn't like the thought of Digger poking around her home.

'Just looking around the old girl. Nice boat.' Digger winked and downed the Coke in one gulp, handing the plastic cup back to her. 'Well, when you find Alex, tell him I said hello.' Digger held on to the shroud with his left hand and stepped back into his boat. He reached down to start the motors and checked to make sure the lines were untied. Digger spun the wheel of the boat to starboard. '*Mañana*, Miss Kevyn Morgan.' He tipped his head and waved a pinkie and thumb in her direction.

Mañana. God, she hoped not.

The speedboat pulled away and circled back toward the island leaving a wake of white foam in the otherwise clear blue water. Kevyn stood, holding the empty cup, thankful Digger had left without incident and wondering what on earth had just happened.

*****

Chapter Fourteen

The soft breeze of morning stirred, billowing quietly through the sails.

Kevyn stretched out and stared up at the whiteness of the material, feeling like she was on a cloud. Turquoise water rippled past *Wander*'s green hull as it had for the past three days since leaving the Turks and Caicos. The sailing had been easy. The wind had blown just enough kisses to *Wander*'s sails to keep them filled – not too heavy, not too light.

She watched snow-white terns soar overhead, as the pastel yellow sun began its climb into the morning sky. She looked out on a brand new world and sighed. Today was the day they would make landfall in the Virgins. Today was the day she would arrive in her father's world.

As he had done every morning, Sam stepped out wrapped only in a towel. He leaned over the tiller and planted a kiss on Kevyn's cheek, handing her a mug of black coffee in the process. As he reached for the hose, he dropped his towel in her lap, and rinsed the night's sleep away on the deck, avoiding the claustrophobia of the head's cramped shower. He shook his head, spraying Kevyn with droplets of water before he wrapped the towel back around his waist without a hint of shyness. Only the terns and the flying fish soaring past the boat caught a glimpse.

'Are you ready to face the world again?' He took the tiller from Kevyn as she scooted ahead to the front of the cockpit.

'Do we have to?' She shielded her eyes from the glare of the sun as it intensified. 'I kind of like having you all to myself.'

Sam laughed. 'Next stop could be the Azores if you want, but you would be awful sick of canned soup by then. Fresh vegetables are almost gone.'

'Guess we better stop then.' Kevyn tried to pout dramatically, but the laughter of freedom and exhilaration came instead. 'A quick stop in St. John's and then on to Anegada tomorrow.'

'Fine by me.' Sam shrugged. 'I can spend all winter bouncing around these islands with you.'

'As great as that sounds, I hope it doesn't take that long.' Kevyn's pulse raced at Sam's easygoing flirting, but she had her father on her mind. 'I just want to talk to Trista's divers and get a sense of what Alex has been doing down here. From all the stories I've heard, I still can't decide if he's a good guy or not.' She hadn't told Sam about Digger's visit to the boat or his insinuations of Alex's insurance fraud. She wasn't sure why, but she was embarrassed to even think of one more shady thing linked to her father, and she didn't want to give Sam any more ammunition to hate him. Leaving his children behind and his past of drug running accusations was enough.

Sam grabbed her hand. 'Well, let's go find out.'

Sam dropped the anchor off the small emerald island of St. John's. The Virgin Islands curved like a hook around the eastern edge of the Caribbean Sea; St. John's was located on its post and Anegada at its tip. They'd sailed south just to turn north again the next day, but it felt like a stop Kevyn had to make. She wanted a little more information before facing her father.

The view from the bow was of undulating tropical hills. Shadows fell across the dips creating a tie-dyed pattern of green. The water mutated from navy in the deep to blue-green to aquamarine as the view moved closer to shore.

It was a tropical kind of day. A hot, sultry breeze blew over the brilliant blues of the Caribbean carrying the smell of frangipani in the air.

Len was out diving when Kevyn called the number Trista had given her. The voice on the phone said he probably wouldn't come in until nightfall, so they decided to spend the day exploring.

The open-air Jeep they rented bounced crazily over the mountainous winding roads. They snorkeled in Cinnamon Bay and hiked through the cactus and scrub looking for Taino Indian hieroglyphs.

Now that they were here, a part of Kevyn was reluctant to leave at all. She hoped that once they found her father she could return to these islands and spend more time slowly getting to know the mysteries and beauty they held.

By early evening the sun dropped. The sky was awash in lilac and Kevyn was famished from the day's adventures. They decided to stop at Island Blues for a drink and dinner before heading over to where Len's boat would dock. The sounds of a stand-up bass enticed them to enter.

'Do you do this often?' Kevyn asked Sam once they had sat at the far end of the bar, looking out over Coral Bay. 'Rescue young women in distress and sail away with them?'

He grinned. 'Couple of times a year. Whenever I'm in need of a Caribbean vacation.' Sam asked the bartender for two margaritas. A man in shorts and a Hawaiian shirt stood playing a bluesy version of 'Ring of Fire' on a guitar in the corner. 'I'm glad you're here.' Kevyn bent the straw out of the way and took a sip of the pale green drink, shuddering at its tartness. 'You may have been right about me needing help.'

Sam shook his head. 'No. You'd have been just fine. But, for what it's worth, I'm glad I'm here, too.' Sam smiled. 'Anyway, there's no better way to learn long passages than being thrown in head first.'

'Into sailing or into the sea?' Kevyn was glad it hadn't come to that. Overboard was no place she wanted to be.

'Either way, you learn pretty fast what not to do again.'

'Either way, I'm still glad you came.' Kevyn wanted to say more, to put into words how much she'd changed since meeting him – how much more she enjoyed life with him by her side. But how could she put into words how much Sam had come to mean in such a short time? 'I don't want this adventure to end.'

Sam grabbed her hand. 'When you meet Alex you'll have a lot of catching up to do. My guess is you won't just make small talk and then turn *Wander* around to sail home the next day. This adventure could continue for quite a while.'

'Would you still be here if it does?'

'I'll be here as long as you want me to be. I'm not going anywhere.' Sam looked at Kevyn. 'What about you? Do you *have* to return to Savannah?'

'Eventually. Grandfather is there, and my mother...but now with Kyle in the Keys and Trista's illness...' Kevyn let out a breath. 'And you in Lauderdale...I'm not sure where I want to call home anymore.'

'That's the great thing about a sailboat.' Sam wiped the salt from the rim of his glass and took a sip. 'You can call a whole lot of different places home.'

Kevyn played with the straw in her glass. 'That's true. I could move back and forth between the two. It's not like I keep nine-to-five hours with the restoration business.'

'And Alex?' Sam asked.

'I may be dreaming of a perfect reunion, but I certainly don't think that we'll return to Savannah and become one big happy family. Too much has happened; too much time has passed.' Kevyn bit her lip. 'Besides, he's the one who turned his back on me. He's known where I was for the past thirty years and has never once come to see me. He chose this life for us. I can't expect him to change his mind overnight and suddenly want to be a father. I'm not even sure I want him to want that. I don't know what he was thinking.'

'You could ask him.'

'Yeah, if we ever find him.'

'No, you could ask him now.' Sam used his head to gesture to the end of the bar at the man who'd just entered.

A faded blue tattoo of a sloop peeked out of a Tommy Bahamas shirt that'd definitely seen better days. A shot glass was already on the bar as he approached. He nodded to the bartender, shut his eyes and tipped the glass back. Swiping the back of his sun-drenched hand across his goatee, Kevyn's stomach seized. He looked the way her grandfather had years before.

The man looked across the bar, focused on Sam, and nodded his head. 'Sam, what brings you down here?'

Kevyn grabbed Sam's forearm and dug her nails into his skin.

'Is that him?' She had trouble getting the words out.

Sam nodded to Kevyn but spoke to the man across the bar. 'It's been awhile, Alex.'

The man started to round the bar. Kevyn swung her head from left to right in disbelief that this was happening – right here – right now. He was supposed to be on Anegada. She wasn't ready to meet him yet. She hadn't even thought of what to say. Shit, he was catching her off guard. She had wanted to be in control of their first meeting.

She clutched at the wooden bar hoping it would steady her nerves, and swallowed hard in an attempt to remove the dry lump that'd formed in her throat.

Her father approached Sam on his right, allowing Sam's broad shoulders to block Kevyn from view, giving her another few moments to think – or, rather – panic. She could hear their conversation but it sounded like it was underwater, muffled and far away.

'What are you doing here?' Sam asked. 'I heard you were searching for *La Victoria*.'

'Who told you that?' Alex sounded surprised. 'You still working for Trista? Deadman's not doing well?'

Sam nodded his head and stole a glance at Kevyn. She sat staring straight ahead, hands clamped tightly to the bar.

'Shop would be better if my sellers wouldn't keep disappearing.' Sam's voice was laced with acid, his anger at Alex apparent again.

Alex avoided looking at him and signaled the bartender for another drink. The man on guitar switched to 'Like a Rolling Stone'. 'You looking for me?'

'I was just in the Keys and spoke with Trista.' Sam's voice softened.

'I didn't think she knew I was here.' Alex and Sam's conversation continued as Kevyn gathered her nerves. She heard Sam's animosity evaporate and wondered if hers possibly could.

For the first time in her life she was hearing her father speak. He didn't sound like a drug smuggler. He didn't sound like a man who'd abandoned his children either, but he was.

'She thinks you're on Anegada,' Sam said.

Alex nodded. 'I am usually. Just here picking up some supplies.'

The normal chitchat seemed surreal to Kevyn. Here he was – the man who had left her, alone, without a word for over thirty years– yet he was as comfortable as could be. Perhaps his demons had been put to rest a long time ago. Finally, Kevyn heard the question she knew was coming.

'And who is this?'

Sam twisted slightly in his chair to reveal Kevyn. She sat wide-eyed staring at Sam, pleading for more time. He searched her eyes like he was seeking permission. 'Alex, I'd like you to meet Kevyn.'

Alex's hand was half-extended when Sam spoke her name. He held it there, paused in mid-air.

Kevyn dared not look him in the eye for fear of crying. So she sat, rigid, staring at his hand. It was long and thin like her own. Wrinkles cut deep around his knuckles and tributaries of blue veins throbbed under the skin. Those hands could tell her his life story if she dared to study them for too long.

What seemed like a lifetime later, Alex yanked his hand away and called for another rum. He stared straight ahead at the bartender. 'Nice to meet you.'

Now that his focus had moved away, Kevyn looked up at the man who was her father. He was taller than she imagined. Older, too – no… maybe just worn. Thirty years in the tropics had drained Alex's youth. He looked like a man who'd spent his life under the blistering sun. He had the same skin tone that she had, and probably the same dark hair at one time; it was more of a salt-and-pepper now.

'You look a lot like Grandfather.' It was the only thing she could think to say.

'And you look like your mother.' Alex's gaze remained straight ahead. He had already thrown back his second rum and another was being poured for him. 'How is Brianna?'

Brianna? Brianna! That's who he was asking about? Kevyn had just sailed fourteen hundred miles to find this man and he couldn't even look her in the eye. She jumped to her feet, knocking the bar stool over in the process.

Crash! The whole bar turned to look at what the trouble was and the guitarist stopped mid-strum.

'Not so great, thanks to you. You ruined her life!'

Her father clenched his glass tighter and stared straight ahead. 'She knew what she was getting into.'

Kevyn slammed her fist against the bar. 'She knew you were no good. She even warned me to stay away. For the first time in my life, I wish I'd listened to her.' She turned on her heel and ran from the bar, unsure if her outburst had really been about her mother or herself. Tears ran down her cheeks and clouded her vision as she raced through the parking lot. She ran right into the side of a car that was parked on the grass as she headed for the road, but barely felt the pain shooting through her knee.

There was no sidewalk or shoulder so she stumbled to the center of the road. She had only gone twenty feet when a car came whipping around the blind curve. Kevyn froze in its headlights unable to move. The tires squealed as the car lurched to the side, narrowly missing her body. Stones spit from the tires, spraying her ankles like bullets.

A man with dark dreadlocks leaned out the window and shouted, 'Get out of the road, lady!' The car's stereo thumped out reggae beats that faded as he sped away.

Kevyn stood still, shaking violently from fear and frustration.

Sam ran up and grabbed her by the shoulders, spinning her around to face him. His eyes wide with fear, he began to shake her. 'Are you nuts? What are you doing?' He yanked her to his chest, wrapped his arms around her neck, and breathed hard against her hair. 'Are you alright?' Pushing her away, he looked her up and down checking for scratches, bruises, or breaks.

'I'm fine. I just couldn't stay in there. I can't face him.' Kevyn buried her head in his chest.

'It's okay. You don't have to do anything you don't want to do.'

'I left my purse in there,' Kevyn sniffed, taking a deep breath and wiping her tears. 'I have to go back.'

'I'll go get it for you.'

'No, I came all this way. It's time to get some answers.' Kevyn pulled the front of her shorts down and tucked in her t-shirt. Wiping her eyes, she looked up and saw Orion shining overhead. 'Okay, let's go.'

Sam grabbed her hand and they walked back into Island Blues. The bar had emptied out. There was a man Kevyn didn't recognize from earlier slumped in the corner, and the musician was packing his guitar into a beat-up leather case. The bartender wiped the far end of the bar. He watched Kevyn and Sam return, but respectfully turned away to give them some privacy. Her father was nowhere in sight.

'He left? *He's gone?*' Kevyn glared at the spot where Alex had been just a moment ago. 'He can't even stick around long enough for a conversation?' Kevyn exploded. 'I'm not even important enough to him to talk to in a bar? Not even a, 'Hi Kevyn, what have you been up to?'

No! He didn't even stick around long enough to wonder what I was doing here.'

She began to wring her hands, swiftly moving one over the other like a mouse running in a wheel.

Sam grabbed her to stop the neurotic movement. 'You just surprised him, that's all.'

'Surprised him? Surprised *him*? What about me? What about the surprise of finding out that I actually have a father after thirty years?'

And for the second time that night, Kevyn stormed out the door.

Kevyn didn't sleep much that night. All she felt was stupidity and disgust for coming all this way for nothing. It wasn't like she thought she and Alex would run into each other's arms like long lost friends when they met, but she *had* thought that she'd at least rate an explanation for why he'd stayed away.

Along the way she'd started to defend his actions. She had no reason to, but she'd been excited to finally have a father in her life. But, like he'd done thirty years before, he'd slammed the door to that possibility.

In the morning, Sam suggested they go for breakfast. 'Coffee and Miss Lucy's Eggs Florentine makes everything seem brighter.'

Kevyn highly doubted that, but put on her sunglasses and followed Sam into the tender without a word. She sat up front and stared out over the water while Sam untied the lines. They puttered across the bay and pulled up on the rocky beach. Kevyn ducked her head under the limb of the sea grape tree, barely missing the low hanging branch, and walked listlessly to the far table.

Pulling out the wrought iron chair, she flopped into the seat. 'Just coffee,' she mumbled when the server came around.

'Come on, Kevyn. Miss Lucy's is an island tradition. Her breakfasts are legendary.' Sam's voice was full of strained cheer. When Kevyn didn't respond, he ordered for them both. 'Two Florentines and two orange juices.'

Kevyn stared at the water. The sun was halfway through its climb. A two-foot lizard scurried across the pebbles and suddenly froze at an unheard noise. Stretching his front legs and chest skyward, like an infant pushing himself up to crawl, he seemed to be listening. The prehistoric fan of spikes that ran down its spine began to tremble. Whatever the noise was that stopped it in its tracks must have finally been deemed safe, as a minute later he continued his scattered dash along the beach. Kevyn stared at the event blankly.

When the coffees arrived she propped both elbows on the table, cupping the mug between her hands. She leaned into the table and held the mug just inches from her lips.

'I think I made a mistake. I want to go home.'

Sam put down his coffee and placed his hand on Kevyn's knee. He squeezed gently. 'You just took him by surprise. He wasn't exactly expecting you.'

'Of course he wasn't. He expected to walk away and never look back. Heaven knows he's done it before, and that's just what he did again.' There was very little emotion in her voice. 'He's living the life he wanted. I'm the intruder here. I'll call Grandfather and tell him I found him then leave him alone to live his life.'

'I'm sure if you talk to him—'

Kevyn cut him off, 'No! He wanted to be thought of as a dead man and I did that for thirty years. I'll do it for another thirty.' She took a sip of coffee and winced. It was strong and bitter. 'He wasn't even a part of my life. I shouldn't feel any different than I did a month ago, before I knew he was alive.'

'That's not the way these things work.' Sam grabbed her hand. 'You know that. You now know he's out there, *here*, on this island. You can't just pretend he doesn't exist. Can you honestly come all this way and not find out why?'

'He likes living in a world where I don't exist.'

Sam sighed. 'Maybe. But I bet he never forgot.'

Kevyn didn't have a comeback for that. 'I just want to go home,' she said quietly.

Sam didn't say anything. He picked up his fork and broke into his eggs. The yellow yolks poured onto his plate offering a vibrant contrast with the bright green spinach. He skewered a piece of English muffin on the tines and pushed it around the plate, creating a road of white through the pool of yellow. 'You'd go back to Savannah?'

'That's where my family is.'

'What about Kyle?'

'I don't know. I could go and help Trista, I suppose. Get to know him better,' Kevyn thought out loud.

'And…me?'

Kevyn looked at him; tears lined her eyes, threatening to spill over. She swallowed and opened her mouth to speak, but nothing came out. She swallowed, trying to gain her composure.

But only a deafening silence remained.

The sky was softening by the time Sam and Kevyn approached *Wander* in their inflatable. The sun cast a warm orange glow over the bay, and offered a beautiful spotlight on Alex– standing in *Wander*'s cockpit.

As he watched their approach, Kevyn clenched her fists; her nails dug into her palms. What was he doing standing on her boat? *Wander* was no longer his to climb aboard. He'd given her up, just like everything else in his life when he'd left.

Sam threw him the bowline, which Alex caught effortlessly. He bent down and wound two figure eights over the cleat and tied the line off once. He held his hand out to Kevyn to help her aboard.

Kevyn felt her face burn. She stared at the man standing on her boat like nothing had happened, like the past thirty years were not only forgivable but no-big-deal. She ignored his offering and stepped around him onto the deck. 'What are you doing here?'

He dropped his hand and cleared his throat. 'Last night I behaved badly. I came to see if you were okay.'

'Now you're concerned about me?' Kevyn's voice was cold as she placed her hands on hips, ready for a fight.

'You looked pretty shaken up.' Alex shifted his weight from foot to foot and looked down at what would've been his shoes if he hadn't kicked off his flip-flops before climbing aboard.

'Geez, I'm sorry. Did I ruin your evening? Forgive me, but it was a little upsetting to see a ghost standing in front of me for the first time.' Kevyn couldn't keep the sarcasm from her voice.

'Ghost?' Alex looked from Kevyn to Sam and back to Kevyn.

'Yes. Ghost. I'm quite new to the fact that you're still alive – not to mention living down here in paradise. I've always thought you died in a car crash. It's only been a couple of weeks since you've come back from the grave.'

'Who told you I *died?*' Alex looked bewildered. 'I didn't just disappear. Your mama and grandfather both knew I was leaving.'

'Yeah, it seems everyone knew but me.' Kevyn flung her bag on the bench. 'Nobody told me a thing about you.'

'Kevyn…I'm so sorry, but I had no idea you thought I was dead.' Alex's eyes pleaded with her to believe him.

'Yeah, it's much better that I grew up thinking you just didn't care enough to get to know me.'

'That's not what…' Alex grabbed his goatee in his fist and pulled. 'I didn't think…' Shifting his weight he took a deep breath, opting for a different approach. 'The old boat looks good. You've kept her in great shape.'

'It's my boat now.' Kevyn narrowed her eyes. Did he want *Wander* back after all this time? 'Grandfather gave it to me.'

Alex held his hands up. 'No argument from me. You obviously belong on her. You sailed it all the way here?'

Kevyn squinted at Alex through suspicious eyes. 'I sailed to Lauderdale, and then Sam and I sailed here together.'

'How'd you two meet?' Alex's voice was light and inquisitive. He was obviously trying to stick to a calmer subject.

'Grandfather sent me to see Pete. He directed me to Sam.'

'He sent you to see Pete? Why?' Alex looked confused.

'Oh, for crissake!' Kevyn threw her hands up in the air. 'He was worried about you. For some strange reason he still cares what happens to you. He got a call about the *K Sea* sinking and he began to worry. That's when he finally told me that you weren't dead and sent me down here to find you.'

Alex stared at his hands. 'How is he?'

'He's old. He's frail. He's all alone. How did you expect he'd be? You abandoned him, too.'

Alex bowed his head and scuffed at the teak deck. 'I just couldn't stay.'

'That's odd…I feel the same way about this place.' Kevyn straightened; her spine was rigid. 'Apparently we *do* have things in common. Now, if you'll kindly get off my boat. We're about to set sail.'

*****

Chapter Fifteen

'I hate to tell you this, but customs will be closed by the time we get there.' Sam stood in the doorway of the cabin.

Alex had left without much more than a mumbling, and Kevyn had stayed on deck watching his tender return to shore. The boat was long out of sight before she went downstairs. She sat on the side of her bed snuggling Athens under her chin. 'I know.'

'He came out here to see you.' Sam crossed his arms over his chest and leaned on the frame, his shoulders barely fit the narrow opening.

'I know.'

'You didn't tell him about Kyle.'

'I know!' Kevyn flung herself back down on the bed and stared up at the ceiling.

The next morning, she was down below checking the charts and plotting their return to Florida while Sam sorted out lines on deck. She was hoping to make landfall in Key West and spend some time with Kyle before heading north. The sound of a motor approaching and Sam's muffled voice alerted her to Alex's return.

'She's downstairs. I'll get her.'

'I heard him.' Kevyn came out of the hatch. She held a rolled up chart in one hand and the other she used to shield her eyes to the sun. 'What do you want?'

'I came to say goodbye.' Alex held a burgundy velvet pouch in his hands; he twisted it over his knuckles, around and around. As if he suddenly realized it was there, he thrust the bag at Kevyn.

'I brought this for you.' Kevyn's hands trembled while she opened the bag and poured its contents into her palm. A clunky gold chain slipped between her fingers. She turned the necklace's pendant over and stared at a gold cross the size of a deck of cards. Set with a cluster of emeralds; there must have been two-dozen stones sparkling up at her. It wasn't polished, and the grooves of the cross were tarnished, making it look like mould, yet Kevyn had never seen anything so beautiful.

'Is this my sweet sixteen present? Graduation, maybe? You know you missed a wedding, too.' The barb hung heavy in the air, like the smell of the remover she used to clean old paint off wood. Even Sam winced. Why was she doing this? She sounded like her mother. She didn't want to be this bitter.

'It's not to make up for anything. It's something I would like you to have. It was your grandmother's once.' Alex looked over the water.

'I gave it to her long ago but it was returned to me.' Kevyn recalled Grandfather saying he'd thrown it back in Alex's face believing it ill-gotten. She turned it in her hands now, wondering the same thing.

He traced the line of teak with his toe. 'I haven't been a father to you, Kevyn. I've given you nothing, nothing of myself. If you leave today, I would like to think that at least a little something goes with you.'

Kevyn bit her bottom lip. Did she really want to leave now, without finding out more about the father she'd never known?

'We aren't leaving today.' She took a deep breath.

'There are things to say.' Alex looked up with a hope in his eyes.

Sam nodded once to confirm the decision.

'Well, that's great.' Alex's smile widened.

'Why don't I put on a pot of coffee?' Sam excused himself, went downstairs, and shut the hatch.

Kevyn stared at the closed companionway, not sure of what to say or how to begin. All she really wanted to know was why, but at the same time she was afraid to ask. She shifted her weight from one foot to the other as the silence grew uncomfortable.

'I like the green hull. When I first got her she was white.' Alex avoided the subject of what he'd been doing for the last thirty years.

'Billy helped me update a lot of the systems on board.' *Wander* wasn't what she wanted to talk to him about. Questions flashed through her mind. *Where have you been? Why did you leave? Why didn't you come back?* But as soon as one question formed another took its place.

'Billy always looked out for her.' Alex ran a hand over the life stays. 'I never thought I'd see her again.'

Kevyn managed a nod. 'She's a good boat.'

'Didn't give you any trouble getting here? She's got to be getting old by now. I bought her when I was just a kid.' Alex sat down on the port cushions. He leaned back and crossed an ankle over his knee.

'We cracked the tiller but pulled into Turks and Caicos for a few days while we got the part.' The connection dawned on Kevyn. 'Actually, we visited with a guy who knew you…Digger. I forget what he said his real name was. Sam knew him.'

'You talked to Digger?' With the mention of Digger's name Alex sat up and leaned his body forward.

'We had a drink with him at some tiki bar.' Kevyn took a deep breath. 'And he came by the boat for a few minutes to talk to me about you and the *K Sea*. He thought maybe it hadn't sunk.' Kevyn searched her father's face for an answer while she skirted around a direct question of whether he'd faked an insurance claim that sent her on this goose chase.

He ignored her question and shot to his feet. 'He was on this boat?' His voice grew loud. Sam came through the hatch carrying steaming mugs of coffee. 'Who was on the boat?'

'Digger.' Kevyn took a mug and passed one to Alex. 'What's the big deal?'

'Did he give you anything?' Alex paced in the tiny space.

'What would he give me?' Kevyn was confused by Alex's nervous movements.

'Alex? What's going on?' Sam put down his coffee. His face wore a serious look.

Alex ignored him, keeping his focus on Kevyn. 'You're *sure* he didn't give you any packages to carry?'

'No. I would remember. Besides, he was only here a few minutes.'

'Where exactly was he?'

'What's the matter with you? He was here in the cockpit for ten minutes. I got us drinks and he left two minutes later.'

'He was on deck alone?' Alex looked around like he had lost something. He bent down and began lifting up the cushions.

'What are you doing?' Kevyn's eyes darted around the deck while she tried to understand what her father was so worked up over.

'Why didn't you tell me he was here?' Sam sounded worried now.

'It was no big deal. He was here for ten minutes to talk about Alex and then left.' Kevyn felt like a teenager again being interrogated by her grandfather after he had found marijuana in her backpack.

'Listen, you two know that the *K Sea* sank.' Alex grabbed Kevyn's wrist as he spoke. 'It wasn't an accident that sank her.'

Kevyn's stomach lurched. 'What do you mean?'

'I sank the *K Sea* myself.'

'What? You sunk your own boat? Why?'

Alex took a deep breath. 'I used to run through the Turks every couple of months. I knew Digger. I knew he wasn't operating a hundred percent above the law. He always had gold and gems that he needed delivered somewhere. He had papers for them, but I've dealt with authentic papers before and his never looked right.'

'I heard rumors that he was smuggling something. I thought it was drugs.' Sam pushed his sunglasses to the top of his head. His eyes showed concern.

'Drugs, guns, stones – he does it all,' Alex replied.

'What does that have to do with the *K Sea*?' Kevyn threw her hands in the air.

'I made some deliveries for him. Just the stones and *just* the ones I knew were legit. I took them to St. Thomas and dropped them with the dealer there.' Alex watched Kevyn closely as he continued, 'The last trip I made through the Turks we met at the bar. He didn't have any stones for me, so we just had a few drinks. I was headed down here the next day. Halfway across the Puerto Rico Trench the air conditioner conked out. I pulled out the wall to crawl behind the unit to repair it and found bricks and bricks of cocaine.'

'*What?* On your boat?' Kevyn felt ill. The stories she' had heard were right. Her father was a drug smuggler.

'I think he had his crew stash it while I was at the bar with him. Anyway, I didn't want to mess with that stuff.'

'Why not turn him in?' Kevyn wondered if that was the truth, or just what he wanted her to hear. Pete had talked about Alex's boat being confiscated, as well as being linked to heroin in Vietnam. Could her father really expect her to believe he was innocent in Digger's drug running scheme?

Alex dropped his eyes and lowered his voice, 'I've had my share of run-ins with the local authorities and I wasn't convinced they would believe me when I said the drugs weren't mine. I didn't know what to do. All I knew was that they would never find the boat in the trench because it's so deep. So I sunk it, drugs and all.'

'You really sunk it?' Kevyn's mind was reeling, wanting to believe her father. 'What did Digger do?'

'Nothing...yet,' Alex said. 'I made it look like an accident. Technically, he doesn't actually know I had any knowledge of the drugs being there. I've kept a low profile and not been to the Turks since.'

'He knows we were headed to Anegada to see you,' Sam said quickly, warning Alex that he was no longer hidden.

'I don't care if he comes for me, but if he was on this boat then I want to search it and make sure you aren't carrying his shit as well.'

'On *Wander*?' Kevyn looked around at the thirty feet of space. Her kayak crowded the deck. Hatches were stuffed full of extra sails, lines, and covers. The only unclaimed space was the shower and she knew there were no drugs in there.

'Let's just look around to be sure.' Sam opened the hatches under the seats in the cockpit. He pulled out the lifejackets and threw them on the teak floor. Uncoiling the extra lines, he dropped those in a heap at his feet. They pulled every last piece of equipment out of its storage spot. Reams of sail fabric and Rubbermaid containers full of spare parts soon littered the decks.

Kevyn stood where she was and watched the odd *Law & Order* search going on around her. She blew out a sigh and ran her hands through her hair, pulling it tight off her face. This wasn't the reunion she had thought it would be. Had searching for Alex made her a drug runner, too?

'I don't understand why you sank your boat. Why didn't you just turn the drugs in?'

'Kevyn, I've been bouncing around these islands for the past thirty years – running around during the heyday of drug smuggling. I'm a treasure hunter, which most people associate with pirates. Do you think anyone would take a look at my life and believe I was innocent?'

'But to sink your own boat?'

'I loved the *K Sea*, but it's not the first time I've had to start over from scratch.'

Athens sauntered up from below and headed for the bow.

Kevyn watched him stretch out and remembered hearing Digger banging around up there when he was on board. She headed forward and opened the front hatch. It looked the same as it always had. Bottles of boat soap lined a shelf beside bins of chamois, sponges, and wiper blades. Extra lifejackets were stuffed in the corner.

She was about to close the hatch and move on to the next one when she spotted a bundle of bubble wrap taped to the top of the compartment.

'I've found something.' She reached in and yanked a package the size of a baseball out of its hiding spot.

She walked down the side of the boat and joined Sam and her father in the cockpit. It was tight for three people with little clear space left on the floor, so she perched herself on the side of the hull and put her feet up on the cushions trying to act calm. Her stomach felt empty and began to involuntarily contract as she handed the package to Sam. It was becoming a familiar feeling ever since she first discovered that her father was still very much alive. 'What is it?' Alex asked.

'It's too small to be drugs. Digger wouldn't bother with such a small amount.' Sam began unwrapping.

A bubble popped and Kevyn jumped. Her nerves were on edge.

Sam whistled as the last wrap of plastic peeled away. 'Alex, take a look at this.' Green rays of light reflected the sun from Sam's hand. He held up a cut oval stone the size of a magnolia flower; he had to stretch his fingers wide in order to hold the gem, and even then it surpassed his fingertips.

'That's the biggest emerald I've ever seen.' Alex tore the stone from Sam's hand. He lowered his sunglasses on his nose and peered over the top to get a better look.

'That's got to be million dollars.' Sam pursed his lips and whistled low.

'If not more. Look. It's one solid stone.' Alex held it up to the sunlight. 'Superior quality…this thing is flawless.'

'I'm sorry, a *million* dollars?' Kevyn couldn't believe that any one thing could be that expensive. 'For one emerald?'

'They are the most expensive gems in the world.' Sam's eyes never left the stone. 'It's an incredible jewel. Could make all our troubles go away.'

'Once you start thinking like that, it's a hard road back.' A funny look came over Alex's face. 'You'll spend the rest of your life running and looking over your shoulder.'

Kevyn wasn't as mesmerized by its presence. When Alex handed it to her she studied it looking for its value. It was large and a beautiful color of green but hardly looked like more than a colored piece of glass. Maybe she was missing something? It was cool in her hand and smooth. She'd never held something so valuable before and couldn't see what all the fuss was about. 'Why the hell would he give it to us?' She passed it back to Alex.

'I doubt it was a gift.' Alex turned the stone in his hand. 'My guess is that he was coming down here to retrieve his drugs when I sunk the *K Sea*. It's probably the same with this. You transport it somewhere and he comes in clean and retrieves it from you.'

'You think he's here?'

'If he isn't already he will be soon.' Alex nodded. 'You said that he thinks you're headed to Anegada? Then, that's where he'll go.'

'What do we do with this thing now?' Kevyn couldn't believe this was her first real conversation with her father. 'I don't want it on my boat. And, I don't want Digger here if he's coming for it.'

'We could turn it over to the authorities.' Sam's voice held little enthusiasm for the suggestion.

'Here?' Alex shook his head. 'You'll be tied up in paperwork and official channels for years. It would take forever for any of us to be allowed to leave the island.' Alex pulled at his goatee; the muscles in his forearm rippled. 'And it brings up the same questions about what I've been doing for the past thirty years.'

'What *have* you been doing?' Kevyn finally asked.

'Not smuggling.' Alex grabbed her hand. 'And, I don't want anyone thinking you are, either.'

'But we're innocent. We just got here. We can't be held accountable for your past.' Kevyn's eyes shot from one man then back again.

'But you will be. Whether you knew it or not, you are my daughter and you are tied to me.'

Kevyn suddenly felt ill. 'I just met you.'

'It won't matter. To them, you're my daughter.'

Frustration filled Kevyn. In the past two days she had found her dead father and become a criminal – not exactly the father-daughter reunion she had envisioned.

'The way I see it, getting rid of it is our only option.'

Alex sat at the table in *Wander*'s galley with Sam; the emerald lay between them. Kevyn didn't want to touch it, but she couldn't keep her eyes off it.

'Do you mean dump it or sell it?' Kevyn was still not sure what side of the law her father walked. She stood beside the two men at the counter mixing up a jug of margaritas, and set the pitcher down beside the jewel.

'We could sell it but that takes time, and without authentic papers a sale would invite a type of person into your life that I'd rather avoid.' Alex ran his finger around the rim of his glass, knocking the salt off. 'I suggest just dumping it. It's what I did with the *K Sea*. Digger must have found it while diving a wreck somewhere. It came from the ocean and it should stay in the ocean.' Kevyn's head shot up. She replayed the timing in her head. Digger had stashed the emerald but it was Alex who suggested searching for it. Had he already known it was there?

'So you can go find it when we've gone?' Kevyn placed her glass down on the table. Was he trying to keep the emerald for himself? Was he really so innocent in all of this?

Alex shook his head. 'So we can all go back to our normal lives.'

'The life before I came looking for you?' Kevyn gripped her glass tight. The ice cooled her hands but not her suspicions.

'I didn't mean that.' Alex looked directly at Kevyn and she felt a rush of emotion overtake her. 'I meant without Digger in our lives.'

'He'll come looking for it.' Sam drained his glass.

'I've been thinking about that, too.' Alex spoke to Sam directly, laying out his plan. 'Leave *Wander* with me and fly out tomorrow. I'll deal with Digger. He can search *Wander* high and low but he won't find it. Above all, I don't want Kevyn here when Digger comes back.'

Sam stared at his empty glass and spoke low. 'You want us to trust you with another boat and the emerald.'

'What? Leave *Wander*? No way!' Kevyn threw herself into the conversation. 'There is no way I'm leaving.'

'You don't know what this guy is capable of.' Alex reached out to grab Kevyn's hand. It was only the second time in her thirty years she'd felt her father's touch.

'I'm not going.' He wasn't getting rid of her, or getting *Wander*.

'Why don't we just give him back the stone?' They'd been over this already, but Kevyn still couldn't understand why calling the police wasn't the best option. In Georgia, in what seemed like a lifetime ago, she would've just let the authorities handle everything. But down here, where her father was involved, the waters were beyond murky.

'We can't just give it back because then he'll know we know about it,' Alex explained again. 'And Digger doesn't like any loose ends.'

'So we put it back and pretend we never found it. He comes and gets it and leaves us all alone.' Kevyn stared at her empty glass. 'He gets his stone and we get to leave.'

Alex rubbed his chin. 'That's not a bad idea.' He leaned back in his chair and then thudded forward. 'Okay, so here's what we do.' He sounded like a man who was used to making all the decisions. 'We put it back. But I don't want either of you aboard *Wander* when he comes looking for it. You'll stay with me. We'll leave for Anegada in the morning and moor *Wander*, out in the open for him to find. He comes, retrieves his emerald, thinks he's pulled a fast one on us, and leaves.'

It sounded too easy to Kevyn. 'How do we know he'll come?'

Sam laughed. 'It's a million dollar emerald. He'll come.'

Kevyn eyed her father with suspicion. 'How do we know you won't come back and grab the emerald yourself?' *Was he in cahoots with Digger?* So far, all she had was his claim of innocence, but his word didn't mean a whole lot to her. Brianna probably thought she'd had his word that he'd stick around all those years ago. 'It would mean a lot of money to finance your search for *La Victoria.*'

'You don't know.' Alex looked her straight in the eye. 'You just have to trust me.' Kevyn passed her empty glass back and forth between her hands weighing whether she should trust him or not.

Sam got up from the table and stood by the sink washing his glass. Finally, he broke the awkward silence. 'I think it's our only option.'

Kevyn couldn't find fault with the plan, other than the fact it involved Digger walking on her boat again…and trusting her father.

Alex put his hand on Kevyn's and looked her in the eye. 'It's not that I want you to leave. I want you safe, and that means you'll stay with me at my place until it's all over.'

Both men looked at Kevyn for her approval.

She twirled the end of her ponytail around her fingers. She hated the idea of Digger getting away with it, but she didn't want any of them involved anymore than they already were. Sam was right; there were no other options. Kevyn nodded her head. 'On to Anegada.'

It looked like she was going to spend time with her father… whether she liked it or not.

Kevyn tried to concentrate on cleaning up the mess the search had produced, but she had trouble staying focused. All she could think about was what Alex had said. Did he really want to protect her?

Sam finished preparing the boat to sail and dove into the water to scrub the hull free of any barnacles and algae that'd accumulated. The warmth of the Caribbean waters produced more growth than *Wander* was used to in Savannah.

Alex had gone ashore late the night before to grab his bag. While he was gone, Kevyn picked up her cell phone and called her grandfather. 'I found him. He's here in St. John's and he's okay.'

'Oh, Kevyn, you don't know how good it is to hear you say that.' Her grandfather sighed. 'How are you? How are you taking all this?'

Kevyn's eyes filled with tears. It was all too much. Warm salty tears spilled over her eyelids like the infinity pools decorating the mansion lawns in Ft. Lauderdale. 'I'm okay. I can handle it.' She briefly wondered when she'd started to lie to the ones she loved, too.

'Is he coming home?' Her grandfather's voice shook with emotion.

'We haven't got to that part yet.' She couldn't bear to tell him the truth about how tenuous the connection between father and daughter really was. With the discovery of the emerald, she hadn't had a chance to talk about why he left or what he would do in the future. She hadn't mentioned her grandfather's desire to see him again, or Trista's request that he come to Key West to learn about his son.

'There are a few things happening here at the moment. I'm not sure he can leave just yet.' She wiped her face with the back of her hand.

'He's in trouble.' It wasn't a question so much as a foregone conclusion. 'Not really trouble, but there is a situation.' Kevyn hoped her grandfather wouldn't hear how scared she was. As confused as she was about her father, she hadn't forgotten there was real danger in the fact that Digger wanted his emerald back. 'We're going to sail to Anegada this afternoon. I'll talk with him then and figure what to do.'

'Kevyn, don't you go getting mixed up in anything.' Her grandfather's voice was stern. 'I know I asked you to do this, but it's not worth getting yourself in trouble for. You are more important to me than bringing him home. I know he's safe now. That's all that counts.'

Kevyn heard a woman's voice in the background. 'Is that Kevyn? Did she get there?'

'Who's that?'

'Brianna's here.' He took a raspy breath. 'She's been here every afternoon this week.'

'What's she doing there?' Kevyn's face burned where the slap had landed.

'It's time we all put this behind us and moved on. We are trying to do that. Forget the past and mend some fences.'

Kevyn couldn't believe what she was hearing. 'Is she okay?'

'She isn't drinking, if that's what you mean. She has yet to beat me at Scrabble, but that hasn't sent her to the bottle.' His gruff laughter made him sound good, like he was being taken care of.

For a second Kevyn wasn't sure if she was glad her mother was his caregiver, or jealous that Brianna had taken her place. 'I never thought I'd see this day.'

'As I said, the past is the past. I'd say the same to Alex if he came home. But, most importantly, I'm saying it to you. It's time for all of us to start fresh.'

As Kevyn hung up, she wondered if it was that easy. Could she have a fresh start? It was all there in front of her: A new boyfriend, a new family, a new life – it was all hers for the taking. Could she forget all her pain and start again as a brand new person?

Grandfather could. After all, when she returned she would bring news of an unknown grandson. Brianna could. Apparently she'd already stopped drinking and was now mending fences. Alex could just go back to the Keys and start a life with Trista and Kyle. But could she start a life with Sam? With *all* of them?

There was one thing Kevyn knew for sure. There would be no fresh starts for anyone if they ended up in jail for smuggling emeralds. The jewel was the first thing that needed to be buried.

It didn't take them long to get ready to sail. It was only a few hours down the Sir Francis Drake Channel through the British Virgin Islands to Anegada, and their only task was to sign out of the U.S. Virgin Islands with the immigration department in St. John's and then sign in with the British in Tortola. Kevyn made a wry note that she would be getting yet another stamp in her passport. She just was not as excited this time around. This time, she was transporting an illegal item into another country. She was as bad as her father.

Alex met them on the dock with a single bag. He raised his arms up to hug Kevyn and they both leaned to the left. His right arm bumped into her left and bounced up, knocking his hand into the side of her head.

Mumbling an apology, he settled for a handshake. 'Ready?'

Sam grabbed his bag and tossed it into the tender. 'Let's go.'

They motored out to *Wander* in silence. Once aboard, Kevyn sat on the starboard bench with Sam beside her, ready to sail.

Alex looked around uncomfortably and pointed to the far port side bench. 'I'll just sit there.'

Sam took the tiller. 'Ready to raise anchor,' he called out.

Kevyn started forward to comply just as Alex jumped up on the seat to help. They both made for the bow and then stopped. 'I...errr...' Alex muttered awkwardly.

'I've got it,' Kevyn said, a little too loudly. Her voice held a sharp edge, making sure he knew that she was the rightful owner of *Wander* now.

'Of course...I was just trying to help.' Alex retreated back to the bench. Kevyn climbed up on the superstructure over the main cabin, wincing at the way she was acting. She raised the anchor, glad for the distraction to keep her on the bow.

Sam raised the sails and turned the boat into the wind to exit the bay. The prongs of the anchor had brought up strands of seaweed and sand. Kevyn reached into a hatch to retrieve a bucket, tied a line to the handle and lowered it over the side of the bow. She hoisted a bucket of seawater over the lifeline to douse the anchor. The white sand filtered away easily. Then she reached down to remove the seaweed and stowed the anchor. Moving slowly, Kevyn stayed on the bow, coiling lines and rearranging the locker. She was too embarrassed to go back in the cockpit just yet.

The muffled sounds of Sam and Alex talking blew in the wind. Kevyn couldn't hear what they were saying but the tone was evident: they were arguing. Kevyn watched as Sam reached out and grabbed Alex's elbow, shaking his arm as Sam leaned in close and said something to Alex.

Alex wrenched his arm from Sam's grip, looked up at Kevyn, and shook his head. Sam threw his hands up and said something else.

Again, Alex shook his head as his vehement 'No!' carried over the wind.

'Hey guys, what's going on?' Kevyn jumped down from the bow and sat beside Sam, putting her hand on his bicep. 'Everything okay?'

Sam's glare at Alex turned to the water ahead. 'Yeah, just catching up.' He gripped the tiller tight in his hand, his knuckles turning white.

Kevyn looked across the cockpit to Alex searching for more of an explanation.

He rubbed his elbow where Sam's grip had been and shrugged. 'Sam was just asking about my latest search.'

'You're sure that's it? It seemed awful intense.'

Neither man offered any more of an explanation. Kevyn looked from one to the other. What was going on here? Why were they lying to her? It was time she started asking questions and getting some answers.

'Trista said you've been down here working the *La Victoria* site.' She started her questions with the facts she already knew.

'You did your homework.' Alex nodded. He apparently wasn't hiding the treasure he was searching for. 'I've been working on that ship for a long time now.'

'But you haven't found it, yet?'

Alex shook his head. 'It's out there. I'm close.'

'How do you know?' Kevyn stole a glance at Sam. He wasn't contributing to the conversation but he was following it. 'Have you found anything?'

Sam leaned forward, his eyes on Alex.

'I can just feel it.' Alex tapped his stomach with his index and middle finger.

Sam settled back in his seat.

'Feel it?' Kevyn raised an eyebrow.

'I can't explain it, but it's this knowledge, this feeling I have that I'll find it.' He looked at Kevyn under the boom. 'I felt the same thing right before I found my first treasure in Georgia and now I feel it here.'

'Confidence?'

Alex shook his head slowly. 'No, more like the ocean is willing to let me in on some of her secrets…like she and I have an understanding. I don't rob her and she lets me stay.'

'But aren't you raking her bottom? Ravaging her?' Kevyn couldn't believe she was talking this way.

'Some see it that way, but I try not to be one of those guys.' He leaned back in the seat and crossed his long, tan legs at the ankles. 'I always try to leave more than I take. I salvage just enough to piece together the story of what happened. It's like putting together a puzzle from the ocean floor. I find the pieces and fit them together with the research in order to tell a story.'

'You leave the rest?' Kevyn's voice was full of doubt.

Alex nodded. 'It's an agreement we made long ago.'

'You and the ocean?'

'She hasn't let me down yet.'

'And now?' Sam asked. 'You think you've found *La Victoria*?'

Alex stared out at the ocean and a mystical note filled his voice. 'Not yet. Progress has slowed with the loss of the *K Sea*, but she's out there. Waiting to tell me her story.'

140

They sailed close to the islands and Kevyn watched the green of the islands as she thought of her next question and where she wanted the conversation to go. It felt like they were on a tour of the British Virgin Islands. After they had left immigration in Tortola and sailed down the passage they passed Norman Island on their left and Peter on their right.

Sam stood up from the tiller and stretched.

'I'll be down below if you need me.' He shut the companionway hatch behind him as Kevyn switched seats and took the tiller.

'So, here we are.' Alex stared out over the rail to the beaches beyond. 'Can't say as I thought this would ever happen.'

'What, seeing *me* again?'

'Ouch.' Alex sat straighter on the bench. 'I guess I deserve that. What I meant is that I didn't think we'd be sailing *Wander* together.'

Kevyn took a deep breath; this was her opening. She searched his face. 'What did you think?'

Alex leaned forward. Placing his elbows on his knees, he studied his hands as if the answers to everything could be read on his palms. A light breeze blew through the sails as the minutes slowly passed. The only noise to be heard was the clanging of the rigging. Finally, Alex spoke, 'You know, I saw you in the bassinet in the hospital. You were so beautiful and innocent. For a moment I thought I could do it. I loved your mama and I loved you.' He continued to stare at his hands. 'But I was flailing and I couldn't bring you down with me. I wanted you and your mama to live in peace.'

'You think leaving us gave Mama peace?' Tears burned her eyelids. 'She's a mess. She drinks to forget you left her.'

Alex hung his head. 'When I met your mama she was beautiful. She had long dark hair, just like yours, and the deepest brown eyes.' He looked up at Kevyn and smiled, possibly remembering a better time. 'I used to say I could taste chocolate by staring into those eyes. I'd been going to the crab shack every night trying to get up the nerve to talk to her. I'd spent most of my teenage years on the water, and then the last four years in Vietnam surrounded by hell. I didn't know what to say to a beautiful woman.'

Kevyn couldn't help but be fascinated. She'd never heard this story of her parents meeting. It was the story of a boy she never knew and a girl she'd only glimpsed during her lifetime. 'You must've said something right.'

He laughed. 'This one night I was in there and four or five drunken fishermen came in and started hassling Brianna. Regular jokes that shouldn't ever be told in the presence of a woman. Everyone in the bar was uncomfortable and felt bad for her. I got up and said something, but your mama stopped me. She didn't need rescuing.' Alex shook his head. 'She was a strong woman, and she set them straight way better than I could have. It's what made me think she could handle my baggage.'

'So what happened?' Kevyn tightened the sheet that had begun to flutter in the wind.

'Brianna *could* handle my darkness. Problem was I couldn't.' Alex stole a quick glance at Kevyn. 'She shone so bright when she told me she was pregnant.' Kevyn leaned in closer and felt her heart begin to race. This was it; this was the story she wanted to hear.

'I could see how much she loved the idea of us being a family, and I wanted to give that to her.' He rubbed the back of his neck. 'I really did. I wanted to be a new man for her...and for you.'

Reaching out, he placed a hand on Kevyn's knee. She jerked back, recoiling from his touch. 'But you left.'

'I really tried to make it work. All through her pregnancy I thought I could do it. But the night you were born the nurse let me hold you while Brianna slept. You were so tiny. You had a mess of dark hair and looked just like your mama. You had your eyes shut tight for the first few minutes, but then you yawned and opened those green gems of yours.' He stared into those same eyes, and continued, 'They were my eyes.'

He took a breath and paused. 'The nurse said you were just like me and I panicked. I knew I couldn't contaminate anything so innocent and perfect.' Sighing, he went back to studying his hands. 'So, I put you back in the bassinet and left. It was the only gift I could have given you.'

'You took the easy way out and left us to fend for ourselves.' Kevyn's ice cold words shot through the searing heat of the tropics, cooling the air around them. 'I've got news for you. Mama wasn't strong enough to handle you or me. Your leaving broke not only her but that innocence you claimed you were trying so hard to protect. You didn't protect me, you threw me straight to the gators.'

Silence erupted. It seemed even the wind had gone quiet. Kevyn watched other sailboats cruising in the distance. Their white sails were just dots in the intense blue. A tern circled slowly above, soaring wide sweeping circles in search of lunch in the water below.

Kevyn took deep breaths filling her lungs with the warm salty air. Anger was getting her nowhere. Finally, she spoke, 'I know about the little girl in Vietnam.'

Alex looked up with tears in his eyes. 'That little girl deserved more out of life than I gave her. You all did.' He stared out over the water. 'I ruined her life.'

'Why was she there?'

'It was a crazy time. It had been for years. I was supposed to be taking the boat from Saigon to Thailand to patrol. The woman who sold noodles on the corner where I bought my cigarettes found out and begged me to take her child with me.'

'To Thailand?'

'Her sister lived there and would take the girl. The woman couldn't get an exit visa and with everything in the city crumbling around her she wanted her daughter to have a better life. She begged me to save her and I couldn't say no.' His voice was quiet and seemed as far away as Vietnam itself.

'You were trying to help her.'

'I made everything much, much worse.' Alex stared over the water.

'Were the drugs on board yours?'

'Everything was happening over there – drugs, prostitution, gambling – and a lot of soldiers were mixed up in it. We're talking about majors and generals too.'

Kevyn pushed, 'And you?'

He shrugged. 'I figured each man had his own path to walk.'

She took a deep breath and tried again, 'The drugs on board, were they yours?'

'No. They weren't mine.' Alex returned his gaze to the floor of the cockpit. 'I wasn't the one delivering them, but I did guess that they were there. I never saw them but I should've checked before we left. I might not have put them there, but that boat and those soldiers' lives were my responsibility.' Alex's voice was barely audible over the breeze. 'I didn't stop the guys when I suspected.

'Besides…taking that little girl to what I thought was safety was just as wrong. I didn't have clearance to do it. I just had the pleading look in her mother's eyes when she held her out to me.' Alex choked on his words. Tears sprung to Kevyn's eyes but the wind whisked them away.

Alex cleared his throat and straightened in his seat. 'So, I was smuggling, too. The only difference is my cargo was an innocent little girl instead of heroin. Who was I to judge what others did? I got that little girl killed.'

Kevyn grabbed his hand. 'The war killed her. It killed a lot of people. You were only trying to help.'

A haunted look filled Alex's eyes as he finally raised his head. 'My help only destroys people. That little girl, those Marines….they were my friends.'

Emotion washed over her and Kevyn squeezed his hand. 'Why'd the boat go down?'

'Why did anything happen over there? I have no idea. One minute we were leaving port and the next we were under fire, a hole was ripped in the side of the boat, and we were sinking.'

Athens strolled up on deck, plopped down on the bench beside Kevyn, and began cleaning himself with his tongue, totally oblivious to the tension around him.

'It all happened so fast. I couldn't get to the little girl or any of the men.'

'It was an accident.'

'It was a nightmare.' Alex whispered.

'And it's haunted you.'

'I thought I had it under control when I met your mother, but when I saw you in the hospital it all came flooding back.'

'And you've been running ever since?'

Alex hung his head. 'I thought about you. A lot. But, as time went by, it seemed it was too late.'

Kevyn's stomach fluttered. It didn't excuse his absence but she understood how hard his life had been and how hard it would have been.

'What about now?' Kevyn looked into her father's eyes. 'Are you ready to let people into your life now?'

Alex nodded slowly. 'I'd like to try.' His tone turned to one of pleading, 'Kevyn, you've got to believe me. I left for your own good and your mama's.'

'I know you think that.' Kevyn took a deep breath, hoping she was making the right decision to trust in his words. 'What are we supposed to do now?'

'Look, I can't ask you to forgive me, but maybe you and I…we could just get to know each other.'

Kevyn wiped the tears from her eyes with the back of her hand, and adjusted the main sail as she thought about what he'd said. There was no way to change the past. She couldn't forget it, true, but she had to deal with it. And she saw no other way to do that then open the door and get to know her father. She took a deep breath, 'Well, let's start… see where we go from there.'

Alex sank back into the cushions and heaved a sigh of relief. 'I'd like that.'

Leaning forward, she held out her hand. 'Hi. My name is Kevyn Morgan.'

*****

Chapter Sixteen

It was late afternoon when they approached Anegada, and Kevyn found herself amazed by how different it was from the other islands. Where Tortola and St. John had been full of hills and valleys jutting out of the sea, this island was completely flat. The white sand beaches were still highlighted, but this island offered no backdrop of green shooting into the sky.

'I suggest we head to the north side of the island to anchor.' Alex looked through a set of binoculars before handing them to Kevyn.

Sailboats lined the bay in front of them, like soldiers that swung in unison to face the wind. 'There are too many here,' he explained. 'I don't think you want an audience when Digger comes a callin'.'

'Is it safe on that side? I don't see an anchorage.' Sam smoothed a chart out on the bench between himself and Kevyn. A reef circled the island like an undone necklace; its chain ran the length of the area that Alex had proposed. 'We wouldn't want to be another shipwreck.'

'There's not a designated anchorage but I know that area well. I've spent the last year there looking for *La Victoria*.' Alex reached across the cockpit and pointed to a spot on the chart close to the reef. 'It'll be away from other boats, so Digger should feel confident about grabbing the stone.'

Kevyn bit her lip. 'I don't want to get in trouble. Are we *allowed* to anchor there?'

'Don't worry,' Alex replied. 'I'll deal with that. I just think it's better to be away from all eyes – prying, or otherwise.'

Both men turned to Kevyn. Her nerves fluttered. Alex seemed very comfortable playing loose and easy with the rules which made her think that running drugs might not be completely out of the question. He said he was innocent, but what proof did she have? What he did have, however, was a good point – dropping anchor away from the rest of the boats. She certainly didn't want to endanger other sailors when Digger came looking for his emerald.

'Okay, if you think it's safe,' she said hesitantly. 'But I better not wake up tomorrow to find the authorities have confiscated *my* boat for something *you* did.'

Alex looked sheepish but assured her that wouldn't happen.

Sam turned to Kevyn. 'I'd feel more comfortable if Alex took over piloting.' He held up the tiller. 'He knows the reef better than you and I.'

Both men looked to Kevyn again. No matter how much they'd been through, this was still her boat and her decision.

'I think that's a good idea.' Kevyn forced herself to smile. She had to start trusting her father at some point, didn't she? 'It's all yours.' Clearing her throat she added, 'For the time being.'

It was another two hours around the island to the spot Alex proposed. Alex took the tiller, allowing Kevyn and Sam to relax and watch the scenery. It was strange sailing with Alex. Kevyn and Sam had developed an easy routine that they'd grown used to, but now they were the passengers.

Alex worked the tiller and the sheets effortlessly. Kevyn watched him trim the sail until it fluttered only slightly. Sam nudged her in the ribs and thrust his chin in Alex's direction. *Look at him,* he seemed to say.

Kevyn gave a light nod and continued to study her father's movements. Alex watched the clouds above for signs of the wind's direction and adjusted the sails accordingly. He studied the ripples on the water and steered carefully using the varying shades of the water around them instead of the chart. Against her will, Kevyn felt that rush of pride. It was obvious Alex was born to be on the water. Snuggling closer, Kevyn rested in the curve of Sam's arm and smiled.

Once they reached the northern side of the island Alex lined *Wander* up to pass through a cut in the reef.

'Are you dropping sails?' Kevyn stood up to help him with the task. But Alex shook his head. 'I'll sail her in.'

Kevyn scanned the water ahead. It was lighter than the deep blue they'd been sailing through. The sandy bottom was visible and littered with submerged coral heads. This was the reef that'd claimed more than three hundred shipwrecks, including Alex's *La Victoria*.

'I hope you know what you're doing,' Kevyn muttered, as she scurried to the bow to act as lookout.

It was late in the day and the sinking sun made it hard to see the reef. On either side of the hull sharp, hard coral shimmered close to the surface, making navigation tough. The entrance was tight and Kevyn pointed to the nearest jagged edge she saw. 'Ten feet to port,' she shouted over the wind.

Alex ignored her and watched the water ahead. Waves broke on the reef all around them.

Kevyn swung to starboard and pointed again, calling over her shoulder, 'Twelve feet.'

Once again Alex seemed not to hear her. 'It's okay. I've done this a thousand times.'

The current pushed *Wander* closer to a large outcrop of coral. The distance between the hull and the reef decreased rapidly. 'Veer to port!'

Kevyn's stomach lurched. 'Eight feet!' She held her breath as they kept moving forward. 'Five feet!' The wake of the boat distorted her view and for a moment she couldn't see the coral head. *Was it under the hull?* Her heart thundered in her chest; it felt like it would explode with the pressure.

Her eyes darted everywhere. *Were they going to hit the reef?* Finally, she spotted the last of the coral clumps to the stern. They'd made it through the pass. The water that now surrounded *Wander* was turquoise blue, an indication of just how shallow the water was.

Alex stood at the tiller, beaming. 'Drop anchor.'

'*Here?*' Kevyn jumped down from the bow, her body still shaking as Sam scrambled forward to comply. 'Aren't we a little close to the reef?'

'If things go south with Digger, I want to be close to the cut in order to sail her out of here in a hurry.' Alex laid a hand on her shoulder. 'It'll be okay. I promise.'

Sam's stomach growled loudly.

Alex laughed. 'How about dinner at The Big Bamboo?'

Sam rolled up the chart. 'Sounds good to me. A cold beer after a day of sailing always gets my vote.'

What the hell? Kevyn thought. *Wander* used to be his boat once. He must know where it would be safe?

While Alex and Sam stowed the sails, Kevyn straightened up the cabin. She moved piles of personal things from one drawer to the next. She didn't like the idea of Digger returning.

'What about Athens?' She didn't feel right about leaving him alone.

'Let's go grab some dinner,' Sam said. 'I'll come back, stash the emerald, and pick up Athens once we're settled at Alex's.'

Kevyn reached down and picked up the notebook she'd been using to jot down all the information about the trip and Alex. She flipped the pages to the start and ran her fingers over the words, *Sam Strider, Deadman's Chest.* How long ago that seemed now. The rest of the pages were filled with directions to Trista's, notes on Henry Morgan, and a list of places they'd been. Kevyn opened her bag. It was empty save for a tube of lip balm, a couple of pennies, and the emerald. She put the notebook inside. It was a diary, after all, and she didn't want Digger going through it.

Bending down, she kissed Athens on the head. 'We won't be long.'

Sam pulled the tender in close, and Alex steadied the inflatable as they all climbed in. Kevyn sat on the side of the rubber tube cradling her purse with the emerald inside for comfort. She curled her spine around the bag and rested her head on its cool leather, turning back to stare at her beloved home as they motored away.

It wasn't far to the beach. In fact, *Wander* was much too close to the beach for Kevyn's liking. Looking back, it seemed like the boat was practically washed up on shore. Too close to the beach, too close to the reef. Anchored where it shouldn't be. Nothing about this felt right. The wind had picked up and *Wander* rocked back and forth. She looked so stoic and strong. Kevyn said a quick prayer, hoping they would find her in the same condition after Digger's visit.

The Big Bamboo was a beach bar like any other. A series of wooden shacks with concrete foundations sat in the same white, powdery sand Kevyn had seen on all the beaches that ringed the island. Sea grape trees lined the shore and a hammock was strung between two coconut palms, standing sentinel over the place. The patio and open walls looked out over the bay.

Kevyn had decided she needed to tell Alex about Kyle that evening. They had so much to talk about. She hadn't even begun to ask him all she wanted to know, or told him all he needed to hear. The discovery of the emerald had pushed a great deal to the back burner.

They walked up the green and blue concrete path from the beach and selected a plastic patio table set in the sand away from other ears. The bartender brought a round of Carib Lagers for Kevyn and Sam and a strong painkiller for Alex. They ordered lobster from the grill and a platter of conch fritters and sat quietly, listening to the collapse of the waves over the reef.

'Will you be staying on this island after all this is over, Alex?' Sam asked, making small talk until their food arrived.

He shrugged. 'I've rented the cottage for another six months. If I can't turn up anything on *La Victoria* by then, I'll have to consider my options.'

Kevyn downed a gulp of her beer. Picking at the label on the bottle with her fingernail, she tried to form the words she needed to say. 'Grandfather would like you to come home. He wants to see you.'

Alex nodded.

'We could all spend some time together.'

Again, Alex just nodded. He sat quiet, twirling the straw in his drink. The sound of ice swirling and bouncing off the sides of his glass filled the awkward silence. Finally, Alex asked, 'What about you? Where will you head after this? Lauderdale with Sam, or home to Savannah?'

Kevyn dipped a fritter into the creamy sauce and popped it in her mouth while she gathered her nerve.

'I thought maybe we all could head back to the Keys for a while.'

Alex's right eyebrow shot up. 'Well, you shouldn't be stuck here too long. I'm sure you want to start sailing for home soon.'

Kevyn's jaw clenched.

Alex winced, like he suddenly realized what he'd just said. But it was too late. The words were out there, hanging in the air like icicles in the warm Caribbean air.

Kevyn had said *we*; Alex had said *you*.

They ate the rest of their meal in silence. The lobster was tough and infused with the woodsy flavor of the barbecue. Red beans and rice and coleslaw dripping with dressing were served, but Kevyn didn't really taste the food. She wanted this adventure over. If her father didn't want her here, then she wanted to sail away and never think about him again, just like he had thirty years ago.

But she couldn't. There was the emerald to deal with before freedom was an option.

The mosquitoes began to bite. 'How about we head to my place?' Alex swatted at his ankles. 'It's just down the road three minutes, at the other end of the beach.'

Sam stood up. 'I'll get the check and meet you in the parking lot.'

Alex and Kevyn walked in silence through the sand. The parking lot was made of harder packed sand and held a few scraggly trees. Lit by a solitary bulb perched on the top of a pole by the dumpster, a rusted white Ford pick-up sat parked at the far end. *Captain Morgan's Treasure* logo was stenciled in powder blue on the door. 'Is that you?'

'The one and only.' Alex nodded. 'I'm just borrowing it from Denise, the cook who works here. She drives it mostly, but it makes the government think I'm stable.' He laughed. 'Being established on the island helps me hunt for *La Victoria* without anyone becoming suspicious.'

Kevyn remembered what Sam had said about treasure hunting being a game of secret locations. No salvager wanted to alert others to a possible site before they'd identified a wreck and claimed a lease on it. They often moved around a lot to throw others off the trail. Or in this case, she supposed, made it look like they were just living on the island and not searching its waters. It was yet another slightly shady thing her father did.

They stopped by the tailgate to wait for Sam.

Alex reached out and grabbed her elbow. 'Listen, Kevyn. Back there... I didn't mean...'

She pulled her arm away. 'It's okay. I didn't expect you...'

'It's just that this is all happening so fast,' he said quickly.

'For me, too.' Kevyn turned her head and stared into the back of his truck at a mess of dive tanks and gear. 'Maybe we should just...'

The sound of sand shifting under the weight of approaching feet stopped her train of though.

'I'll be taking my half of the treasure now, Alex.' Both Kevyn and Alex whipped their heads around at the sound of the voice. It was a voice she recognized, but not the one she'd been expecting to hear.

'Lemon! You scared me!' Kevyn put her hand over her heart. 'What are you doing here?'

Lemon emerged into the light from the shadows of the sea-grape tree, his eyes looking wilder than ever. In his hand he held a knife that resembled the one Sam strapped to his calf before each dive.

'I'll do more than just scare you.' Lemon raised the weapon. 'You ain't so hard to find, Alex. I listened to the girl and followed her down here. Now I *want* my treasure.'

'Lemon, I told you, there is no treasure. I haven't found it yet.' Alex stepped in front of Kevyn blocking her from Lemon and his knife.

'We had a deal. I want my half.'

'What treasure?' Kevyn looked from Lemon to Alex, unsure of what they were talking about.

'Your pops and I had us an agreement. He talked big and promised treasure. Said it was a sure thing.' Lemon turned the knife in his hands while he spoke; the blade gleamed in the moonlight. 'Said we'd be rich as millionaires.'

Alex held his hands up, his eyes never leaving the blade. 'Lemon, you know as well as I do that these things aren't as easy as all that.'

'You took my boat and my money and sailed off without ever comin' back.' Lemon's eyes narrowed. The bartender was right; he did look like a shark.

'Lemon, I've looked. I've been beyond that reef every day.' Alex gestured to the water, far beyond where *Wander* rocked in the wind. 'I found nothing so far.'

Lemon's eyes were on fire. 'You took my boat and my money!'

Kevyn's stomach churned. The pieces of the puzzle were sliding together. 'Lemon owned the *K Sea*?'

Alex nodded. 'Half.'

'We had a deal! You promised me treasure!' Lemon waved the knife, forcing both Alex and Kevyn to take a step back. Kevyn pressed her body against the truck's rear bumper.

'Yeah, we had a deal. But the ship's not there. I can't find it.'

Alex shook his head; his grey hair skimmed the top of his collar. 'There's no money. No treasure.'

'Alex, you ain't listenin' to me. I put everything I had into that boat and you sailed away with it. You took my money and my life, and I want it back. I don't care one bit if you found the treasure or not. I want my money. Now!'

Alex looked out over the water; the waves crashed loud and strong. He flinched before he spoke, 'It's gone, Lemon. It's all gone. I don't have anything left. The boat sank. I haven't found any treasure. All my money is gone, too.'

Lemon tightened his grip on the knife. His eyes were cold, dead steel. 'Wadda you take me for? You're living down here in paradise drinking fruity drinks with umbrellas in 'em, and I'm left holding the bag in a shitty one-bedroom old ladies' condo in Laudy with no treasure, no glory, and no family. I want my half.'

Remembering what Sam had said about Lemon's estranged daughter, she took a step forward. 'This won't bring Carly back. She doesn't care about the money. She cares about how the money changed you.'

Lemon's eyes shifted to her. 'What do you know about Carly?'

'I know what I would think if you were my father. I know that I wouldn't care about treasure or glory. I would care about having my father around. I would care about having him in my life, not drinking his sorrows away or chasing ghost ships.' Kevyn shot a glance at Alex, as she continued, 'You may not have been down here, Lemon, but I'm guessing you were just as obsessed with treasure as Alex. You started out as Carly's father, but just look at what all this obsession has turned you into.'

Lemon looked down at the knife in his hand. 'She doesn't want me around. He stole my money and did this to my family.' Lemon strengthened his stance and waved the knife in Alex's direction. 'He's the one who should pay.'

'I know how Carly feels, living without her father. I know she must wish things were different. That she could just know you and talk to you…talk to the man you used to be.' Kevyn moved closer to Lemon. Her voice fluttered with nerves. 'You have to fight for Carly. Nothing comes easy. You have to quit this life you're living and work hard to go back to the man you once were. If you want Carly back in your life you have to put in the time. Show her you can change. Show her you don't care about money, you only care about getting to know her. If you want her in your life, you have to make the effort.'

Kevyn could see Lemon struggling with her words. She softened her tone, 'You were Carly's father – her rock, her protector. You were a family. But look at what chasing treasure has done to that family.'

Lemon hung his head, kicking at the sand. 'She ain't talked to me for the last year.' He looked more beaten and worn than he had in Lauderdale, wrung out like the ratty old t-shirt he wore.

'Carly's just a little girl who needs her father. She's lost. She needs to know you're still there for her and care about her.' Kevyn moved even closer. She and Lemon were now face to face. 'No matter how hard it is, you're still her father.'

'I miss her. She's my little mermaid,' Lemon's voice quivered.

'Then tell her that.'

Lemon looked into Kevyn's eyes and lowered his knife slightly, relaxing his grip on the handle. He shook his head as if trying to clear away the scrambled thoughts. 'You think she'll talk to me?' His wide eyes pleaded for an answer. In that moment, he looked more like an innocent child than the knife-wielding, greasy threat he'd been just a moment ago.

'It's worth a shot. You have nothing to lose.' Kevyn laid a hand on Lemon's arm. 'Why don't we go find a phone and call her right now?'

Lemon hung his head like a scolded puppy. 'Yeah, that's a good idea.'

Kevyn turned Lemon towards the bar, putting an arm around his shoulder. She plucked the knife out of his hand like it was a soiled diaper and dropped it in the sand.

As they walked away, she turned her head to see if Alex was okay. He stood rooted to the same spot as tears rolled down his cheeks.

'I'll be right back...Dad,' she said.

Lemon suddenly stopped. The blood vessels in his neck pulsed and Kevyn felt the muscles in his forearm clench. 'Son of a bitch,' he said in a raspy voice.

Like a running back avoiding a tackle, Lemon pivoted around Kevyn and lunged toward Alex. He bent down and scooped up the discarded knife and plunged it deep into Alex's belly, just below the ribs.

'No!' Kevyn screamed.

'You bastard! You ain't got the right to have a family when mine's gone!' Lemon withdrew the knife as Alex fell to one knee. He held his hand over the wound. Bright red blood oozed between his fingers and ran down his hand. Alex stared at his stomach like he was unable to believe what had just happened. Looking up at Kevyn, his eyes were that of a scared little boy.

As the first drop of blood soaked into the sand, she ran to Alex, gathering him in her arms.

'I...ugh...' He tried to speak as he sunk onto her lap. His eyes fluttered closed.

Kevyn frantically searched the empty lot looking for help.

Lemon backed away. 'He ain't gettin' a family.'

'Help! Sam! Someone help!'

Sam bolted out of the bar, crossing the parking lot in four long strides. 'What the hell happened?' He dropped to his knees and felt Alex's neck for a pulse.

'Lemon,' was all Kevyn could say. 'It's okay, Dad. We'll get help.'

Alex gazed up at her. 'You called me Dad.' Closing his eyes, he passed out... his lips still set in a smile.

Sam ripped open Alex's shirt, popping the buttons as he did so.

'Shit.' He pulled his own t-shirt over his head, bunched it up to a ball, and pressed it to Alex's side. 'Hold this.'

'Is it bad?' Kevyn leaned over the man she barely knew and put pressure on the wound, praying he wouldn't bleed to death in her arms.

'It's not good. We've got to get him to a doctor.' Sam scanned the parking lot; his eyes focused on the truck with the *Captain Morgan* logo. 'Get his keys.'

Alex groaned while Kevyn kept one hand on the wound and stuck her other in his pocket and fished out a set of keys. She handed them to Sam. 'Down the road toward town...' Alex said before he passed out.

Kevyn slapped his face. 'Stay with me, Dad.'

His eyes fluttered but stayed closed.

'Help me get him in the back of the truck.' Sam swung Alex's arm over his shoulder.

From her crouched position, Kevyn tried to do the same.

The ride to the clinic was like a rollercoaster, reminding Kevyn of the one at Disney that thunders through a pitch black building so that no one sees what twists and turns lay ahead. Bumpy Caribbean roads at night are not the best way for a man with a slit in his stomach to lie still.

Sam wound his way through the unlit roads. One arm cradled the back of the seat, and he constantly pivoted his body from concentrating on the road ahead to checking on Kevyn and Alex in the bed of the truck behind him. The night was full of shadows; the crescent moon barely shone through the blanket of clouds that covered it.

Alex lay on his back drifting in and out of consciousness.

Kevyn cradled his head in her lap, trying to soften the jarring of the truck when it made contact with yet another pothole. Empty air tanks rolled back and forth in the grooves of the truck bed clanging together with every sudden corner. She pounded on the window. 'Hurry!'

Sam picked up speed and Kevyn felt the tires lose their traction in the fine sand. The back end of the truck fishtailed, and she was thrown from one side of the truck bed to the other.

Alex groaned and pulled his knees up to a fetal position causing the wound to seep more blood.

'Hold on, Dad. We're almost there.' The wind felt cold on Kevyn's skin as it whipped over her body. Strands of her hair flew from her ponytail and slapped her across the face and neck.

The tiny island clinic didn't resemble any hospital Kevyn had ever been in. Anegada had a population of two hundred and fifty people year round, so they hardly needed a full-blown hospital. This building looked like a simple cottage – someone's home.

They pulled up to the dark building and Sam jumped out and banged on the door three or four times before a light finally clicked on inside. An island woman in a royal purple nurse's uniform decorated with penguins answered. She looked like she was wearing her pajamas.

'Sweet Jesus. What's going on out here?' She stood blocking the door, her thick pudgy arms crossed over her ample bosom.

'I've got a man with a knife wound.' Sam gestured to the truck where Alex struggled to sit up. Kevyn knelt behind him, supporting his back as he swung his legs over the bed.

'Bring him in.' The woman turned from the door letting it swing shut behind her, not offering any assistance at all.

With Kevyn on one side and Sam on the other, they carried Alex from the truck; he let out a groan of pain as they pivoted in order to fit through the small door.

Not only were there no ambulances or waiting rooms, but there also was no clinical smell of ammonia that met their senses. Posters warning of sunstroke hung on one wall and an ad to prevent AIDS from spreading decorated the other. There were six plastic chairs, like the ones used in grade schools, lined up along the far wall. Other than that, the space looked like someone's living room.

The nurse moved behind a large wooden desk in the corner. 'How you doin', Alex?' She barely looked up as she pulled a file from one of the four cabinets behind the desk.

'Been better, Marilyn.'

Kevyn looked from one to the other with wide eyes. 'You know each other?'

Her loud laugh echoed through the quiet room. 'Shoot, yeah we do, girl! Alex here is always comin' by with a broken bone or dizziness from too much divin' in the hot sun.' She smiled at him, revealing two gold-rimmed front teeth. 'He's one of our regulars.' Her laughter filled the room. I ain't seen him with a knife in his belly before, though.' Marilyn came around from the desk and pulled Alex's Hawaiian shirt open. She removed the t-shirt Kevyn had been using to stop the bleeding and replaced it with a clean bandage. 'I'll have to call the doctor for this one.' She sighed and shook her head. 'He's gonna have to get out of bed.'

Sam helped Alex to a chair after he refused to lay on the gurney Marilyn had begrudgingly wheeled over to them.

'Lay down.' Her dark face showed that there was no room for negotiation.

'No, I'm fine.' Alex tried to sit straighter. He drew a lungful of air through his teeth, wincing with the effort.

'Suit yourself.' She shrugged. 'You're the one bleeding.' Shuffling back to her desk, Marilyn picked up a tattered copy of *Ebony* magazine and proceeded to ignore them.

Kevyn gnawed on her lower lip. 'Why did Lemon come after you like that?'

Alex winced when he spoke, 'Lemon's got a right to be mad.'

Kevyn sucked in a deep breath, bracing herself for another tale of the nefarious deeds he'd been up to. 'What'd you do to make him mad enough to try and kill you?'

'I told you, the *K Sea* was half his boat.' Alex held the bandage tight to his side. 'We were partners...until I sunk it.'

'So he loses everything and thinks you're down here in paradise diving the reefs?'

'Something like that.'

'And all those reefs are what sank *La Victoria*?' Kevyn tried to keep his mind off the pain by distracting him with conversation.

Alex nodded. 'You saw. The reef is long and sits just under the surface. Even in good conditions it's hard to see until a ship is practically on top of it. During hurricanes or runnin' from pirates,' he grimaced with pain, 'ships had no chance.'

'And you think *La Victoria* is one of those boats out there?'

'That's the beauty of it. All those wrecks down there are different. Some are new and intact, others are ancient and scattered. You may find a few pieces here when the bulk of the ship is way over there.' Alex pointed to the corner of the room. 'You just keep diving and researching and eventually you hope to put all the pieces together. It's like building a jigsaw puzzle.'

'And that's what you want? To stay down here and find out what happened to that ship?' A clearer picture of her father was forming in Kevyn's mind. 'Sounds like you could use some help.'

'I sure could. Especially now.'

He pointed to the bloody bandage. 'I'll need help diving and cataloging all the information to launch a proper search.'

Kevyn thought about the best way to phrase her sentences. She didn't want to scare Alex away again. 'Trista would be perfect for the job of cataloguing.' Kevyn watched Alex's face to gauge his response.

The right side of his mouth turned up in a slight smile. It was hard to tell if he was interested, or if it was another wave of pain.

Kevyn took a deep breath. 'She could come down with her son, Kyle, and spend some time with you.'

'She already has a life. Why would she want to come down here?'

Was he really that oblivious? Had he never questioned the timing of Kyle's birth? 'I bet if you asked, she would come.'

Sam had discretely walked to the other side of the room, feigning interest in a medical journal sitting on a table along the far wall.

'Kyle is quite taken with the whole idea of ships and sailing.'

'He's a great kid.' Alex smiled broader now, settling into the conversation.

'Have you spent much time with him?' Kevyn skirted a direct statement about parentage.

'Not much.' Alex stared at his knees. 'The few times I've met the little guy, I always wondered if that was what you were like at his age.' His voice dropped. 'I've missed a lot.'

The irony of the statement was not lost on Kevyn. 'Maybe you should ask them to join you.'

'Here…with me?' Alex seemingly mulling her idea over. He shook his head. 'She doesn't need to be chasing me around.'

'Maybe she'd like to.' Kevyn let the statement dangle in the air. 'Maybe you should stop deciding what's best for other people, and what they can handle, and let them decide what's best for them.'

He ran his hand through his hair to pull it off his face. He looked calmer than when she first saw him in St. John's. His features seemed softer in the dim light, not as rugged and worn by the elements.

Alex rubbed the day's growth on his cheek and pulled his hand through his goatee. 'Do you think she'd come?'

'Only one way to find out.' Kevyn pulled out her cell phone and handed it to him. He took it from her and was about to dial when the doors of the clinic flew open.

The doctor had arrived.

*****

Chapter Seventeen

It took the doctor an hour and a half to stitch Alex up. He'd bled a lot, but the knife had missed all his major organs and arteries. He was lucky, the doctor said. What could have been a bloody end was declared an unfortunate flesh wound that would need to be cleaned and dressed daily until it healed. He was given a tetanus shot and some painkillers and told to return in a week to have the stitches removed.

It was late by the time they got to Alex's cottage and the weather had deteriorated. They helped him up the dirt path. Sam searched Alex's pockets for the key, seeing as that the drugs they'd given him were taking effect. Sam struggled to get the key in the lock while still holding Alex up; the lone bulb on the porch covered in flying insects blocked any helpful light.

Inside, the cabin was quiet. A small kitchen was decorated with a rickety aluminum and Formica table circa 1970. A weathered couch sat in the open living area and the opposite corner held a tiny bathroom with a toilet and pedestal sink.

'Welcome to paradise,' Alex slurred.

Sam and Kevyn exchanged an amused look. The painkillers were seriously strong.

Alex's head dipped low. But just when Kevyn thought he would pitch forward, his neck snapped back. 'You stay here,' he spit the words out before his jaw went slack again.

'Thanks, Alex.' Sam placed the keys to the truck on the lone table on top of a pile of charts.

'It ain't much, but it's all I got.' Alex stumbled two steps forward and three back across the wooden floor as Sam and Kevyn helped him to the couch.

'It's still more room than *Wander*.' Kevyn pulled a blanket off the back of the couch and wrapped it around her father's body.

'I once had a boat called *Wander*.' Alex closed his eyes and his face broke into a smile; it was the same smile Kevyn had seen on Kyle's face when she gave him the fire truck. 'My daughter sails her now.'

Kevyn and Sam exchanged looks, and he smiled down at her. She didn't know if she wanted to smile back...or burst into tears.

The wind blew hard and rain began to fall. The weather came in bands, raining hard for twenty minutes before subsiding for half an hour just to come again. The noise echoed through the cottage like the sound of thundering drums.

'Why don't you wait here with Alex while I go plant the emerald?' Sam stood up, grabbed his rain jacket and reached for the bag with the emerald. 'It's getting rough out there.'

Kevyn's body went rigid. Her mind raced with warning bells. With all the excitement of finding Alex she'd pushed aside her questions of Sam and why he was here. Was Sam's shop in real trouble? Was he here to collect money owed from Alex just like Lemon? Was he going to take the emerald and flee while she stayed behind nursing Alex? She was tired and overwhelmed and didn't know who to trust anymore.

Glancing over at her father, she mulled the questions over in her head. Nothing Sam had done so far had been overtly suspicious, but she didn't want to be played for a fool.

Alex dozed on the couch, completely out of it. It had been a long night for all of them, but the effects of his painkillers had put him into a deep sleep.

'No,' she decided. 'I'll go, too. I want to check on *Wander* and get Athens.' She put on her own foul-weather jacket and grabbed the bag from Sam. 'Then we'll all stay here until the storm passes.' She slung the bag over her shoulder. 'Together.'

She bent over Alex to check that he wasn't bleeding through the bandage. Her St. Christopher pinned to the collar of the jacket jingled as it slid on the hook.

Alex's eyes fluttered open for a brief moment and focused on the medallion. He reached out to it. 'My pendant.'

Kevyn was only confused for a moment. Of course it was his. She'd found the medal in Alex's old treasure workshop.

Reaching up, she fingered the metal, her hand grazing her fathers. All these years and she *had* carried a piece of her father without ever knowing it.

Smiling, she kissed him on the cheek. 'We'll be back soon.'

They waited for a break in the rain.

The cottage sat facing the Loblolly Bay where *Wander* was anchored. Conch shells lined the narrow path leading from Alex's back door to the beach, and their dingy lay on the sand where they'd left it. The wind whipped through the sea-grape leaves hanging over the water. The surf crashed on the sand, flooding the beach area where the dingy sat before rushing back out and leaving a line of seaweed and grass to mark where it had been.

It was a short ride from the beach to the anchorage, but the rough water slowed their progress. It may have stopped raining for the time being, but the seas were tumultuous. The dingy crept toward the sailboat as it rode up and slammed straight down off the white-capped waves. Both Kevyn and Sam were thoroughly drenched within minutes.

Neither said much during the ride, both exhausted by the night's events. The waxing crescent of the moon shifted in and out from behind the clouds giving just enough light to direct them.

Wander rode the waves of the storm, bobbing up and down with each roll of water. Her anchor light flashed in and out as the dingy dropped in the waves. Kevyn hoped her home was okay so close to the reef and to the shore. Dragging anchor with the wind would be disastrous.

Sam lassoed the bowline to the stern of the boat in an attempt to hold the inflatable steady. Even with his strength, the boat rode up and pulled away from *Wander* as the swells hit the side of the hull.

Kevyn held on tight as she slid onto the wet deck. She lay on her stomach and held the dinghy's line, her hands wet and slippery with the spray.

Sam scrambled aboard then turned his back to tie another line to secure the dingy.

Kevyn looked around her boat. This was the first time in her life she felt awkward stepping onto *Wander*. Not only was it rough from the weather, but she also now knew it had transported an illegal item. It no longer felt like her safe haven; it felt tainted…violated. Digger had soiled the boat in her mind and she felt uncomfortable.

Looking around the deck, she couldn't quite put her finger on what had changed. The cushions were the same; the teak deck still creaked when she shifted her weight; the lines clanged loudly against the mast with the wind.

'Where's Athens?' she asked Sam, looking around. 'He didn't come out to greet us.' Even in bad weather, Athens would always stick his head out. The hatch was shut like they'd left it, but Athens hadn't come out the cat door.

She reached to unlock the hatch but the lock was broken, dangling from one side of the hinge. Her breath caught in her throat as her heart raced faster and louder, ringing in her ears.

'Sam.' She had trouble making her voice work. Her throat constricted as she called in a voice that was barely a whisper. The sound was lost in the howling winds. She couldn't take her eyes from the latch; her hand froze in mid-air.

Sam was still securing the dingy, when suddenly the hatch door flew open and Digger lurched forward. He held a gun in his right hand as he stepped out onto the small, now crowded, deck.

'Hello, darling.' He waved the gun in her direction. 'How convenient to find you here.' Digger was dressed like the night: black boots, black cargo pants, black t-shirt. If Kevyn didn't know any better she would've thought he was part of a SWAT team.

'I think you have something to give me, Kevyn Morgan.' He flashed a sickly sweet smile.

The Caribbean Sea slammed into the reef only a few feet away, forcing them to shout above the noise.

'Christ, Digger, put that thing away.' Sam jumped up, holding onto the boom for support. 'We've got your emerald. Nice of you to have us transport it.' He stepped off the side of *Wander* and onto the cushions. There wasn't much room on the floor, so he towered over Digger and Kevyn standing on the port bench.

'Not so fast, cowboy.' Digger swung the gun toward Sam, directing him to step down onto the deck with Kevyn as he climbed on the starboard benches to gain the upper hand. The cushion was wet from the rain and the black boots Digger wore slipped out from under him. His body jerked as he stumbled forward.

Clenching the revolver tightly, his thick finger squeezed the trigger.

A hollow *bang,* followed closely by a metal *clang,* split the noise of the storm. 'No!' Sam screamed. In a lightning fast move, he threw his arms around Kevyn and pushed her to the bench, smashing both of them into the cabin bulkhead as she buried her head in his chest.

Kevyn didn't feel any searing pain but Sam's body on top of her crushed her and her shoulder throbbed where she hit the boat. She could feel her fast beating heart drum against his chest. He wrapped around her so tight she couldn't see his face.

She placed her hands on his chest and pushed him off and to the side. He rolled to the cushion they had fallen on, his eyes closed, his body dead weight.

Kevyn's hands flew over his chest searching for an entry hole. 'What did you do?'

Sam's eyes fluttered opened and he shook his head, clearing the momentary daze. He pointed to a place above Kevyn's head.

She craned her neck and squinted to see through the rain. The bullet had lodged itself in the boom.

Digger laughed. 'Oops.' He reached out to steady himself by grabbing the metal stays running from the mast to the aft of the boat.

'You bastard!' Sam lurched up and lunged at Digger. 'Get off this boat!'

'Or what Sam? You'll kill me?'

Digger brandished Sam away with the gun. 'You and I both know that you don't have the guts. Besides you couldn't save Beth, remember? What makes you think you can save Miss Kevyn Morgan?'

Digger pointed the gun at Kevyn, his index finger back on the trigger. 'Now, about that emerald.'

Sam pulled Kevyn back and stepped in front of her. 'This doesn't concern her, Digger. Let her go.'

Digger straightened his arm and gripped the gun tighter. 'Oh, she's not going anywhere.'

'I won't let this happen again,' Sam seethed through clenched teeth. A vein in his neck stood out, pounding as if his whole body was ready to fight.

Digger rolled his eyes. 'Relax, Sam. We're all friends here.' He reached down and grabbed a roll of duct tape. 'Just not friends who trust each other.' He tossed the roll to Sam. 'Will you do the honors?'

Sam stared at the tape in his hands.

Digger waved the gun. 'Come on, Sam. Don't go getting all sentimental on me. Just tie the lady up.'

Sam's eyes turned to steel.

Digger tapped the boom with the barrel of his gun. 'Hands above the head. Right here will do nicely.'

Sam looked Kevyn in the eye. She couldn't read his thoughts but could see the torture in his eyes.

Wind ripped past her as she raised her arms, extending her wrists to Sam. She wanted to reassure him that this was different than Beth, that they had no choice and this wasn't his fault. No longer worried about Digger, all she could think about was what Sam must being going through. She could see it all over his face. He was reliving a nightmare that he could not shake.

Kevyn held his look and tried to communicate everything with her eyes. It was okay. She understood.

Digger nodded. 'Nice and tight, cowboy.'

Sam's eyes never left Kevyn's. He clenched the roll of tape tight in his hand and took a deep breath.

Digger tapped the boom with the gun again. 'Anytime, Sam. I don't want to be here all night.'

Sam broke his gaze with Kevyn and turned to Digger. His eyes turned from blue to steel. 'I don't think I want to do that.' He tossed the duct tape overboard, and it fell into the rough water below.

Digger held the gun up straighter. 'Now, why did you go and do something foolish like that?'

Reaching up, he grabbed Kevyn by the arm and pulled her to him.

The cold nose of the gun pushed against her throat and Digger's forearm mashed her breast. She kept her hands up high and tried to control her body from shaking, not from the cold driving rain but from fear.

'You can have the emerald, Digger. We don't want anything to do with it.' She shouted the best she could with a gun shoved under her chin as *Wander* rocked back and forth like a pendulum.

'Oh yeah, is that why it's no longer where I left it?' He waved the gun toward the bow with one hand and held onto the lifelines with the other.

Kevyn's eyes darted to the hatch that was open. She hadn't seen it when they approached. Lines and bottles of cleaning products were strung across the deck.

'You already took it ashore to pawn?' Digger asked. 'Maybe you gave it to Pops to sell? Where *is* Alex anyway?'

'He doesn't have it.' Kevyn shouted to be heard over the rain that pounded the cabin top. 'He doesn't even know about it.' She thought quickly. 'We have it here. It's in my bag.' She held up the black messenger bag that was slung across her chest. The movement pushed Digger's gun closer to her chin. She slipped the strap over her head and held it up. 'You can have it back. Just leave my boat.'

'Leave?' He loosened his grip on her so he could grab the bag allowing her to inch as far away as she could into the small space. 'Aw, darling. That's no way to greet an old friend of Sam's.' He held the bag in his left hand, no longer able to hold on to the gun, Kevyn, and the lifeline all at the same time. He chose the gun and emerald and bent his knees to balance on the cushions while he dropped his hand from the stays.

'We were never friends, Digger.' Sam's seething tone hung in the air. Rain lashed down around them; large fat drops hit the deck and stung Kevyn's face.

'See? That's the problem, Sam. You always thought you were better than me. Smarter in school. Higher values. But look who's holding the money.' He thrust the bag into the air. The movement set his balance off and he had to grab for the lifelines with his left hand to steady himself. The boat rode up and slammed down with a vengeance.

'You're right, Digger,' Sam's tone was now resigned. 'You win. Just get out of here.' He slipped an arm around Kevyn, sheltering her from the storm and Digger. He dug his knees into the seat to support both of them as they braced against each other with the rocking of the boat.

'Just waiting for my ride.' Digger switched the bag from his left hand to his right, trying to balance the gun and the strap. He dug into his tight black jeans and pulled out a flashlight. He flicked it on once and then straight off again. The light beamed into the darkness and then vanished. He hit the button again.

Athens sprang from the cabin and bounded up the stairs to where Kevyn stood. He arched his back and curled his lips, hissing as he bared his sharp teeth. Digger laughed and pointed the gun at the cat.

'No!' Kevyn screamed and jumped out to grab Athens. She curled him close to her chest to protect him. He was wet and shaking. ...Or maybe that was her?

'Bang,' Digger said and brought the barrel up to his face. He pursed his lips and blew like he was a television character. His eyes never left Kevyn's and she shuddered as he laughed maniacally.

He lowered the gun and aimed it at Kevyn.

'No!' Sam yanked Kevyn away and blocked her body from Digger.

'Aw, ain't you the gentleman?' Digger said. 'Protect the girlfriend... even though you couldn't protect the wife.'

'Get off this boat!' Sam shouted. 'I will not tell you again.'

Athens leaped from Kevyn's arms and bolted back downstairs.

In the distance, Kevyn heard the whine of a boat motor over the sound of the pounding rain. All three of them turned in the direction of the noise. In the sliver of moonlight, Kevyn could see the shape of a boat bouncing over the waves. There was a lone driver, but through the rain she didn't recognize whether it was one of the goons she'd met in the Turks or not.

Digger turned back to face Sam and Kevyn. He reached down and grabbed the bag. Again he struggled to hold the gun, the bag, and the lifeline. He reached inside and pulled out the emerald with his right hand. The big, heavy gem had smooth edges that made it hard to hold along with everything else. Digger held it up, balancing it in the palm of his hand. 'Too bad you didn't claim this, Sam. Would have put that store of yours on the map.' He pulled his arm across his face to whisk away some of the rain. 'Would get you outta that money trouble I heard you were in.'

'I don't want anything to do with that thing,' Sam seethed through gritted teeth.

The boat pulled up behind Digger. Sam's broad shoulders blocked most of Kevyn's view. All she saw was the white fiberglass bow approaching in the darkness. Coiled at the front was a rusted metal anchor. 'Thanks for the shipping.' Digger let go of the lifeline and turned around just as the man in the boat leapt onto *Wander*.

The man from the Whaler knocked Digger off balance, and he swayed before crashing forward. Sam pushed Kevyn back. She lost her balance as her knees buckled against the port seating. Her hair fell in her eyes, blocking her view of the newest man to join the party.

Digger's hands shot out and he fell into *Wander*'s cockpit. The gun flew from his hands and slid across the wet deck into the corner below where Kevyn knelt.

Kevyn brushed the hair out of her eyes in time to see the man from the boat hold up the emerald. It had stopped raining and the moon had crept out from behind a cloud. The gem shone in the moonlight, and the man looked deep into it like it was a crystal ball holding all the answers.

'Lemon?' she said in surprise. 'What are you doing here?'

'I came to apologize.' He didn't take his eyes off the prize. 'But I see I don't have to. Alex lied to me. He did find treasure.' Lemon's ragged hair flapped in the wind. Strands pulled free of his ponytail and whipped in the wind. He stood on the starboard seating where Digger had been, his boat tied close alongside.

Lemon's eyes darted wildly about the now overcrowded deck. Digger lay in a heap in the cockpit, dazed from his fall but coming around. Sam stood aft by the tiller holding the boom for support. Kevyn crouched on her knees on the starboard bench.

'Where is he? Where's Alex?' Lemon screamed.

'He's still in the hospital where you put him,' Kevyn lied, not wanting to reveal her father's whereabouts to either of the men. The gun was out of Digger's hands and lay in the corner, but they were hardly out of danger.

'Hospital? I didn't mean to hurt him.' Lemon broke his stare at the gem and looked at Kevyn. He once again looked like a hound dog; bags of skin pooled under his eyes. His long straggly hair had fallen from its ponytail and now lay in wet ringlets plastered to the side of his face. He lowered his arm, bringing the emerald back down by his side. 'That's why I came back...to see if he was okay.'

The two boats clashed together in the swell. The crunching sound of both hulls colliding filled the air. Lemon hadn't taken the time to secure the Whaler tightly. A constant *thump, thump, thump* sounded over the wind as Lemon's boat banged into *Wander*.

The roar of another boat motor alerted everyone to Digger's real ride approaching. Kevyn scanned the water but saw nothing; they were running without lights again.

'Well, all this reminiscing sure has been nice.'

Digger's eyes flared demonically at the emerald in Lemon's hand. He bolted straight up from where he'd fallen and lunged at Lemon, making a grab for the emerald.

Lemon jumped back. The emerald slipped from his hand as he held onto *Wander*, clinging to the lifeline. Seeing the emerald fall to the cockpit, Digger contorted his body to catch the jewel…but it was too late. The momentum of his lunge hurled him over the side of the sailboat toward the Whaler. A loud *thunk* filled the night air as Digger fell, hitting his head on the anchor of Lemon's boat. It was a hollow splitting sound like that of a melon smashing on the floor. He ricocheted off the bow and plunged into the water with a splash.

Kevyn watched in horror as the approaching boat roared right over the splash Digger's body had made. Her hands flew to her mouth, and she screamed. The driver must've seen what happened because he swung his head around, frantically looking for Digger.

Sam jumped for the gun that lay by his feet. He came up, pointing it at the driver of Digger's boat. With just the light from the mast, the man's face registered the danger and he swung the boat back out to sea and fled.

Sam dropped the gun to the cushion, bent under the boom, and scrambled out between the rail and the stays to grab Digger. He was too late, though. There was no body in sight. Sam untangled himself from the rigging and stripped off his shirt. Kevyn climbed on the starboard seating to lend a hand.

Sam dove into the water and disappeared from sight into the blackness.

Waves slapped *Wander's* hull and splashed up at Kevyn, drenching her further. She hung over the side trying to gauge where Sam was just as another wave soaked her and sent her scurrying back to the relative shelter of the cockpit. *Wander* rocked back and forth.

'What's happening?' Lemon asked.

Kevyn ignored him. Thirty seconds passed. She peered nervously at the point where Sam entered the water. Forty-five seconds…

Lemon asked again, 'Where is he?'

Finally, Sam's head broke the surface of the water. He let out the breath he'd been holding and gasped for air. Flinging his head back, he sprayed water at the side of *Wander* and simultaneously removed the hair from his face. A wave crashed over his head, and he had to repeat the process.

'Did he surface?' he shouted, looking wildly around.

'No.' Kevyn scrambled back to the railing to help him aboard. 'I can't see anything.' The night was still dark, another hour until sunrise.

Sam ignored her outstretched hand, took two quick breaths and one deep one before ducking under the choppy waves.

Kevyn held her breath as he disappeared from sight.

'Who was that guy who fell overboard?' Lemon asked.

Kevyn ignored Lemon for a third time.

It seemed like an hour passed. Kevyn tried holding her breath as long as Sam was under but had to gasp for air. Sam had not yet surfaced. Kevyn stood up and climbed out on to Lemon's boat to get closer. The smaller boat rose up and down in the chop and she scurried like a frightened crab across its bow to peer over the side into the dark water. She rolled on her belly to lean over and her hand touched something sticky along the rim of the bow. Everywhere was wet, but this was thicker than water. She brought her hand closer to see what it was and dark, tacky blood met her gaze.

Sam surfaced again, empty-handed. 'I can't see anything in the dark.' He grabbed the side of Lemon's boat and pulled himself up and in. 'It's too rough to look for him. We'll have to wait for morning's light.'

'He's bleeding.' Kevyn held her hand out to Sam to show him the evidence.

He gave her fingers a squeeze. 'Let's hope we find him before the sharks do.'

They climbed back on *Wander*. Kevyn grabbed a towel for Sam and he began drying off. The wind had settled and the water seemed to calm all around them.

'What about that?' Lemon pointed to where the emerald lay in the corner of the boat, discarded like garbage.

'That thing is more trouble than it's worth.' Sam completely ignored it. Kevyn's heart leapt. He *wasn't* just chasing fortune.

'I'll go radio this in. There will have to be police involved.' He looked at Kevyn. 'I'll let Alex know what happened.' He stepped into the cabin to use the radio.

Kevyn watched Lemon, and thought for a moment. There was no way she wanted the police to think the emerald was hers, and there were too many questionable things in Alex's past to convince the police he was innocent in all this. She didn't want him to go to jail. If he got into trouble for this, it would be because of her. She had brought the emerald into their lives. She gnawed on her bottom lip while she weighed her options. 'It's yours.'

'*What?*' Lemon sounded like he hadn't understood her words.

'The emerald. It's yours.'

'What about Alex?' Lemon looked leery of the offer.

'I think he likes the diving far more than the actual treasure.' Kevyn thought about all that'd happened in the few short days since she'd found her father. 'Besides, it isn't from his site anyway. He won't want it.'

'You sure?' Lemon raised an eyebrow, still suspicious.

'I don't know him that well yet, but I think he would want you to have it. Payment for your boat and all. Maybe you can share it with Carly?'

'I'd like that.' Lemon's predatory smile scared Kevyn less than it had month ago. He looked a little more hopeful in the morning light than the sharks he was named after. 'I sure am sorry about all this.'

'That's alright, Lemon. I think you just saved us from that man. Let's say we call it even? It's time we all had a fresh start.'

Sam returned from down below. 'Authorities will be here within the hour. They're sending divers from Tortola, and Alex is on his way.'

'It will be awful crowded on this boat,' Kevyn said. 'And they'll confiscate the emerald as evidence.' Kevyn looked out over the water hoping she was making the right decision. 'You better take it and go now,' she said to Lemon, 'It's easier to say it fell overboard.'

Lemon looked at Kevyn and then at Sam. He hesitated.

'You heard the woman, Lemon. This is your treasure.' Sam reached down to untie Lemon's boat. He held the line in one hand and gestured with his other. 'It's now or never, man. You don't want them finding you fleeing an accident with blood all over your boat and a million dollar emerald in your possession.'

Lemon snapped out of his daze. He leaned over and kissed Kevyn on the cheek. 'Thank you.' He breathed deeply and spoke into her hair. It was the first time he touched her without sending her recoiling in disgust.

'You're welcome.' She hugged him back. 'Good luck…to you and Carly.'

He shook Sam's free hand as he stepped past him. In the cockpit of his boat, Lemon looked once again at the emerald before placing it on the seat beside him and starting the engines. He half saluted as he twirled the steering wheel in his hand and pulled away from *Wander*. The only sound in the air was that of his engine as he roared off into the night.

The storm was over.

*****

Chapter Eighteen

The sun lit the sky in the east as it climbed above the horizon. Pastel pinks and blues weaved in and out in a dramatic display. The storm from the night before had settled, and the water was now calm and clear.

Kevyn leaned over the side of the boat as Alex pulled his skiff alongside where Lemon's Whaler had been. She wasn't sure if she hoped to see Digger's body or not, but there was nothing but blue.

'What happened?' Alex held the bowline out to Kevyn. He looked better in the morning light than he had the night before. 'Are you alright?'

'I'm fine.' She tied off the bow and reached out to help Alex on board. He held his side with his right hand as he stepped gingerly over the railing and into the cockpit. He hugged Kevyn tight.

'Digger's dead,' Kevyn whispered, hugging him back.

'No loss there.' He held her out at arm's length, looking her up and down. 'Are you sure you're alright?'

'I'm fine, Dad.' Kevyn took a big breath and swallowed. 'But the emerald's gone.'

Alex paused and looked around the cabin. 'Good riddance.' He kept his hand on Kevyn's shoulder and squeezed. 'I'm just glad you're okay.'

A smile spread slowly across Kevyn's face. *Those* were the words she wanted to hear.

'It's lighter now. I'll go get Digger.' Sam grabbed his BC from the hatch. For the second time that morning, he pulled his shirt over his head to enter the water.

'Shouldn't you wait for the police?' Kevyn held the discarded shirt to her chest. Sam's coconut scent wafted up at her.

'It's a long way from Tortola for them to get here.' He slipped his mask over his head. 'There won't be anything left of him if we leave him down there for too long.'

'You'll need a dive buddy.' Alex handed him his fins. 'Why don't you go with him, Kevyn?'

'Are you sure? How's your side?'

'I'm fine. You guys go. I'll stay and watch *Wander.*'

'I can always use a dive buddy.' Sam reached back into the hatch and pulled out the gear Pete had given Kevyn in Lauderdale.

Pushing her hair off her face, Kevyn lowered the mask over her eyes. With the all-clear signal, she leaned over the boat and splashed into the water. It took no more than five seconds for Sam to find Kevyn in the sea, and he immediately reached out to hold her hand as they descended into the depths. The water was warm and visibility was poor; she could only see a few feet in front of her. The storm had stirred up all the sand on the bottom.

Kevyn held her nose to clear her ears and blew against the pressure. She looked at her gauge – they were fifteen feet below the surface. They dropped slowly and within thirty seconds she could see the bottom. It was a truly eerie feeling, waiting to see a dead man. Kevyn shuddered despite the warmth of the water.

Sam pointed north, and they began to swim.

Horseshoe Reef, the cause of all the shipwrecks, lay another thirty feet in front of them. Clumps of Elkhorn coral signaled its beginning, and it rose from the sand like a wall blocking their way. Two eagle rays soared overhead between them and the shafts of sunlight above. Down here, it was as if the drama from above had never occurred.

Kevyn floated for a moment, staring at the reef in wonderment. How could something so beautiful be the cause of such sorrow for so many people? This reef had claimed over three hundred ships and countless lives. How many other children grew up without fathers on account of this one force of Mother Nature?

It was hard to imagine terror and destruction being part of this scene. Right now all was peaceful and tranquil, but four hundred years ago this had been a place of agony and death. The sailors on board the ships that sank would've panicked, the decks would've been a place of mayhem. Some most likely knew they would die here, in this very spot, as the ship hit the reef and the loud smashing of the wooden hull sounded over the crashing waves and thunderous rains. Others would have thrashed about and tried to swim for shore when they hit the water, leaving still others trapped inside whose fate was to go down with the ship trapped inside. This reef offered nothing more than a chaotic and terrifying death.

But not this morning. This morning the scene surrounding Kevyn was beautiful and calming. A school of sergeant majors darted around the reef and waves of their yellow and grey stripes swarmed past. A larger black angelfish floated ahead as if guarding the entrance of the reef.

On the far side, a bull shark cruised past – the grey muscular body propelled by the swaying of its powerful tail. Kevyn pointed to it and squeezed Sam's hand tighter. It was a good distance away and totally oblivious to their presence, but still her heart beat faster.

Kevyn searched the reef. Digger's body wasn't there. Maybe he'd drifted farther away with the tide, or maybe the shark had smelled the blood and had already dined. Kevyn had read they didn't usually attack people, but if that person was already dead and covered in blood, then she assumed he'd be fair game.

Sam swam ahead, up and over a strand of purple fan corals that swayed with his motion.

Kevyn lingered behind, not wanting to get close to where she last saw the shark. She swam twenty feet down the face of the reef, watching the small tropical fish dart in and out of the protection of the coral. Maybe Digger's body had already washed out to sea. She left the protection of the reef and swam over the sandy bottom away from the island. She turned to make sure Sam was following and kept her eyes alert for both hungry sharks and bodies being buried in their ocean graves.

Ahead, to the right, something caught her eye. A clump of coral sat by itself in a stretch of white sand. She looked back to signal Sam, but he faced the other way investigating under a lone rock. She swam over to the coral to see what it was attached to. It looked so out of place sitting in a wide expanse of ocean floor with nothing around it.

Kevyn fanned the sand with her gloved hand. The movement revealed an orange-hued object encrusted in the rock and coral. Bands of rusted metal reinforced what looked like a corner of a box. Purple and yellow coral spread over most of the exposed side like moss on a rock.

Scooping more sand away, Kevyn found that it was indeed a corner of something large. Gently, she pushed the sand and tried to get a grip on the object to wiggle it out. It was buried deep, and she could not budge it from this angle. She looked up. This time Sam was looking at her, and she waved him over.

As he swam up she pointed to the object. She watched as his eyes grew large behind his mask. He, too, fanned more sand. Kevyn again tried to dislodge it, but Sam shooed her away. He dug his hand into the sand beside the box and pulled. It moved, but would not dislodge.

Sam raked his gloved hands into the sand beside the object, brought them up in front of Kevyn, and spread his fingers. Fine specks of sand flowed through them like a waterfall of earth. His smile widened as Kevyn watched three silver coins emerge from the pile of silt. They were dull and crusted with tarnish but they were definitely coins – old coins – just like the one Grandfather had given her on the porch.

Kevyn's heart thundered in her chest. She thrust her hand into the sand beside the box and repeated Sam's motion of filtering the sand through her fingertips. Revealing two more coins, she screamed into her regulator making a distorted sound of muffled excitement that came out as a stream of bubbles. She wrapped her arms around Sam in all his gear.

Using his hands to push the sand over the object, Sam looked around, played with the watch on his wrist, and signaled that it was time for their ascent.

Kevyn ignored him and started to dig further in order to retrieve more coins. *She'd just found a treasure chest and wasn't going to leave it behind.*

Sam grabbed her arm and shook his head, pointing at her air gauge. It was time to head back to the surface. She was out of air.

Kevyn kicked toward the anchor line of *Wander*. She swam back up over the reef, this time not noticing any of the fish darting in and out of the coral. She grasped the coins in her hand tightly. No wonder Alex was so intrigued by all of this. She kept looking back over her shoulder, unable to believe what they'd found.

Breaking the surface of the water with her hand held above her, she looked like Superman flying through the air. Kevyn ripped the mask from her face. 'We found it!'

Alex leaned over the side of the boat. 'You found Digger?'

'No, we found the wreck.'

Alex looked confused. 'What wreck?'

'*Your* wreck.' Kevyn treaded water so hard that her upper body lifted out of the water. '*La Victoria!* It's out there.' She pointed to the sea.

'The whole ship?' Alex laughed while trying to grab Kevyn's gear.

'No, coins and a chest...a treasure chest.' Kevyn barely drew a breath between sentences as she continued, 'Just like the stories!'

Sam grabbed the side of the boat beside where Kevyn flailed. 'It's true.' He held up his gloved hand and showed Alex their find. 'I'm not sure what else is down there, but these doubloons came out of a broken trunk. There's way more to be found.'

Alex held one coin between his thumb and forefinger. He squinted and studied the piece.

Kevyn slapped the water to get his attention. 'I'm going back down.'

'Hold on there.' Alex lowered the ladder on the back of the boat to allow the divers aboard. 'You're out of air – the tanks need to be refilled.'

Kevyn's excitement bubbled up and out. 'So let's go ashore! Let's get more tanks and go back! Sam and I can bring up the treasure.'

Alex laughed. 'Just like that? You think it's that easy?' He turned to Sam. 'You know where you found these?'

'I marked the spot on the dive computer.'

Sam held up the watch on his wrist. 'Last night's storm must've uncovered them.'

Alex nodded. 'I guess Digger found his gold after all.'

'He went overboard right on top of the site.' Sam floated his tank to the swim ladder. 'I don't think he'll get to see any of it though.' He climbed out of the water. 'He's long gone.'

Kevyn stayed where she was. 'Come on! I want to look for more!'

Alex shook his head. 'The authorities are on their way to look for Digger.'

Kevyn couldn't believe what she was hearing. Wasn't he supposed to be the treasure hunter? 'But it's down there. We found it!'

'It's not going anywhere.' Alex stretched his hand out to help Kevyn aboard. 'I've got equipment, and we'll need a bigger boat with blowers and metal detectors. Just because you found coins doesn't mean that the ship is sitting right beside them.'

Sam helped Kevyn shrug out of her BC. 'It'll take a lot of time to bring it up if that *is* the *La Victoria*.'

Alex nodded his agreement. 'It could be *La Victoria* or a whole new mystery to uncover. Either way, there's a lot of work ahead. We're going to have to start carefully documenting everything, and I'll still be laid up for a few days.'

'You'll need help.' Sam passed a dry towel to Kevyn.

Kevyn bounced on her toes. 'We could do it! Sam and I, we could help you.' Kevyn looked at Sam for approval but kept right on talking, 'I could stay. I'll call Grandfather and tell him. And Sam…' she paused. 'Oh…the store. Maybe you need to go home?' She spoke fast, trying to think it all through.

'Ginny can run the store,' Sam said with a laugh. 'She likes it better when I'm gone, anyway. I just end up losing money. She's better at handling it all then I am.'

Kevyn chewed on the side of her lip, her eyes darting between Sam and Alex. 'Did you lose money because of Alex?'

Sam laughed and clamped Alex on the shoulder. 'Quite the opposite, actually. I still owe him for his last shipment.'

Kevyn thought it through. It was true that Sam had never said Alex owed him money. 'But, I saw you arguing.'

Sam lowered his eyes. 'I was trying to give Alex back the money I owed him, but he won't take it.'

Alex laid a hand on Sam's shoulder. 'You're looking out for my little girl, making sure she was safe coming down here, doing something I couldn't. That's enough payback for me.'

Sam put his arm around Kevyn and squeezed her shoulder. To Alex, he said, 'Maybe you'll let me work off the money I owe in exchange for help finding the rest of what's down there.' He motioned to the water around them.

Kevyn frowned and turned to Alex. 'Maybe you don't want us to help.'

Alex limped over to where Kevyn stood and grabbed her hand. 'I'd *love* it if you stayed.'

Looking from Sam to Alex, Kevyn knew she'd struck gold.

The local police sent two sets of search and rescue divers down with lights and a mesh body bag to bring Digger up. Another officer stayed on board asking the same questions over and over. After hours of telling the same story over and over to the detective, Kevyn watched the divers' bubbles shimmer to the surface as they grew close to the back of the boat. The officer in charge had warned her not to look at the body if she was squeamish. After all, if the sharks had gotten Digger it wouldn't be a very pretty sight.

But the gruesome warnings were wasted. The divers came up with nothing more than a turtle sighting.

'None of you are leaving the island?' the officer in charge asked.

Sam, Kevyn and Alex all looked at each other and smiled.

'No, my daughter is staying here with me,' Alex replied.

She smiled and wrapped her fingers through his, giving his hand a squeeze.

The police left with a promise to be in touch, but since Digger hadn't been cleared into the country through immigration, and there was no record of him being in the area, there wasn't much they could do unless a body turned up. The emerald or the coins were never mentioned.

Later that afternoon, Kevyn watched Sam as he cleaned the coins in soap and water and rubbed them gently with a soft cloth. He held one up and squinted at the raised markings in order to check the dates. Logging them into a ledger that Alex had given him, he compared the treasure to Alex's notes he'd kept on *La Victoria*. He reminded her of Alex. Sam may be a more responsible and reliable version, but he still was a boy who dreamed of sunken ships. Maybe every man did? Perhaps it was the one dream from childhood they still held on to.

The coins they found that morning held Sam's interest. There was no doubt this was a once in a lifetime opportunity for him. Kevyn looked around *Wander* and once again thought about all she had done in such a short time. She stood beside a man she was starting to fall in love with, and a man who was finally trying to become a father. She had a new family she needed to get to know, and a new life that Kevyn desperately wanted to see where it took her. But something was missing.

Pulling her cell phone out of her back pocket, she called her grandfather to tell him the news. Brianna was at the house once again and reassured Kevyn it was okay to stay. 'I'm going to take care of James.'

'Thanks, Mama.' Kevyn hardly knew what to say. This had been a long time coming. Kevyn felt guilty about abandoning her grandfather, but maybe this was what they all needed...time.

Sam stepped on deck as she finished the phone call. He stood behind Kevyn, wound his arms around her, and kissed her ear.

Her heart beat just as fast as the first time he kissed her and goose bumps popped out over her skin. She smiled and hugged him close to her.

To Alex, he said, 'You know, this is a big operation. We'll need a lot of time and people, not to mention more resources.'

Alex nodded, lost in thought.

Kevyn held the phone out to Alex. 'Perhaps Trista and Kyle would like to come down here and be a part of this? Her connections with the museum would be invaluable.'

A slow smile stretched across Alex's face. 'You know, I was just thinking the same thing.' He took the cell phone and walked to the bow.

Kevyn spun to face Sam.

'It's never dull with you, is it?' He placed his left palm flat against her ribcage and pulled her close with his other arm. His eyes were the color of sapphires as he stared deep into hers.

She could feel her heart vibrate. 'I was going to say the same about you.'

He ran his fingers through her hair, clutching it in his fist and pulling her head gently back as she looked up at him.

'I'm glad you're here,' Kevyn whispered.

Me, too.' He leaned down and kissed her with his soft and salty lips.

Kevyn felt more anchored than she ever had before. 'Will you really stay?'

Sam held her tight. 'I'm not going anywhere.'

Standing on *Wander*, with Sam's arm wrapped tight around her, Kevyn knew that no matter what they found on the ocean floor, she had already found her very own treasure.

*****

Lightning Source UK Ltd.
Milton Keynes UK
UKOW02f0345011214

242434UK00017BA/711/P

9 780994 169594